Dr. Cornelius
vs. Countess Petrovska

BY THE SAME AUTHOR

The Return of Captain Vampire

Dr. Cornelius
vs. Countess Petrovska

by
Brian Gallagher

with an epilog by
Brian Stableford

based on characters created by
Gustave Le Rouge
and
Arnaud d'Usseau & Julian Zimet

A Black Coat Press Book

Acknowledgements:

Stories and Afterword Copyright © 2024 by Brian Gallagher except for *Malbrough s'en va-t-en guerre* © 2024 by Brian Stableford.
Foreword Copyright © 2024 by Jean-Marc Lofficier & Brian Stableford.
Cover illustration Copyright © 2024 by Mike Hoffman.

Visit our website at www.blackcoatpress.com

TABLE OF CONTENTS

GUSTAVE LE ROUGE

LE MYSTÉRIEUX
DOCTEUR CORNÉLIUS

L'ENIGME DU CREEK SANGLANT

LA MAISON DU LIVRE 28 R. MONSIEUR LE PRINCE PARIS

Foreword

Le Mystérieux Docteur Cornélius by Gustave Le Rouge (1867-1938) was a serialized novel originally published in eighteen weekly parts by the Maison du Livre Moderne in 1912-13.[1] It proved to be the author's most successful work, even inspiring a cycle of poems adapted from his work by the author's friend and first enthusiastic champion, the avant-garde poet and novelist Blaise Cendrars.

By 1912, Le Rouge was already a highly experienced writer of popular works in the long tradition of French feuilleton fiction—having begun his career in that field, after a period of near-starvation as a Latin Quarter poet and publishing an assortment of short stories and items of non-fiction—by working in collaboration with Gustave Guitton on a series of sprawling endeavors, begun with what was intended to be a four-volume novel (it was actually split into eight by its publisher) collectively entitled *La Conspiration des Milliardaires* [The Billionaires' Conspiracy] (1899-1900)[2].

---

[1] Available from Black Coat Press in three volumes: *1. The Sculptor of Human Flesh*, ISBN 978-1-61227-243-6; *2. The Island of Hanged Men*, ISBN 978-1-61227-244-3; and *3. The Rochester Bridge Incident*, ISBN 978-1-61227-245-0.

[2] Available from Black Coat Press as *The Dominion of the World*, in four volumes: *1. The Plutocratic Plot*, ISBN 978-1-61227-095-1; *2. The Transatlantic Threat*, ISBN 978-1-61227-096-8; *3. The Psychic Spies*, ISBN 978-1-61227-097-5; and *4. The Victims Victorious*, ISBN 978-1-61227-098-2.

Guitton and Le Rouge wrote three more long novels before going their separate ways, after which Le Rouge became far more successful than his former friend, whose solo career faded away and whose eventual fate—and, indeed, his entire life—remains mysterious.

Le Mystérieux Docteur Cornélius is a deliberate return on Le Rouge's part to the milieu and genre of *La Conspiration des Milliardaires*, with the exception that American billionaires are here the victim of a vast conspiracy rather than the makers of one. Whereas the earlier series had a band of American plutocrats hiring a scientific genius to provide them with the weapons necessary to conquer Europe and hence obtain economic world domination, in *Le Mystérieux Docteur Cornélius*, the partners in a Trust monopolizing American production of corn and cotton become the targets of the insidious criminal association of the Red Hand, whose three mysterious Lords are the scientific genius Cornelius Kramm, his brother Fritz. and the renegade son of one of the billionaires.

The sympathy accorded by the overarching plot of *Le Mystérieux Docteur Cornélius* to billionaires in general is an ironic reflection of literary convention. Le Rouge's own political sympathies were on the far left of radical socialism, but in his fiction, he was consciously following in the footsteps of numerous French anarchists who had turned to popular fiction as a means of making a living—the most conspicuous examples being Jules Lermina and Michel Zevaco—and who embraced its conventional prejudices with an apparent wholeheartedness while retaining their tongues in their cheeks.

The notion of "organized crime" has now become so commonplace that it is not easy for modern readers to appreciate, without an imaginative leap, how unusual that concept was in 1912. It was not original, of course, and *Le Mystérieux Docteur Cornélius* has a much more remote but even more obvious model than *La Conspiration des Milliardaires* in Paul Féval's pioneering series of seven romans feuilletons featuring *Les Habits Noirs* (1863-74)[3], but Le Rouge's updating of the notion was considerably more adventurous and spectacular than any of the other revisitations of the idea produced before the Great War.

Cornelius Kramm is, in essence, an equivalent figure to Féval's Colonel Bozzo-Corona, and several other characters in the Le Rouge series also have near-equivalents either in the Colonel's coterie, or in the extensive cast of his victims and adversaries. The fact that Cornelius is an experimental scientist rather than a mere bandit, however, has numerous logical ramifications, which transform the fundamental nature of his conspiracy and its procedures. Arguable, they do not transform it nearly enough, because the logical ramifications in question are not extrapolated to what would nowadays be considered an adequate extent, but that is the inevitable fate of many pioneering enterprises; the writers who are boldest in taking first steps are often found wanting when it comes to developing more disciplined and far-ranging explorations.

---

[3] Available from Black Coat Press in seven volumes: *'Salem Street*, ISBN 978-1-932983-46-3*; The Invisible Weapon*, ISBN 978-1-932983-80-7*; The Parisian Jungle*, ISBN 978-1-934543-03-0*; The Companions of the Treasure*, ISBN 978-1-934543-26-9*; Heart of Steel*, ISBN 978-1-935558-05-7*; The Cadet Gang,* ISBN 978-1-935558-45-3*;* and *The Sword-Swallower*, ISBN 978-1-61227-024-1.

In spite of its limitations, however, the particular criminal conspiracy featured in *Le Mystérieux Docteur Cornélius* does have some intriguing precedent-setting features. The notion of a criminal scientist employing his genius in the service of a vast criminal enterprise was not entirely new, and it must have seemed only logical in 1912 that anyone who was actually to undertake a large scale twentieth-century enterprise in plunder, making virtual war on a technologically-progressive society, would need scientific expertise in order to secure the necessary melodramatic inflation of its enterprise. That logic was, however, conspicuously lacking in much of the crime fiction of the era, and remarkably tentative in many of the instances in which it was manifest. Le Rouge is tentative too, but was nevertheless in the forefront of the early-20th century evolution of what was eventually to become a major literary mythology, fated to undergo an extraordinary elaboration and sophistication in the course of the century.

Jean-Marc Lofficier & Brian Stableford

The Doctor of Sarajevo

Sarajevo, 28 June 1914

Countess Sophie Chotek was relieved. The assassination attempt on her husband, Archduke Franz Ferdinand, had failed. A grenade thrown at them earlier had clattered over the roof of their car and damaged the vehicle behind them, causing casualties.

Her husband had a premonition of trouble, and it came true. He was thinking of creating a new province within the Austro-Hungarian Empire, encompassing Croatia-Slavonia, Dalmatia and Bosnia-Herzegovina, with the city of Zagreb likely being its capital. She remembered him discussing it with her. His ideas not gone down well in Serbia and with various radicals, and this attempt on his life had clearly been a response to it. Still, they managed to get to City Hall for a speech by the mayor, in which her husband interrupted with a sarcastic remark about his welcome to the city. She was proud that he later gave a speech in which he thanked the people of the city for the failure of the assassination attempt.

They were now on their way, by car, to the hospital to see the casualties. They were accompanied by Oscar Potiorek, Governor of Bosnia-Herzegovina. Suddenly, she heard him exclaim:

"This is the wrong way! We are supposed to take the Appel Quay!"

She sensed danger immediately and saw a man on the street, with a pistol aimed right at them. She heard two shots ring out. She felt pain in her stomach. She turned and saw blood ooze from her husband's neck. She fell sideways, her head coming to rest on the Archduke's knees. The last thing she heard was the heir to the throne pleading with her not to die, for the sake of their children.

The Serb assassin was tackled to the ground by the crowd that had come to see the Archduke. The gendarmerie took charge of him. He was delighted. He was sure that he had just assassinated the man who would have prevented the union of Slav lands under the control of Belgrade by carrying through reforms.

It was unfortunate that so many people in these lands—including those who had restrained him—were not convinced of this, preferring the Empire over union with Serbia. Only a few Croats and Muslims were radicalized. *They did not know what was good for them*, he thought.

The gendarmerie had his pistol—a 9mm Browning, supplied by the Serbian Black Hand organization. They had trained him to shoot in the Topčider forest, in Serbia. He was grateful, the training had worked well. Now, he would face a trial. He cared only for his cause, and soon everyone would know his name: Gavrilo Princip.

Berne, Switzerland, August 1914

Dr. Cornelius Kramm warily regarded the man who had summoned him to what was referred to as the British Envoy Extraordinary and Minister Plenipotentiary to the Swiss Confederation at 50 Thunstrasse. This Percy Phelps was clearly not interested in a medical consultation with the man now known as "Dr. Malbrough." At least, not on medical matters.

"Perhaps I had better come to the point, Dr. Kramm," Phelps said. "His Majesty's Government would like to employ you to obtain a certain item from the General Philippovich barracks in Sarajevo. You would be well compensated,"

Dr. Cornelius responded, deciding to affect ignorance of his name.

"I fear you are mistaken; there is no Dr. Kramm at my practice. I, Dr. Malbrough, am the sole practitioner there, along with my staff. And we certainly do not work as couriers—if that is what you are asking. However, we do some facial surgery," he waved gently at Phelps's face, "and certainly, I think I could help you in that respect."

Phelps was affronted. How dare this man—a criminal—be so insulting to him? He would put on his cross face and put this damnable fellow in his place.

"Now, look here. You are the criminal known as Cornelius Kramm, one of the former leaders of the Red Hand organization. After its destruction, you fled to Australia where you worked as Dr. Malbrough, before leaving to set up a branch of your practice here in Europe, which is a front for your criminal-for-hire activities."

Phelps sat back, most satisfied.

Dr. Cornelius said nothing, leaving an awkward pause.

"You were recommended to us by your fellow criminal, Professor Moriarty, Dr. Kramm," an exasperated Phelps continued. "But we can make life difficult if you do not cooperate."

Dr. Cornelius was pleased. Not by the threat, but by how easily he had drawn the man out. Now he knew that the British were not entirely trustworthy, but also that they were serious about their offer. He also knew that he was not in a position to antagonize them in any serious way. He put his hands up in a placatory gesture.

"My dear Mr. Phelps, you don't expect me to admit to such things, do you? It is clear you are well informed, and your mentioning my colleague, Professor Moriarty, gives me great confidence. Please, give me further details about your proposal."

"As I have said," replied Phelps, placated, "we are in need of a certain liquid, for scientific purposes, you understand."

Indeed, Dr. Cornelius did. This was something of military value that the British did not want their Austro-Hungarian foes to retain.

"A phial of this liquid is kept securely in the General Philippovich barracks in Sarajevo," Phelps continued. "It is well guarded in a special section. We want you to steal it, and hand it over to our agent who will verify it is real. This will be done in Sarajevo. At that point, you will be paid £20,000 into your Swiss bank account."

"Hmm. Yes, it can be done," responded the Doctor. "I have one question, however. You clearly know me. Therefore, you must be aware that one of your country-men, Lord Burydan, is an enemy of mine. I can't imagine he would approve of your hiring me."

"We know all about that," replied Phelps, waving that away. "The good news is that, on the declaration of hostilities, Lord Burydan swiftly enlisted and is an infantry Major—he was in the army previously. He's in France. He will not get in your way, Dr. Kramm."

"Good," said the Doctor, nodding. "Before we discuss further details, firstly I am usually referred to as 'Dr. Cornelius.' In my specialized field, people seem to prefer my Christian name. It's become something of a trademark, shall we say. Secondly, there is the matter of my compensation. Your offer is derisory to be frank…"

They eventually came to an agreement and Dr. Cornelius left. Phelps was pleased with the result. Certainly, the Doctor had upped the fee somewhat, but it would be worth it. With Professor Moriarty refusing the job—the unpatriotic swine!—this sinister doctor was the only option. Physically, the Doctor had looked thin, indeed almost emaciated – did he not eat? However, if he was successful, Allied possession of this liquid would be the last part of a weapon that would end this war before it had barely begun.

Evidenzbureau[4] facility, Vienna, September 1914

"My dear Countess, how wonderful it is to see you," said the man who headed this particular *Evidenzbureau* department. "I have a new mission for you. I have made some preparations."

Countess Irina Petrovska sat opposite him. She was unimpressed by his tone.

"Your Serene Highness Prince Wilhelm, please remember that I do not work for you; I carry out some of your missions for the good of Poland and the Empire."

The Prince realized that he had been presumptuous.

"Of course, I do recognize your independence," he rushed to add. "However, this is a mission of great importance; one that could decide the outcome of the war. Please, you may call me Prince Wilhelm."

---

[4] The Habsburg Empire's military intelligence service. Formed in 1850, it was the world's first such organization.

The Countess nodded and gestured for him to continue.

"We are concerned over the General Philippovich barracks in Sarajevo. It has been reported to us that questions are being asked about them and, in particular, their security. These questions are being asked at all levels of society, not merely the lower classes. This is of concern to us. We would like to find out who is behind them."

"Surely," the Countess replied, "that is the sort of thing that happens in war? Why do these particular barracks concern you so?"

"The barracks have a special significance. There are a number of special items kept there that could be of great value to our enemies. We are giving thought to moving them elsewhere, but for all we know, that would tip the advantage the other side. We want to find out who in Sarajevo is making inquiries before any decision is made on relocation.

"Discreet inquiries on the ground have produced no results and we can hardly arrest leading members of society or pull them in for interrogation—that could cause any number of problems. Essentially, we would like you to visit Sarajevo and mix with the higher echelons of society and find out what is going on. Naturally, we will provide appropriate recompense. I know you would prefer to be operating against the Russians at the moment, but believe me, you will be serving the war effort better in Sarajevo."

"Very well," said the Countess, nodding. "It would be interesting to see Sarajevo at the very least. Certainly, I would wish to pray at the Catholic Cathedral there for the soul of Archduke Ferdinand, a man who promised much for the Empire when he took over. I will leave at once."

"Excellent!" exclaimed the Prince. "You remind me of a fine woman I once knew..." he looked wistfully out of a window.

The Countess felt weary suddenly. Surely, he was not going to bore her with the tale of Irene Adler once again? She had come across the woman and considered her a bit dull. How she had managed to confound the famous Sherlock Holmes was beyond her. It amused the Countess that this Adler had caused the Prince any problem at all—a woman in his past that he thought could trouble his ludicrous claim to be the King of Bohemia. Well, Emperor Franz Joseph, the actual King of Bohemia—amongst much else—dealt with the "Grand Duke" most firmly. He was fortunate that the Emperor had given him this job with the title of Prince. The Adler thing was meaningless in the end.

To the Countess's great relief, the Prince reverted back to the mission.

"We must make arrangements. We have already set up a social occasion for you to attend…"

After the Countess had left, an aide came into the office.

"The Countess has accepted the mission. She will soon be leaving for Sarajevo," the Prince told him.

The aide, a young army officer, responded, "Your Serene Highness, I understand that the Countess has done many services for the Empire."

The Prince bade him to sit. "Yes," he replied. "As you know, this department deals with matters of an unusual scientific nature. The Countess is well suited to such things. She was involved in an incident on the Trans-Siberian Express in 1906 in which a creature from beyond our world was running amok."

The officer looked startled.

17

"Ah, I see, you have not been fully briefed. I will see to it that you will be. Since that incident, in which her husband died, the Countess has had a number of adventures. She is motivated by Polish patriotism. She wishes to see the parts of her homeland ruled by Russia liberated and unified with our Galicia within the Empire. There is heavy fighting there with the Russians at the moment.

"She was born in Galicia, and thus is our citizen, and married the Count Petrovski, who was resident in the Polish lands occupied by Russia." Here, the Prince paused. "You have been with us for only a couple of weeks? Seconded from the 96th Karlovac Infantry Regiment?"

"Yes, sir" the aide replied.

"Ah!" said the Prince with a pleased look. "I must tell you all about another remarkable woman, one named Irene Adler..."

September 1914, Sarajevo

Dr. Cornelius was most satisfied. In only a few weeks of opening his new practice in Sarajevo, he had attracted some wealthy clients from the city, Croats, Muslims and Serbs, and the rest of Bosnia-Herzegovina, and beyond. He recalled with amusement one dignitary's comment:

"How good of you to set up here, Dr. Malbrough, in order to promote our city after the assassination."

The "sculptor of human flesh" cackled. What a naive fool that man was! He had even referred some customers to him. And it was not long before some of them were revealed to not have the money to pay for his services...

One such person now knocked on the door of the practice. The Doctor let him in, and they went silently to his consulting room, where they sat down.

"Now, Baron von Kuffner," said the Doctor, what have you for me?"

Baron von Kuffner, a thin tall man in his fifties, looked nervous as he answered:

"What is this information for, Doctor? We are at war... The information you seek could be used by my Emperor's enemies."

Dr. Cornelius drew breath. "That is hardly your concern," he replied. "I have completely healed those scars on your face, and you failed to pay me, due to your unfortunate debts. If you prefer, I could simply start proceedings to recover my fee, which would disgrace you. No doubt, someone will offer you a pistol and a bottle of whisky..." Then, he added menacingly, "Perhaps me."

Baron Von Kuffner there and then that told him everything he had gleaned from his contacts in the General. It was good information, but not enough.

"I need more, Baron," said Dr. Cornelius.

The Baron looked concerned. "That is all I know. What else can I do?"

"I advise you to think harder."

The Doctor beckoned to someone, seemingly behind him. Suddenly there was a knife at the Baron's neck. He had not even realized that there was anyone else in the room. So he did as instructed and said:

"There is a reception in three days' time, being held by the mayor in honor of the military. There will be some officers there. I could perhaps talk to them?"

The Doctor waved the man with the knife away.

"More than talk. You will gain the precise location of the item I want. And passwords. And you will help me to make their acquaintance."

The Countess was pleased with the reception at City Hall, known as Vijećnica. Ostensibly, it was being held to honor the Austro-Hungarian armed forces. In reality, it was an opportunity to observe those who had been asking questions about the General Philippovich barracks. Aside from the military officers, the elite of the Sarajevo society was there: civic dignitaries, members of the local cultural societies, and leading members of the religious communities of the city. There was a small orchestra playing *Die Bosniaken Kommen*[5] always popular with the troops. She had received many admiring looks from men interested in this elegantly dressed, auburn-haired, beautiful woman.

She turned respectfully to the man she was with.

"Your Excellency, I must thank you again for your hospitality,"

"It is my pleasure. The Emperor himself wrote to me. I understand that your work is of importance. I am of course also pleased that you have attended church, and your grasp of my language is impressive."

The Countess was pleased that she had his favor. This was the Catholic Archbishop of Vrhbosna[6], the Croat Josip Stadler. She was staying at an apartment arranged for by the Church. Her cover was that of a journalist writing for a Catholic newspaper—being a Coun-

---

[5] *The Bosniaks are Coming*, a military march composed in 1895 by Austrian composer Eduard Wagnes.
[6] The Roman Catholic diocese of a large part of Bosnia-Herzegovina, including Sarajevo.

tess gave her work a certain celebrity value. It was an invaluable cover for much of her work. And the Archbishop, who had dabbled in politics with his own Croatian political party, was well known as being loyal to Vienna.

"Yes, I know a number of languages. The example of our multi-lingual Emperor is a great example. It certainly helps with my article on the Church here. I was very impressed by your Sacred Heart Cathedral. I felt at great peace praying there."

"I am pleased to hear it," the Archbishop said.

He looked over to a small group of men. There was Baron von Kuffner, talking to two military officers.

"Countess," he said, "I believe one of the gentlemen you wish to meet, Baron Von Kuffner, is in discussion with two military officers. Should I introduce you?"

The Archbishop was aware that the Countess had a special mission, although he was unaware of the precise details.

"Yes, now would be an excellent time," replied the Countess.

Baron Von Kuffner was one of those identified by the secret police as having asked indiscreet questions.

The Archbishop guided her toward the group. The two officers were members of the Bosnian-Herzegovinian infantry, in dress uniform complete with cutlasses. The Archbishop made the introductions, then moved away, to let the Countess do her work.

"I'm sorry to interrupt your conversation, but I was curious to meet some of our gallant soldiers, and yourself Baron—I have heard so many good things about you."

"You flatter me, Countess," the Baron replied. "I wholeheartedly support our soldiers; I only wish I could fight alongside them. I am a reserve officer, but despite my protestations, due to an old liver complaint, the doctors will not let me return to active duty."

"How devastating for you," the Countess replied, knowing full well that her information was that it was *his* protestations over his 'liver complaint' that had prevented his return to the military.

"Yes, however, I do give the troops some moral support!" the Baron said. "Now, I must take my leave to pay my respects to the Mayor, but I shall see you gentlemen later."

"Well…" said the Countess.

She was not used to someone just walking off from her. Clearly, there was something wrong with him. Not least as he walked straight past Mayor Čurčic.

"We shall not be leaving you, Countess!" exclaimed the young officer who had been introduced to her as Lieutenant Novotný.

"I should hope not," she replied with a winning smile. "He clearly is more impressed by you two than me. Are you seeing him again later?"

"Yes," responded the other officer, a Captain Hodžić. "He is very interested in discussing the war and politics. He has invited us both to an excellent establishment in the city where we can discuss such matters further."

"Over drinks no doubt?" teased the Countess.

They all laughed. However, she was concerned. She had no doubt now that the Baron was a little too interested in the personnel from the General Philippovich barracks. A number of officers had been briefed about anyone asking questions, but some had not, including these two. However, it would be important to see what happened next. They were not likely to believe her if she told them of her true purpose, and to brief them now may tip off the Baron or anyone working with him, if they were being observant, which she was wise enough to assume.

She continued to talk animatedly with the officers about her work on her article. However, she managed to slip word to a waiter—in reality a member of the secret police branch of the local gendarmerie—about what to do next.

The evening wore on, with a few dignitaries starting to leave. The Countess had met many people, and many more were keen to meet her.

"What was the situation here after the assassination?" she asked Mayor Čurčic.

The Mayor was well acquainted with what had happened.

"There was great anger," he replied. "Regrettably, there were some attacks on the Serbs and their property. The Croats and Muslims are loyal to the monarchy, and there was some over-reaction. However, we have taken action against Serb organizations."

"The Archduke was a great man, with views on reforming the monarchy that would have benefited the people of the Empire, including my own," she observed. "Now we have a war. Belgrade must be held fully to account. It is unfortunate that this man Princip is too young to be hung."

Čurčic nodded. He had heard that the Countess was a woman with firm views. Like many, he found her highly intriguing. She was a woman who seemed not to recognize any second place to men, and appeared to lead a highly adventurous lifestyle.

One of the staff came up to the Countess and said something. The Mayor recognized the man—a member of the local secret police. He had been informed that they would be here, but knew not why; however, it seemed that the Countess was somehow involved. Before he could say anything, she turned back to him and said:

"My dear Mayor, I fear I must take my leave. However, I hope we shall meet again before I depart this city."

And before he could respond, she was heading to the exit.

The gendarme who had spoken to her earlier, was waiting at the exit of hall.

"Countess, the two officers are leaving with the Baron," he said. "We must move swiftly. We shall follow and report back to you."

"No Inspector Lovrić," replied the Countess, "I shall come with you."

The Inspector could see that she brooked no argument; he was also mindful of his superior's order to do whatever she asked. They left swiftly.

Outside, the Countess and Inspector Lovrić were met by another member of the secret police, Sergeant Ahmić. He simply pointed at the spot where the two officers were walking with Baron von Kuffner on the Appel Quay, by the Miljacka river.

The Countess and the officers had little choice but to follow. A horse and cart came up from behind and stopped by the three men. The two officers suddenly reacted as if they had been hit by something.

'Halt! Gendarmerie!" shouted the Inspector.

A shot rang out. Baron von Kuffner collapsed. Two men from the cart leaped out and bundled the now groggy officers in.

The Countess and the gendarmes dashed forward, but the cart was already moving off.

The driver was Dr. Cornelius. He put his gun back within the coat. Von Kuffner had been followed and was now a liability. It was much easier to simply kill him. He had shot the two officers with drugged darts. The Doctor was wearing a hat and some bandages around his face, in order to prevent anyone from recognizing him. He had wanted to make sure that he was present at this vital moment in the plan.

The Countess motioned to the gendarmerie and they followed her to her vehicle—a yellow roadster. She jumped into the driving seat, with the secret policemen getting in behind her. She drove off, headlights glaring in the night, and, within seconds, was behind her quarry.

Another horse and cart rolled up to the body of the Baron, men from the cart picked it up and rode away, much to the puzzlement of onlookers.

In her car, the Countess exclaimed:

"Prepare to fire, officers! I have no doubt that they're about to attack us!"

She was not wrong, as two thugs appeared from under the coverings of the cart. Before they could fire on the car, however, a metal slab slammed up from under the hood, covering the windscreen, with only a small slot for visibility.

The Countess prayed that the bullets would not get through the slots. The two gendarmes behind her were standing up, trying to fire over her, but not getting their aim due to the constant movement of the vehicle and the bullets firing back at them. The thugs fired at the car, but the bullets simply bounced off. Even the wheels seemed impervious.

Both vehicles ceased firing at each other; a momentary stalemate with the Countess only yards away, but unable to overtake, her car being vulnerable on the sides.

One of the thugs informed Dr. Cornelius of the situation. He nodded. He saw that they were approaching a fork in the road. He unhooked the horses and ensured they went along the other road, with the cart barreling along the Appel Quay straight ahead.

The Countess did not know what had happened, but she sensed victory. Then, suddenly, the cart somehow accelerated away, going at a faster pace than her own vehicle. The covering of the cart flew back onto the road. The Countess stopped her car just in time before it hit it.

She and the gendarmes watched what seemed to be a moving platform with wheels, with sheets of metal moving up to enclose the riders, turning off onto another road and disappearing.

The Countess was less than pleased.

"Why didn't they throw out the covering at us in the first place?" Inspector Lovrić said.

The Countess glared at him, but then softened.

"Yes, yes. a good question, Inspector. Our foes have advanced cars, but it appears perhaps not much in the way of common sense? To your headquarters! The city must be searched."

Dr. Cornelius's vehicle disappeared into a small warehouse, with his hired hands laughing and slapping him on the back.

"Well done, boss!" they were saying in their broken German.

The Doctor did not appreciate such familiarity. There was a time—when he was one of the Lords of the Red Hand—when they would have paid for that. However, the Red Hand, once one of the world's foremost criminal organizations, had effectively been destroyed by a group of French adventurers and that lunatic Briton, Lord Burydan. He still employed a few Red Hand people, such as these local louts, but he could hardly lord it over them.

They were laughing and getting out a bottle of the local drink, Rakia. They seemed to have enjoyed themselves. He had not. He felt annoyance at having to be so directly involved, when previously he could have had top quality people to do the job. And he was aware of his lack of experience in more physical matters. He should have had a couple of grenades on hand to throw at their pursuers... He had to learn things fast.

"Enough of the drink. Disguise the vehicle, and then we go to my surgery."

They quickly did as they were told, disguising the vehicle—which the Doctor had made at great cost in better times—as a cart again, along with horses. They left from another exit. If anyone had seen their strange vehicle enter, they would not likely see the horse and cart leave.

The surgery was not far away. They arrived there before the gendarmerie started searching the streets. In the night, however, there was not much the gendarmerie could do. They did receive a report of something that looked like a car entering a warehouse, but when they looked during the daylight hours, they found nothing.

The Countess awoke. She had gone to sleep at 3 a.m., by which point it was clear to her that her quarries had got away.

It was now 7 a.m. She was tired, but she would find some time to catch-up on her sleep later. She bathed and dressed. Her attire was highly fashionable, but probably not the best for running around. However, she had little intention of dressing in a functional way that may attract attention. And anyway, she was a Countess—she would always dress in a manner appropriate to her station.

She looked in the mirror. How her life and changed over the past eight years! Coming across that creature from another world on the Trans-Siberian Express had changed her outlook on life. It was clear that ungodly, demonic forces really did exist. They had to be fought—she could not stand idly by. On that occasion, others had taken the lead in defeating the creature. She would not be doing that again. Further, she felt that a more active role in freeing Polish lands from Russian control would be better than hoping for the best.

Her husband, Count Petrovski, had a different view—even employing a deranged Russian monk as a spiritual adviser, strangely believing this would help in currying favor with the Tsar. The monk had died on that train, and the Countess, having found him repugnant, was less than grieved. Interestingly, she had heard that the current Tsarina was causing concern with a similar character she had around her. *That will not end well*, she thought. Her husband, of course, would have forbidden her newfound assertive activities, but he had been murdered by that creature on the Express in 1910, preventing any such argument. She still missed him, occasionally, despite his appalling arrogance.

There was a knock on the door. It was Ljubica, the maid provided to her by Archbishop Stadler.

"Countess, there is a gendarme waiting for you."

She went into the front room, beckoning the maid to come with her. It was Inspector Lovrić.

"Good morning, Countess. I have urgent news about Lieutenant Novotný and Captain Hodžić."

"Good morning, Inspector," the Countess said, never forgetting to be polite, "Have they been found?"

"In a manner of speaking, Countess. They reported for duty at the barracks this morning, insisting that nothing untoward happened to them last night."

At the General Philippovich barracks, the Countess was received by the officer in charge, a General Auersperg, in his office. As head of the barracks, he himself had been at the reception the night before, and, consequently, had spent the night awake, being kept informed of the search for his two missing officers.

"Countess, thanks to you, I have had no sleep last night. My officers have told me that they spent most of the night at an establishment, no doubt drinking, with Baron von Kuffner. The establishment, the *Crvena Ruka*, has corroborated this. They even let them sleep there for a few hours."

The Countess was puzzled, but did not show it. She had already been told this by Inspector Lovrić. There would be an explanation at some point, but right now, she needed more information.

"General, both myself and the gendarmes with me not only saw your men bundled in a cart, but Baron von Kuffner shot dead."

"As you know, there is some corroboration for what you say," replied the General. "There were witnesses to your chase, and some blood was indeed found where you claimed the body was, but the Baron is alive and well. You no doubt would wish to see the officers for yourselves?"

"Of course," she said.

The General nodded to an aide, who left the room. He returned shortly, with the two officers. They saluted smartly to the General, ignoring the Countess.

"Please tell the Countess where you were last night?" General Auersperg ordered.

Captain Hodžić relayed to the Countess what she had already heard. She looked to Lieutenant Novotný.

"And you confirm this?"

He nodded.

"Please, do confirm it in words."

"Yes, Countess, what the Captain said is the truth. We spent the evening discussing the war and politics and slept at the *Crvena Ruka*. We had permission for the entire evening, so there was no need to return to the barracks prior to when we had to report."

The Countess nodded.

"Your voices sound different, gentlemen," she observed.

The General laughed.

"A good night's drink would do that! Look at them, not a bit of being worse for wear! A credit to the Emperor!"

The men all laughed. The General then said:

"I trust you are now satisfied Countess? Clearly you were mistaken."

The Countess stood up and smiled at the General.

"Thank you, General. I am neither satisfied, nor was I mistaken. I shall take my leave now."

The General had heard of the Countess's assertive manner. Given that he was under orders to cooperate, he thought it best not to antagonize her. He motioned to his aide. They made their polite farewells, and the aide took the Countess out of the room.

"Infernal woman," the General said after she had left. "Now, back to work, the pair of you," he laughed.

Lieutenant Novotný and Captain Hodžić saluted and left. They indeed had work to do.

The Countess drove to the main gendarmerie station. Many of the locals took an interest in her car as she drove past—and the fact that a woman was driving it.

As she was arriving, Baron Von Kuffner was leaving. She was stunned—it really was him! The Baron simply looked at her and walked on. She met Sergeant Ahmić at the entrance.

"Make sure that he is followed," she instructed.

"That has already been done," he responded.

Inside, in a side office, the Countess heard Inspector Lovrić's report.

"We spoke to the Baron; he came to us of his own accord, claiming to have heard that he had been 'killed' last night. It certainly was him, yet we all saw him shot last night. Could we somehow have been mistaken?"

"All three of us, Inspector?" said the Countess. "No, that is not possible. I believe there is some other force at work here. I do not believe that he has come back from the dead, but I certainly believe we may in the presence of something perhaps not part of normal experience. I have had experience of such things."

"What could that be?" asked the Inspector.

"I do not know yet, but I have little doubt matters will become clear soon. I have no doubt that the officers are not quite what they seem. There may well be a threat to the barracks by our enemies. I will attempt to get them quietly removed from duty for a short time. I must contact Vienna."

In the General Philippovich barracks, Captain Hodžić approached a particular locked room, with a heavy steel door. It was a small area dug below the barracks themselves. Outside the door, a bored Sergeant sat at a desk. He longed to get to the front, to partake in the war. The Serbs had committed a terrible act, and they should be duly punished for it. His wife, whilst sympathetic, did wonder if he was too enthusiastic, fearing that he might not come back. He told her it would be a great honor for her if indeed he did die in the service of the Empire. She seemed less impressed than before. There were times he could not understand her. He was jolted out of his thoughts when an officer approached. He leapt to attention.

"Just doing a routine check of the secure area," said the Captain.

"Yes, sir. Please sign in first," replied the Sergeant.

The Captain signed and the Sergeant opened the door for him. He looked around the room. There were a number of items around, many of which seemed damaged or incomprehensible. Next to him was a glass cabinet with what appeared to be something he had seen used to unblock drains—a burnt metallic rod with a cup on the end. The label was German, but he recognized something in his own language—something from far away? Perhaps the military had secret plumbing methods?

He shook his head and looked for what he came for. He found it soon enough. A simple metal phial labeled *Fulgurator explosive fluid*. However, it was locked in a glass cabinet.

He was ready for that. He took out a pick from his pocket, and, within a few moments, had unlocked the cabinet. He carefully took out the phial—he could feel the liquid moving in it—and carefully put it in his tunic. It made a slight bulge, but he did not think it would be noticed. He was entirely correct.

"All in order, Sir?" asked the Sergeant.

"Indeed so, Sergeant."

The Captain signed the book and left. The Sergeant looked after him. *That was a quick inspection*, he thought. And was his voice different? No matter, such is the way of officers.

A short time later, the two officers found themselves at Dr. Cornelius's surgery. The Doctor himself was there, along with another man whom the officers did not recognize.

"We have what you want," said Captain Hodžić.

He handed over the phial to the Doctor. The surgeon looked at it, and then turned to the man next to him.

"Well, then, Monsieur Hart, I trust this will satisfy you?"

"Let us see first," the man replied in French-accented German.

Hart moved to some apparatus on a nearby bench, clearly set up for chemical usage. Whilst he began his test, Dr. Cornelius spoke to the officers. Hodžić told him what he had seen written on the cabinet. The Doctor pondered this. Part of a superweapon? He could, of course, eliminate this Hart and keep the phial. But what use would it be without the rest of the weapon? And did he really want the British—and, it seemed, the French—as his enemies just now? No; it was much easier and profitable to take their money. In his current position, he could not do much else.

"You two," he said to the officers. "Go up the stairs to the operating table. I will now restore your natural features. And I will see to it that the real officers are let onto the streets shortly. They have been drugged and will remember nothing. They will be disorientated, but it will no doubt be assumed they had too much to drink at lunchtime as they had last night. There will be questions, but not as many as two officers really going missing."

Hart looked up and came over at that.

"How is it that you perform such surgery? That you can replicate men's faces so exactly?"

"Come now, Monsieur Hart," the Doctor replied. "You surely do not wish me to divulge my trade secrets?"

Trade secrets, Dr. Cornelius thought, *that had such an origin that even Mr. Hart with his apparent knowledge of superweapons would have difficulty believing.*

"You killed Baron von Kuffner and replaced him. What are you going to do about that?"

"Oh, his corpse shall be found in the Miljacka river. I have his body in my other facility, encased in ice to slow decay. One of my forgers has already written a suicide note, it has been sent to the Baron's solicitor. Of course, the gendarmerie will be puzzled as to why he did not simply kill himself at home, but the fact of the man's debts will override any concerns. At least for the moment. We only need a day or two to complete matters and be on our way. Dr. Malbrough will be returning to Berne very soon. By the time the Austrians, including their agent, this Countess Petrovska, put anything together, it will be much too late."

Hart nodded. He turned back to his apparatus. Whatever he was doing, it was ready. He took out a piece of paper and put it into a small glass beaker of liquid which had been heated to boiling, but had now simmered down. The paper was black.

"You've earned your money, Dr. Cornelius," he said. "This is what we have been after."

The Doctor performed a small bow. One of his minions came in and whispered something to him. His face, never particularly joyful, hardened.

"It seems the gendarmerie have arrested someone from the *Crvena Ruka*, a barman. He works for me, one of my Red Hand operatives. I don't know how they know of his past, but we must move fast. He may not last under interrogation."

Dr. Cornelius noted that Hart had clearly not realized that *Crvena Ruka* meant "Red Hand" in the local language. Some fool had called the pub that name in the past, and he and the other Lords of the Red Hand had not objected, it being a matter for the lower levels of the organization. Technically, he still owned it, but the details were suitably murky to prevent his identification. Nonetheless, this was not a good development.

At the gendarmerie station, Inspector Lovrić had just informed the Countess of the new developments. The two army officers had been followed to the surgery of one Dr. Malbrough.

"I have heard of this Dr. Malbrough," said the Countess. "He is said to perform surgical facial miracles—for a price. I understand he is originally from Australia. Could he be working for the British?"

"It's possible," replied Lovrić. "He's been considered above suspicion, due to his wealthy friends here. However, given the situation, I think we could certainly enter his premises to perform a check and see what the officers are doing there.

"We also did some checks on the staff of the *Crvena Ruka* as requested. One of them had emigrated to America, but returned recently to Sarajevo, and became a barman. Our files contain an American police report sent to us a few years ago. It was suspected that he was a member of the Red Hand, a criminal organization. We have him in custody."

The Countess realized the implications. One of the Red Hand's so-called "Lords" was Dr. Cornelius Kramm, another surgeon with miraculous skills. As for *Crvena Ruka...* She knew what that name meant.

"What does he say?"

"So far, he's corroborated the drinking story of Baron von Kuffner," the Inspector replied.

"Perhaps," suggested the Countess, "you could be more... persuasive? Within reason."

"Of course," replied the Inspector. "I was about to do so anyway. I will also ask Sergeant Ahmić to assemble some men to visit the surgery of this Dr. Malbrough. My gendarmes who followed the officers are already keeping watch there."

The Countess considered driving immediately to the surgery. However, there would only be the surveillance officers there, and who knew what would await them there.

Shortly, Sergeant Ahmić assembled a team of gendarmes outside the station. Inspector Lovrić came out and went over to the Countess, who was standing by her car. She noticed some flecks of blood on his uniform.

"It did not take very long for the barman to start talking," the Inspector said. "He has confirmed that he was told to corroborate the officers' story. They did not spend the night at the *Crvena Ruka*. He was given his orders by a long-time Red Hand agent in this city, despite the fact that the Red Hand has long been dormant.

"Another thing. General Auersperg has called to report that Hodžić and Novotný have been found in some kind of intoxicated state outside of the barracks. He thinks they are drunk, but their medical officer believes they may have been drugged. My men have not seen them leave the surgery."

"That's because the men inside are imposters," said the Countess. "Using whatever unholy means, this Malbrough, who is likely Dr. Cornelius Kramm himself, changed the features of two of his lackeys. For what reason, however? Hold your men for a moment, I would like to talk to the General myself."

They went back inside the station, and the Inspector called the General. Having gotten him on the line, he handed over the telephone to the Countess.

"My dear General," she said in her most charming fashion, "I need your help. I am aware of the functions of the General Philippovich barracks; however, I was wondering if there was anything else that, perhaps, is not publicly known?"

She paused for a moment while he replied. When she spoke to him, her tone hardened.

"Yes, General, I know all about military security and that I am a civilian. However, I should remind you that I operate on the authority from the Emperor himself. Anything withheld from me is being withheld from him."

The General became more co-operative.

"I see, General. You have a vault of precious and obscure items, including weapon components... And would either Captain Hodžić or Lieutenant Novotný have access to it? The Captain does? And did he visit yesterday? You don't know? Please find out at once, and, more importantly, please check the contents of the vault. I see no reason that this should take you longer than fifteen minutes, so call me back. And remember, this task is being performed at the Emperor's behest. Goodbye."

She put the receiver down.

It took the General ten minutes to call back. Lovrić answered and handed the phone to the Countess.

"A phial, containing a liquid for some kind of powerful cannon? Missing? And Captain Hodžić did visit the vault yesterday? What? You say it is useless without the other components? French, you say? Like our enemies on the battlefield, who may very well have all those components already? I fail to be reassured, General, and I doubt the Emperor will be. Let us hope I can retrieve it for you."

She put the phone down.

"To the surgery, at once," she said.

Surreptitiously, the Countess and her gendarmerie colleagues—all wearing civilian clothing—entered the establishment next door to the surgery, a hat shop. The Countess was impressed; the secret police had managed to establish themselves discreetly behind a screen, whilst the shop conducted its affairs, thus not giving rise to any suspicions from the surgery. However, she was a little concerned at being seen to disappear behind this screen with some men. A female shop assistant came over.

"Would madam and her colleagues wish to see our forthcoming catalogue?"

The Countess bowed her head and, led by the shop assistant, they disappeared behind the screen.

"Thank you, Kata," said the Inspector.

The Countess was further impressed; some kind of listening device had been set up, with two gendarmes intently listening on earphones. One of them quickly relayed the situation:

"Dr. Malbrough has been talking to a Frenchman; unfortunately, we have only just set up, and missed what was said earlier. They are talking about leaving Sarajevo, in ways to avoid the gendarmerie."

He went back to his earphone.

"The Frenchman has just referred to the Doctor as Dr. Cornelius," he added.

"We must intervene. Now!" said the Countess, pointing at the next door.

Inspector Lovrić motioned to Sergeant Ahmić and the men ran out. They smashed through the surgery door, glass flying everywhere, cutting some of them. One of the officers took a bit of glass into his eye; he gave a cry and halted his charge, blocking his colleagues' way.

In that moment, Dr. Cornelius grabbed Hart and shoved him towards the back of the premises, waving a gun at the gendarmes. Whilst moving back, he hit a switch underneath a small table.

Lovrić held a gun towards the two men. He barked an order:

"Stay where you are, or I will shoot you both down."

Dr. Cornelius pointed a gun directly at Hart's head.

"Officers, you really do not wish to be responsible for the death of this Swiss diplomat, do you? I assure you it will be portrayed as an act of gendarmerie blundering," he said. "And, given your recent failure regarding the Archduke, this would not look good for any of you, would it now?"

Inspector Lovrić looked uncertain. This man was unfamiliar. If he was a diplomat, he was not one that he had met.

Hart swiftly played his role.

"Please," he said in French, "I am just a diplomat. I am visiting this man to discuss some surgery on my face. He is highly regarded. I know nothing of what is happening, let alone why he has a gun to my head. Please do as he says. And be assured that I will assist in having him be struck off whatever medical register he is on. His behavior is most unethical, and your Emperor shall hear about all of this. I am very well connected."

Dr. Cornelius groaned inwardly. Hart was overdoing it. He swiftly shoved the Frenchman forward. It was best not to let these gendarmes have time to think or allow more theatrics from Hart.

The Inspector waved his men back. Dr. Cornelius pulled Hart onto the street, one arm around his neck, the other with a pistol aimed straight at his head. On the street, there were a few bystanders, a number of whom backed off when they saw the gun.

A strange vehicle appeared on the road, rolling up to outside the surgery—the same one that had previously been disguised as a horse and cart.

But also standing in the street was the Countess. She, too, had a pistol, aimed squarely at the two men. The vehicle door was just a couple of feet away, but her pistol prevented any further movement towards it.

"I am a Swiss diplomat..." started Hart.

"Please refrain from relaying any such nonsense to me," ordered the Countess. "I really do not believe you, not least because I am on excellent terms with Swiss diplomacy and I have no idea who you are—except that you are in league with Dr. Cornelius Kramm here. It would be regrettable if the Doctor shot you, given that we need to interrogate you both, but the retrieval of that phial is my primary concern. Shoot him, by all means, Dr. Cornelius. I will then shoot you, and I will have the phial. I could also just shoot you both anyway."

Dr. Cornelius considered his options. Was the Countess bluffing? He had come across formidable women before… and given she was already pointing a gun at him, he had to assume she meant what she said. Surrender would mean death. He was too notorious. Even if he were not to end up in America, from where he had fled after the destruction of the Red Hand, his crimes on the Continent alone would warrant his execution. No, he would use Hart as a shield and get in his vehicle—that was still his best chance. If Hart got killed, at least he would have the phial to hand over to his clients. He'd worry about explaining Hart's death later.

One of the bystanders was a man named Amar, who had been watching the proceedings. He had worked for the Red Hand for some time, and indeed enjoyed being a henchman. It was something he was good at. He had no time for politics, let alone working for radical groups. The Red Hand paid so much better—or rather Dr. Cornelius did—and the organization's demise had been a real loss to him. He was on his way to the surgery, having been told he may be needed. Now, he was in a quandary. Given where he was, the Doctor had to have seen him. If Amar shot the Countess, as his employer would no doubt wish, he would be executed for that. But if he did not, then what would happen if Dr. Cornelius escaped? He would certainly sign his death warrant if he did nothing—or worse. There had been rumors of foul experiments conducted on those who had failed the Doctor before. He decided upon a compromise.

A shot rang out. There was screaming, and the Countess, momentarily startled, looked behind her. In that moment, Dr. Cornelius and Hart bundled into the vehicle. The Doctor started it up and they drove away.

Three men had wrestled Amar to the ground. He had simply fired in the air, with his gun held low in an effort to conceal where the shot had come from. Regrettably for him, some of the bystanders had seen this and wrestled him to the ground. Now the gendarmerie had him, but he was pleased with himself. A spell in prison, perhaps, given that he had not participated in Dr. Cornelius's murder of the Baron, but a fate certainly better than the noose, or the Doctor's vengeance. Indeed, as the Doctor had escaped, he could look forward to some reward later. What he did not realize was that the Doctor was somewhat occupied with the Countess and her pistol and had not noticed Amar at all.

"A planned diversion, in case of emergencies. My people are well prepared," said the Doctor to his passenger.

"Indeed," said an impressed Hart.

Dr. Cornelius had no idea whatsoever where that shot had come from, but it was good to give the impression that he was behind it. It would help with his business image, now that his Dr. Malbrough identity was finished. He decided to emphasize his planning.

"And of course, the driver here... I was able to alert him to come to us immediately. I plan for every contingency."

Hart looked even more impressed.

"Dr. Cornelius, can this vehicle get us to the coast?"

"Yes, despite the terrain, we can get there within two hours—providing the authorities don't get organized enough to intercept us."

"If I had access to some telegraph equipment, I could arrange for us to be picked up. there any such facilities on our route? I am ignorant of this country."

Dr. Cornelius smiled. He moved over to a locker by his side and opened it.

"I trust this technology is sufficient?" he said.

Inside was a telegraph machine.

The Countess was furious, but there was no time for recrimination. She dashed over to her car and drove in pursuit, not even waiting for the Inspector who was busy with the man with the gun.

Inspector Lovrić saw her drive off and turned to Sergeant Ahmić.

"We need to the get word out. We have to stop that vehicle."

The Countess was in pursuit. Within minutes, both vehicles were out of the city. She was concerned. What if Dr. Cornelius simply decided to stop? She was by herself with only one gun. His vehicle seemed to cope well with the roads, as did hers, but she was not armored like the machine she was pursuing. Her car was something remarkable, British in origin. Her own private mechanics often had difficulty in understanding its advanced functions. Nicknamed "*Elizabeth*," she had been a gift from her friends, the British scientists Professor Saxton and Dr. Wells, in gratitude for her help during an incident in London in 1912. That was before the war. They were on opposite sides now, thanks to a terrorist with a gun. She hoped that the gendarmerie would be able to determine where they were going. She glanced at her compass and a map. They seemed to be heading roughly West.

After an hour of pursuit, they came near the town of Županjac. A barrage of fire came from nowhere, hitting the Doctor's vehicle. The Countess could see some soldiers, but they flashed by—they had only small arms. It seems that Inspector Lovrić had indeed got the word out. The bullets were ineffective, but it seemed that they knew where the vehicle was going. When it stopped, the Countess would not be alone, at least not for long.

Later, she could see where they were going. They were now in Dalmatia, heading straight for the coast, north of the city of Šibenik.

In his vehicle, Dr. Cornelius looked out of a slit at the back.

"The Countess is still in pursuit. Perhaps we should have stopped and dealt with her, but that may have slowed us down. When we get to the coast, it will be a different matter. I trust your friends will be waiting for us, Mr. Hart? And that I shall be escorted to safety, along with my driver, of course."

He cared nothing for the driver; but hiring might be difficult if word got out that he abandoned his hirelings.

"You will be looked after, Dr. Cornelius. You have, after all, given us the key to victory in this war. One thing that I am curious about. This 'Red Hand' that you used to lead. It was criminal, but it sounds political?"

Dr. Cornelius was slightly surprised by the question. No doubt Hart was fishing for any details that may be of use to him and his masters.

"Not remotely," he replied. "In fact, my late brother Fritz and I did consider calling it 'Spectre,' but Mr.

Marx had already used that word, so we thought better of it."

Hart nodded. "Pity, it has a ring to it."

The Countess could see that that the Doctor's vehicle was slowing down. Ahead was the blue of the Adriatic Sea, shimmering in the Sun.

The vehicle slowed down, coming to halt near a cove. The Countess could see some gendarmes nearby. They waved to her and ran to the vehicle. *They must have come from Šibenik*, the Countess thought. One of the gendarmes came over to her. He spoke in broken German.

"Please, Countess, stay back. These men are dangerous. Let us arrest them."

"I am well aware of that," she snapped back. "Very well. Are there more of you? These villains may well have accomplices waiting here."

"Not that we have seen," the officer replied.

He could have been no more than twenty. The Countess softened.

"Nevertheless, please be cautious," she said. "I am grateful for your concern for my safety."

He gave a shy smile and went back to his four colleagues standing around the vehicle. They were banging on it, demanding the occupants come out.

The Countess decided to be patient. It did look like they had captured Dr. Cornelius and this Frenchman called Hart. She had her pistol at the ready, in any event. She looked at Elizabeth, marveling at how the wheels were somehow intact after such a chase.

Suddenly, out of nowhere, came machine gun fire. The five gendarmes collapsed, dead.

From behind some trees came a group of Royal Navy sailors—she recognized the uniforms. Two were carrying a Maxim machine gun. She looked around. There were two men behind her with rifles aimed at her. She dropped her pistol, to their relief. Their apparent leader, a large man, dressed in a civilian tweed suit exclaimed loudly, in English, flexing his fingers:

"Always good to get one hands dirty!"

It was clear that he was the one who had done the firing. He pointed over to the Countess.

"Countess, would you be so kind as to join us?"

He pointed directly at her with a pistol. She looked at the bodies of the young gendarmes, including the one who had spoken to her. He had almost certainly saved her life; the machine gun fire had been indiscriminate. No offer of surrender had been made.

"Who are you?" she asked.

"One moment, Countess," their leader replied.

He turned to the Doctor's vehicle and slammed his palm on it twice.

"Come out! All is safe!"

The door of the vehicle opened, and Hart came out, followed by Dr. Cornelius and his driver. The Doctor stood and stared at the man who had told him to come out.

"Yes, Dr. Cornelius, it is I!"

The leader swung round to the Countess.

"I am Lord Burydan, at your service. I am in command of this operation."

He turned back and looked at the Doctor again. The Countess considered his turning his back on her more than rude. The Doctor looked at Lord Burydan. This man, along with his allies, was responsible for the destruction of the Red Hand. It was because of him that he had to fake his death, first going to Australia, and then to Berne.

"Yes, Dr. Cornelius," said Lord Burydan. "You have been unknowingly working for me. Ironic is it not? It disgusts me, of course, to use a vile criminal such as you. However, this is war, and my role in the Secret Service means that scum such as yourself have to be used. However, you are long overdue for execution for your many crimes against innocents."

"I have done as you asked; I expect safe passage and payment," said the Doctor calmly.

"Safe passage? Of course, we shall not turn you over to the Hun here…" he gestured to the Countess, "but I see no reason why we can't drop you off at an American diplomatic station on our travels."

The Countess spoke, annoyed by this vulgar Lord.

"If you mean by 'Hun' that I am German, might I point out that I am both Polish and a citizen of Austria-Hungary."

Lord Burydan sneered at her. "That makes you Hun," he said.

The Countess remained impassive.

Hart intervened. "Lord Burydan, whatever you think of this man, he was instrumental in getting us what we need to win this war within weeks—even days perhaps. We must ensure his safety and payment."

"Very well," Burydan said, with no enthusiasm. "Now, we must leave. Other policemen are no doubt on their way, along with soldiers. You, Countess, will come with us. I have no idea how much you know, but I certainly do not want the Hun to know it."

"At least, not yet," said Hart.

"I refuse," she responded. "How dare you kidnap a woman! And was it necessary to murder these men? You

47

had a machine gun, you could have asked for their surrender."

"I know you pursued our agents from Sarajevo in that car," he pointed at Elizabeth, "...and I know of your reputation as an adventurer. A fine occupation for a man, but not for a woman. As for these dead men, this is war."

"One moment," said Dr. Cornelius. He entered his vehicle, and then emerged. "It will explode when someone enters."

"But a child could enter it!" exclaimed the Countess.

He smiled at her and gestured to Lord Burydan. "This is war."

Lord Burydan simply nodded.

They moved down towards a cove. There was what appeared to be a fishing boat. The Countess realized it was some kind of camouflaged motorboat. They would no doubt be heading out to a larger vessel.

A few minutes into the sea, and a large explosion took place on the coast.

"It seems your vehicle was found, Doctor!" exclaimed Lord Burydan.

The Doctor looked satisfied. It was unfortunate that the vehicle was destroyed, but he did not want its advanced technology, built by engineers who were rumored to have shared some of Captain Nemo's mechanical secrets, falling into the hands of the Habsburg Empire. He had paid good money for its construction; he would simply do so again after he got paid.

The Countess was assessing Lord Burydan. She knew of his role in destroying the Red Hand. He, too, was an adventurer, and she had heard he had signed up to fight with his old army regiment—clearly an invention to cover for his Secret Service activities. He was right about Dr. Cornelius, of course. However, his manner and his relish in killing those poor men was disturbing. She had noticed the sailors around him appeared to regard him warily. This did not seem to be fear, but rather uncertainty, as if they did not know what he might do next.

She looked at the Adriatic coast moving further into the distance. A thought came to her. She was not being restrained. She stood up and jumped off the boat into the water. She dived underneath, then surfaced. Her dress restricted her moves, and potentially could be dangerous, but she managed to get her shoes off. Then she heard shots.

"Get back in!" Lord Burydan bellowed.

She swam back. One of the sailors helped her on board.

"What were you thinking, Miss?" the sailor asked. "There was no way you could escape."

The Countess knew that. Escape, however, had not been her intention.

An hour or so later, the boat rendezvoused with what looked like a medium-sized cargo vessel, with an American flag. The Countess knew better, and when she got aboard, she could see that it was crewed by men in British naval uniforms. Presumably, there was a strong chance of capture this close to the coast, and the men did not wish to be shot as spies.

"What is to be done with me, Lord Burydan?" asked the Countess, mustering as much dignity as she could in her drenched state.

"Frankly, I think we should take you to London to stand trial as a spy. There is word that such people will end up being executed at the Tower of London."

"Lord Burydan, I can hardly be considered a spy. Might I remind you that I have operated on the territory of my Emperor and have been brought aboard against my will. If anyone is a spy to be executed, it is you, as you were not wearing a uniform when you murdered those gendarmes."

Lord Burydan looked infuriated. Hart quickly intervened.

"We can use her. A witness. We complete our operation and release her to tell the story. Having gained the last component of our weapon from one of their own barracks, it will be a further, devastating psychological blow. She will confirm what we will make public."

Lord Burydan beamed. "An excellent idea. I love the devious French mind! To the bridge!"

Hart gently indicated to the Countess to follow him. He was concerned for her; from what he knew of her, she was an honorable foe. Although he was pleased that his plan would also have a strategic effect.

Dr. Cornelius observed all this silently. He knew well that Lord Burydan had a violent, sadistic streak, at odds with his public image. Once, this Lord had thrown two Red Hand operatives into the sea to be eaten by alligators; yet, the men had been defeated and posed no threat. He would have to be cautious, especially as the Countess had raised the man's ire.

Lord Burydan and Hart led the Doctor and the Countess to the Bridge. There, the ship's commanding officer Captain Huntly looked at her and was horrified.

"This woman is dripping wet, Lord Burydan. She must be given dry garments—although we only have naval clothes."

Lord Burydan looked irritated. "I intend to explain our plans to the Countess!"

"I really must insist, Lord Burydan."

Captain Huntly had orders to follow the commands of this arrogant Lord, but this treatment of a woman was most intolerable.

The Countess raised her hand. "Thank you, Captain. Let us not annoy Lord Burydan. And I am most curious to hear his plans."

Lord Burydan beamed again. "You have heard of the French inventor, Thomas Roch?"

The Countess nodded. "The French weapons designer?"

The Lord nodded. "Yes. He had designed a super-weapon, known as the Fulgurator. In an incident in which Monsieur Hart here was closely involved, he was working for some pirate or the other. This weapon could destroy warships at will, just like that," he clicked his fingers for emphasis. "He, and his pirate friends, ended up dead, along with a British submarine which was lost with all hands. Hart here, having actually been with Roch during that time, has been in charge of a French effort to reconstruct that weapon. We British had some information as to where a crucial element was being kept. Somehow or the other, the Hun—my apologies, the Austrian or whatever kind of Hun—had this fluid in Sarajevo. They were at a loss as to how to use it, given they had no knowledge of how to construct the Fulgurator. Now, we have it and intend to use it."

"Against warships?"

"Oh, no, Countess. Roch had underestimated his own skill. We think we can destroy towns. And we intend to do so today. Our target is Pula. We intend to wipe it off the face of the Earth. My superiors consider it would be uncivilized to destroy Vienna or Berlin, but Pula is less of problem."

The Countess was horrified. Was this possible? Pula was the major naval base for the Austro-Hungarian Navy, with warships and submarines stationed there. It would be a major defeat for the Empire.

"You say the whole city would be destroyed? Including civilians? Women and children? Those are crimes of war, to which you will be held accountable."

"Accountable by whom, Countess? I intend to see Berlin and Vienna destroyed. Why wait for negotiation or surrender? The British and French empires are to use this weapon—as we see fit. We shall conquer all those who look at us the wrong way."

At this point there was a feeling of unease throughout the bridge.

Hart spoke. "Our mission is solely to attack Pula. Berlin and Vienna are not on the agenda. Our orders are clear. In fact, I shall be adjusting the machine to limit the damage to Pula."

"Of course," Lord Burydan replied. "I merely wished to impress our power on the Countess."

"Now that you have, I would like to get into some dry clothes," the Countess said.

Captain Huntly ordered a rating to take her to his cabin and to provide her with whatever dry clothes he could find. He did not like Lord Burydan. The use of his ship as a spy boar was dangerous. A submarine would have been better, but Lord Burydan had insisted otherwise. He may have been right; patrols had left them alone. Risky, nonetheless.

The Countess looked around her as she was taken to the Captain's quarters. This was why she had jumped into the sea; it would mean having to be taken somewhere for dry clothing—a possibility for action. They passed an open door, with a man on telegraph duties. They came to the Captain's quarters.

"Stay inside, Miss" the sailor said, letting her in. He closed the door. "Charlie!" he shouted to someone. "Get some clothes for the posh foreign bird, mate!"

Posh foreign bird? thought the Countess. *These British!*

She hitched her dress up and removed a small pouch from a garter on her leg. She was pleased to see it was still there, given her dip in the sea, and even more to see that it was indeed waterproof as she had been told. Inside, were a number of small items, but it was the three small needles that were of importance.

A couple of minutes later, there was a knock on the door. She opened it and gratefully took the clothes from the sailor. Closing the door, she changed into what was a naval rating's fatigues. Naturally, it did not fit. However, it was at least more practical than her dress. There was not much she could do with her hair, but she put it up, and placed the three needles—very carefully—in it. She opened the door.

"I am ready. Please take me back to the bridge"

"I thought the Captain intended for you to stay here?"

"No, he did not."

The rating looked uncertain. This posh foreign bird could be right for all he knew. Worst that could happen was a bollocking—those were survivable.

He nodded toward the corridor and she got out and walked down. She stopped at the telegraph room, still open. She went in.

"What's in here?" she asked the operator.

She took a needle out of hair and pricked the radio operator on his hand. He was too surprised to stop her and simply gave a small cry and withdrew his hand sharply.

"Miss," said the rating, putting his hand firmly on her upper arm.

Swiftly she took another needle from her hair and scratched his hand.

After a few moments, both men were groggy. She grabbed the rating and pulled him into the cramped room, propping him by the wall. She awkwardly leaned over the telegraph operator and started sending information. It was fortunate that she had invested in being trained in such equipment within the commercial sector; even more fortunate that the *Evidenzbureau* had provided them with the information needed to contact them.

She sent the message and left the communications room. The two sailors were still groggy and unable to move. That would not last long. She walked down the corridor; she thought it best to get off the vessel, fast. She would take her chances in the sea, but only if no one saw her jump in, which would be difficult.

A rating appeared entered the corridor ahead of her, with another behind him. She acted first.

"What kind of ship is this? I have been left by myself in a cabin without any guard to attend to me. Take me at once to your Captain!"

The startled ratings took her not to the bridge, but the bow. There was a strange contraption, looking like a large cannon, but with a box at the base of it with dials on it. A map of Europe with latitude and longitude was nearby, along with a large compass. Hart was looking over it, along with Lord Burydan. The Captain was also there. To the side, watching carefully, was Dr. Cornelius.

"Ah, Countess," said Lord Burydan. "You are just in time. The co-ordinates are set. No sense in hanging around. We merely have to point this thing in the right direction and press a button. And then... Farewell, Pula!"

At sea, all military vessels had received a message from Pula. The *Evidenzbureau* had acted swiftly with the Countess's information.

Captain Jelačić of the U-Boat U-48 looked through his periscope. He could see the vessel mentioned in his orders, with a neutral American flag on it. He hoped his superior officers had gotten this right.

"Prepare torpedoes," he ordered.

"Must we be so close to Pula, Lord Burydan?" asked Captain Huntly. "If this weapon has a long range as you claim, can we not fire this weapon from much further? We may be disguised but we are somewhat exposed."

"No, Captain," replied Lord Burydan. "The first test of the weapon is best done at close quarters to ensure a direct hit. More importantly, I believe some kind of massive cloud may be seen. Have you forgotten why we have a photographer?" he pointed to a rating with camera apparatus.

This man is endangering us all, thought Captain Huntly. As soon as Lord Burydan fired his weapon, he would order the ship to move at speed to safer waters. As far as he was concerned, he would interpret his having to obey this man's orders as having come to an end with the attack on Pula.

The Countess knew she had to stall for time.

"Lord Burydan, surely attacking some land nearby would send the correct message?" she said. "Is there any need for such loss of life?"

Lord Burydan looked at her as if she were mad. He went over to the controls, pushing Hart aside.

"Total and immediate victory is what is required," he exclaimed. "No negotiation. Unconditional surrender. The end of your empire, which our diplomacy aimed at encircling for years, is one of our war objectives. And we will certainly deal with the Kaiser at the same time."

He turned a dial.

"You've turned up the power!" said Hart. "That will obliterate Pula entirely!"

"Quite so. And then, I will fire at Vienna and Berlin. Within minutes, the war will be over, our enemies in ruins. Who will worry about the Hun then? They will not come back from defeat. Britain and France will rule the world, as is our right."

"Are you mad? Those are not our orders!"

"They effectively are. Our masters gave operational control to me did they not? I will interpret that as I wish." He pointed at the map of Europe. "Thanks to you, I know very well how to use the Fulgurator." He took his pistol out of his holster. "And no-one will interfere."

Dr. Cornelius certainly was not going to; he was thinking of potential bases of operations that were not likely to be blown up by this madman. He watched as Lord Burydan moved to the controls.

The Countess took out her last needle and lunged at Lord Burydan. He smashed her across the face with his pistol and she fell back onto the ground. She had just saved Pula.

At that moment, a huge explosion ripped through the ship, as torpedoes from the U-48 hit their mark.

The Fulgurator shifted and fell off the platform. Lord Burydan wildly hit a switch on it. A bright bolt of light soared upwards into the air. Within moments, there was an explosion high in the air, with a blinding flash visible on the coast, disorientating the crew even further. The Countess had done her job. Lord Burydan was scrambling for his pistol, only to find it in the hands of the Countess. Captain Huntly had already barked orders to abandon ship.

"Abandon ship, gentlemen," said the Countess to Hart and Lord Burydan.

She pointed at them with the pistol. She had to ensure that they did not take any part of the Fulgurator with them. The Captain was busy supervising the men towards boarding the motorboat that they had used to bring the Countess and the others to the ship.

Hart moved away, but Lord Burydan lunged at the Countess. She fired at his chest, but the lurching ship meant that she hit him in the shoulder. He fell away. She pointed at the pistol again at Hart.

"Au revoir, Monsieur Hart," she said.

"Au revoir, Countess," he replied, and headed towards the lifeboat.

He considered getting the ratings to come back with rifles, but he did not fancy their chances.

Coming out of a doorway, was the rating and telegraph operator she had poisoned, recovering but still groggy.

"Captain!" she shouted.

Captain Huntly turned and saw her pointing at the men.

"They need help," she cried.

He and a rating rushed over and grabbed the men and took them away to the lifeboats. Men would die on this ship; but she was glad that the ones she had drugged were heading to safety, rather than dying without a chance. Flames came out of the doorway they had used; a fire had started and taken hold. There was a rifle on the deck. She picked it up.

She turned, only to see Dr. Cornelius attempting to take the phial from the Fulgurator. Even now, he tried to seek advantage.

Perhaps an extra payment for saving at least this, he thought.

The Countess fired in the air. The Doctor got the message. He moved away. There was no time to retrieve any parts of the weapon. And she did want to live. She fired some rapid shots into the machine. A bullet hit the phial, and its mysterious liquid splattered all over the deck.

"Join your paymasters, Dr. Cornelius."

It occurred to her that perhaps she should kill him. He deserved death, but only by legal process. More importantly, when the time came, she was unsure she could explain to God why she killed a man in cold blood.

Lord Burydan had gotten back to his feet. The pain of the shot had deranged him more than he already was. The ship was lurching to port, and the platform holding the fulgurator slammed to the side of the boat; the weapon flew off the boat and into the sea.

"Farewell, Lord Burydan!" the Countess cried.

She jumped over the side.

Lord Burydan heard her, but he was not facing her; he was staring at where the Fulgurator had gone over the side. Dr. Cornelius saw a chance. He grabbed him from behind and shoved him into the burning corridor, seeing him fall to the floor.

Captain Huntly staggered back on the bow.

"It is only us left on board, Captain," said the Doctor. "The woman has jumped, and we can do nothing for those souls in the fire. Lord Burydan went in there, looking for survivors… I fear he is lost."

But at that very moment, Lord Burydan came out of the door, aflame. He was clawing at this face.

The Captain rushed over to him and pushed him overboard. Dr. Cornelius was already in the water. He saw the Countess swimming away, avoiding the motorboat. Flames were blasting out of the doorways. There was no more he could do. He jumped into the water, grabbed Lord Burydan—as Dr. Cornelius had not bothered—and swam to the motorboat.

Once on board, it moved off at speed.

The Countess swam hard. She wanted to avoid any possibility of being taken down by the swell the ship would make when it headed to the bottom. She saw a U-boat surface. Men appeared on its conning tower. She did not want to be taken for a British sailor. She cried out in German:

"Help! I am Countess Irina Petrovska!"

Captain Jelačić saw her through her binoculars.

"We were told to look out for that woman; she is on our side. Pick her up!"

He could see the British motorboat heading away. He contacted Pula. His orders were clear: bring the woman back to Pula, other units would pick up the British.

Weeks later, Dr. Cornelius was back in Berne. Not in his office, of course. His cover had been blown, and the Swiss gendarmerie were taking the place apart. Swiss neutrality was irrelevant; it was his criminal activities in their country they were interested in. Instead, he was in a comfortable house, amusing himself with the international press. *The Sculptor of Human Flesh Lives!* screamed one tabloid headline. Somehow, the British eluded the Austro-Hungarian navy and had reached a submarine vessel of their own.

Due to his exposure in Sarajevo, he had been driven underground. But he had prepared for such eventualities. The money the French and British had paid him was substantial. And Lord Burydan was hideously scarred, a wreck of a man now. That also amused him. It was revenge for his role in destroying the Red Hand. He would now plan his next move. This war had, so far, been very profitable indeed.

In Vienna, Countess Irina Petrovska was at the Hofburg palace. She was receiving the Military Order of Maria Theresa from the elderly Habsburg Emperor, Franz Joseph. She was bursting with pride, and was in a good mood, despite news of things going badly in Galicia against the Russians. She believed the Russians would be fought back. She had been complimented on her beauty, but she was more pleased with the praise for her bravery. Any problems about her being woman—and not formally in the military—were set aside. She was happy that the gendarmes from Sarajevo were at the ceremony; given the June assassination, this success would help their reputation.

The Emperor gave her the medal.

"Thank you, my child. You have done well."

He said it in Polish, which for the Countess was a great sign. The heir presumptive, Karl, was present. He had expressed a wish to listen to her ideas on Poland. She was delighted. Perhaps Franz Ferdinand's thinking on reform would still see light. But first, there was a war to be won.

The Telepath of Galicia

Deuxième Bureau,[7] Paris, 21 March 1915

The man in the chair spat out a bloodied tooth. His interrogator had hit him in the front teeth with a truncheon. He had told them everything he knew. Surely his explanation was not that terrible? He looked around him. He was in a small room with just a table against a wall and a couple of other chairs. Two men were standing around. His interrogator was someone he recognized; a policeman seconded to the Deuxième Bureau. His skill in extracting information from criminals was renowned. He looked down at his bloodied military tunic. How could they unleash this man upon him—a French army officer?

The building shook a little. "Release me, let me fight the Hun! They must be shelling us!"

The interrogator was about to hit the man in the chair again, but Simon Hart, the man next to him, dressed in a fashionable suit, raised his hand to stay him and spoke to the man in the chair.

"Maréchal, you are a traitor. Not even worth addressing by your rank. You are not going anywhere."

"I gave a useless liquid to the Russians—our allies!" replied Maréchal. "I was trying to foster good relations!"

---

[7] France's external military intelligence service, created in 1871.

That earned him a truncheon blow in the ribs from the interrogator.

The interrogator, a large thick-set man named Jacquemain, came right up to Maréchal's face. "You *sold* that liquid to the Russians. We know this because you have told us. It was the property of France, and a state secret."

Maréchal nodded dumbly. He had tried to suggest that what he had done was in the interest of France. However, confronted with his bank statements, the blows of the truncheon had made him reveal the truth. He had not slept for some time, and was not thinking straight, and thus repeated his old story. He knew that this would soon be over. He could not imagine they would execute him. He did no harm, surely?

The man in the smart suit spoke again. "Maréchal, why was Professor Ossipoff so interested in the Lynx? You claim not to know, yet you have corresponded and met with him on cosmology. Indeed, it was this hobby of yours that gained you a place here in this section. I recruited you."

"I don't know," said Maréchal, "They just thought it was something they could analyze, given we could not find out why it is now inert. Ask Ossipoff."

"I would, except he has gone back to Russia. In fact, directly after you gave him the Lynx, he boarded a train and left Paris." Hart turned to the interrogator. "I am not sure there is much more to be gained from him. Still, see what you can do, I must make a report."

The interrogator nodded.

"Monsieur Hart, please! I am a French officer! I have a wife and children," pleaded Maréchal.

Hart ignored him as he left. Jacquemain looked at Maréchal.

"I am puzzled," he said. "You sold out France for just 5000 francs?"

"I wished to make sure that my wife could enjoy the finer things in life," replied Maréchal.

"But what of your mistress? Surely some of that would have gone to her? Who is she, we have not found out."

"I have no mistress; I am loyal to my wife!"

The interrogator looked appalled. "I can see you are no true Frenchman—all becomes clear." He pondered for a moment. "I have good news for you," he finally said.

Maréchal looked hopeful.

"You will soon have a mistress," Jacquemain said, "One who has loved many. Soon, you feel the tender embrace of Madame Guillotine!"

Hart headed down the corridor. The building shook a little. Several staff were coming downstairs from above. He recognized the man he was going up to see, General Charles-Joseph Dupont, the head of the Deuxième Bureau. He saluted him.

"General Dupont, I can give you an update on the Lynx situation."

"Good, come with me, Monsieur Hart."

Along with some of the General's aides they headed towards a quartermaster's office. The General sat down on a chair behind a desk and dismissed his aides. He motioned to Hart to sit down. Hart took his chair. The building shook again.

"Zeppelins," said the General. "The Hun are bombing our city from the air, the savages. It is appalling that we must come down here in the early hours. What is the latest from our prisoner?"

"I can confirm what we have previously found out from him and our own observations. Aside from his military career, he had an amateur interest in cosmology and corresponded with Russian academics, one of whom came to Paris, a Professor Ossipoff. Maréchal told us that he met regularly with Ossipoff and discussed the specialized work in my department. This included the fact that we hold the Lynx. The Professor was very interested and was clearly aware that Maréchal was keen on obtaining money to spend on his wife. This was exploited, with the Professor who offered him money and assurances that was all for scientific use. He claimed that petty rules should not come between allies and that they would publicly publish any findings and claim that they had come up with the Lynx formula themselves. The only positive aspect is that no intelligence outside specialist information was divulged."

The General absorbed Hart's words.

"The Lynx," he said, "was used to read minds. However, it is now dormant? Is it possible that the Russians have found a way to activate this serum?"

Hart nodded. "That is my fear. It was created by the chemist Brion at his institute. When the liquid came into our custody, it stopped working after a few days, mystifying both my section and the Institut Brion. I even tried it upon myself, to no effect. It is puzzling that the Russians are so interested. We know the Okhrana have their Vozduhoplavatel research center, set up covertly in 1909 after the previous year's Tunguska event, to see if there is a threat to Russia from beyond Earth."

"I am aware of that, Hart."

"My apologies, General. It is not improbable that they are looking at matters such as mind-reading. I suspect Professor Ossipoff has some connection with Vozduhoplavatel."

"They may think that the Lynx is of extra-terrestrial origin, although we have no doubt that Brion created it. Is it possible that the Russians think they can re-activate the serum?"

"They would not have gone to this effort if they did not think that they could use it," replied Hart.

"We cannot allow any other power to have this knowledge," said the General. "Russia may be our ally today, but they certainly have not been in the past. If they were able to find a way to use it, they could become the most powerful country on Earth; no nation could keep any secrets from them. Only we French can be trusted with its custodianship—and, in the event of making it work again—its civilized use."

Hart nodded vigorously.

The General continued. "The matter is delicate, given that Russia is an ally during this war. Professor Ossipoff is already back on Russian soil—weeks back. It is unfortunate that our own sources in Saint Petersburg only just relayed the information of Maréchal's treachery. We may never have known some of it was missing, let alone that he was responsible..."

Hart felt a little uneasy. He was all too aware that he had recruited Maréchal to his section. It was why, when the report came though of the officer's possible treachery, he had promptly brought in Jacquemain to swiftly extract information.

There was a knock at the door.

"Enter," the General said.

A private walked in, saluted, and gave the General a sealed file.

"I was told to bring this to you at once, General."

The General took the file and read it.

"Hum. It seems, Monsieur Hart, that the Russians not only know how to use the Lynx, but also plan to do so."

He gave the file to Hart to read. It contained a short summary of the information emanating from their source in Saint Petersburg. Hart turned pale. The Russians, at their cosmological facility at Vozduhoplavatel, had made a breakthrough with activating the Lynx, and now planned to use it.

"Our sources will be telling us more," said the General, "and quite possibly, the Central Powers will find out too. Saint Petersburg is riddled with spies."

Saint Petersburg, Fontanka 16,[8] 9 April 1915

Dr. Cornelius Kramm sat outside the office of the head of the Russian Department of Police, who also controlled the feared secret police, the Okhrana. He looked at the thick wooden door of the office. No doubt its thickness was to ensure that conversations within could not be overhead. He did not like to be kept waiting. These new paymasters had not been keen to meet at their headquarters, but he had insisted, to be certain that it was them who wished to employ him, and not some old enemies luring him into a back street to kill him. Perhaps that is why they were keeping him waiting. This would not have happened in the old days, he thought, when he was one of the leaders of the feared criminal organization, the Red Hand. But those days were gone. Now, he sold his criminal expertise to the highest bidder. As al-

---

[8] Headquarters of the Okhrana, the Tsarist secret police established in 1881.

ways, he was professionally known as "Dr. Cornelius," rather than by his full name. On the positive side, he thought, this job would provide a great deal of money. Not rubles, but pound sterling, straight into one of his many Swiss accounts. He had insisted on an advance, which he knew had been paid this very day. The money was such that he had agreed to take the job, but he had never entirely trusted…

"…the Russians," said the young man on the other side of the door, looking at it as if he could see through it, "...since some of his Moscow-based Red Hand agents once tried to break away from his organization and set up a rival group. He will take revenge if we cheat him, but if we pay him the rest of the money after the job is done, he will be content."

"He will get paid and will have no idea that we stole all his secrets," said an overweight middle-aged man seated at a nearby desk. He was A.V. Brune de St Hippolite, the head of the Department of Police.

Another man seated behind the desk spoke:

"Yuri Klebb, is he giving away any secrets at the moment?"

"No, Professor Ossipoff," replied the young man, respectfully. "We need to make him think about them. It needs to come to the forefront of his mind. But I will have plenty of opportunity to have such conversations with him during the mission."

"We know he speaks English, German and passable Russian. What language does he think in?" asked Ossipoff.

"English," Klebb replied.

"Your mastery of languages is why we have selected you for this mission," said Brune de St Hippolite.

"Yuri has done well," said the Professor. "Whilst training with us at Vozduhoplavatel, he mastered the use of the Lynx serum, or rather the abilities to read minds it confers."

"Providing he does not read our minds!" said the spymaster half-jokingly.

"By forcefully concentrating on a particular topic, as we have trained ourselves, we can ensure it is not so. Background thoughts are not heard, but this does not last long, although it should be enough for this meeting!"

"He is thinking random, undetailed, thoughts now about his dead brother," Klebb said, "and something about a favor he is owed by a Russian friend for fixing someone's face... Now he is wondering what has become of a Lord Burydan—an enemy of his..."

"Enough now, Klebb. As you said you can find out more from him in good time," said the spymaster.

"Yes, sir," said Klebb.

"We must finish this meeting quickly, so that the mission begins. Time works against us," said the spymaster. "Professor Ossipoff, you have replicated the Lynx?"

"Yes, our chemical team at Vozduhoplavatel has done so. Of course, the Meyral effect will fade soon."

"This Meyral effect, could it return?"

This was Professor Ossipoff's specialty and he enthusiastically went into it.

"The effect has appeared above the Earth for a few months at time. It can be seen with a good pair of binoculars, as sort of a spiral effect, often mistaken for an *aurora borealis*, which is not surprising, given it's in orbit above Finland. It's appeared before and fades away. Our research into psychic abilities at Vozduhoplavatel investigated if such cosmic phenomena had any effect on the human brain. We discovered that Meyral does indeed emit waves affecting it. Its effect is slight, perhaps momentary. Someone with latent abilities can read a mind for a moment or bend a spoon...

"However, Brion's Lynx serum works in combination with the effect, unleashing a much greater power of the mind. Had Brion not developed the Lynx during that period of the Meyral effect, then it would have been near useless, perhaps being able to mind read for a couple of minutes, if even that! Again, it only works on those who have those latent abilities. The French really did not think to consider any other factors, which is typical of them..."

The spymaster interrupted him. "Yes, thank you, Professor. I'd like to know if the effect will return after its current activity?"

The Professor looked a bit put out, then answered: "We have studied the Meyral effect for years now. With each appearance, it moves further from the Earth, longer each time. Currently, our measurements indicate that its effect on the brain gets weaker each time. We believe there are only a few weeks before its appearance ends. The next time it appears, its effects will be negligible. Eventually, it will leave the Solar System altogether. It is not likely we shall ever know what it is, or why it materialized over Earth a few decades ago. Perhaps there is an intelligence directing it, but we think it more likely to be some natural phenomenon."

"We must then move quickly, as we planned," the spymaster said. "Before I can go to the Tsar with this, we must have a successful operation. Then, we can quickly place agents around the world to find the secrets of the other great powers. And of course, the many revolutionaries at home will soon find all their plans exposed."

Klebb had to restrain himself from reacting. The spymaster's thoughts—his defenses were useless—were clear to him. The reason to delay talking to the Tsar had nothing to do with presenting a successful mission. It was about consolidating control over the entire Lynx project. It seems there were those whom the spymaster feared who would like to gain control of the Lynx, and indeed the whole of the Vozduhoplavatel research.

Klebb caught a couple of names in the spymaster's mind: Rasputin, and one General Boris Liatoukine... The spymaster intended to use the Lynx to read their minds. Klebb could see other thoughts; his superior wanted to improve the reputation of the Okhrana, which had been damaged after a series of scandals, and even expand its domain. Klebb would keep all this to himself, of course. He wanted to remain in the good books of his superiors.

"Let us bring in this Dr. Cornelius," said Brune de St Hippolite. "And no mention of mind-reading!"

They all laughed.

"I had better take my leave," said Professor Ossipoff.

He left via a side-door. The spymaster went to the main door, opening it. He beckoned in Dr. Cornelius and offered him a chair.

"Dr. Cornelius, I take it that what we are offering you is satisfactory? You charge highly."

"I do, but my costs are high, as are my services—including the face changes that we shall need. No one else can do what I do," the Doctor added.

Not for long, thought Klebb.

"You are of German extraction, are you not?" asked the spymaster.

The Doctor took off his gold-rimmed spectacles and cleaned them.

"I am an American," he replied. "But my only concern is myself. I think my reputation demonstrates that."

Klebb read the Doctor's mind and saw that the Doctor really did not care about his roots, just money and power.

The spymaster indicated Klebb.

"Doctor, may I introduce Yuri Klebb. He is one of our finest agents and a superb linguist."

Both men stood up and shook hands.

"I will swiftly go over the mission," continued Brune de St Hippolite. "You are both to go to Galicia, behind enemy lines. Your task, Doctor, will be to bodyguard Klebb. Using your skills, both of you will wear different faces. You will use the contacts you claim to have in the area to assist with the following objectives. One: Gathering intelligence on the German and Austro-Hungarian military plans. Two: Gathering information on those Polish politicians who seek to unite Russian Poland with Galicia under Habsburg control. We desire the opposite, of course. Three: If the opportunity presents itself, assassinating the Austro-Hungarian Field Marshal Franz Conrad von Hötzendorf, or another senior German or Habsburg officer.

"Objectives one and two will be primarily achieved by Klebb using some special listening equipment. Objective three can be done with weapons you, Doctor, claim to have secreted in the vicinity. Klebb has the authority to change these objectives if the need arises, but within reason."

Klebb concentrated on Cornelius, starting with more mundane matters, but always with the covert objective of extracting information about his surgical skills and his underworld knowledge from his mind. The so-called "Sculptor of human flesh" was thinking in English of the equipment he would need. He still had a few contacts left from the Red Hand. He thought that some of them might provide him with surgical tools, travel arrangements, accommodation, etc. Klebb noted that the Doctor realized that, these days, buying loyalty from his former subordinates was more important than instilling fear in them. However, he was not thinking of his surgical skills. Klebb would have to trigger those thoughts by conversation. There would be plenty of time for that later. Dr. Cornelius's thoughts were beginning to fade. It would soon be time for another dose of the Lynx serum.

"If there is nothing else," concluded Brune de St Hippolite, "I suggest you start on your journey."

Austro-Hungarian Army mobile field hospital, Galicia (Poland), Austro-Hungarian Empire, 15 April 1915

The Countess Irina Petrovska looked sadly at the lifeless body in front of her. Private Dabrowski was dead. He had lost an arm in a recent battle against the Russians. His life had been saved, but an infection had taken hold and claimed his life.

"He has gone," said the doctor attending him, although this was already clear.

A military priest was also present. He turned to the Countess.

"Thank you for calling me, Countess,"

She nodded her head. "It was important that he receive the last rites. God played a great role in his life."

Later, after the body had been taken away, the doctor said to the Countess:

"You make an excellent nurse, Countess."

She was already making up the bed for the next patient.

"Thank you, doctor," she replied. "It is only my duty."

"You have a visitor, in my office."

"Who is it?"

"I don't know; he had a couple of officers escorting him."

The Countess then knew who it was.

"I shall see what he wants. Thank you for informing me."

With that, she went off to meet her visitor. The doctor looked at her as she walked away. She was a very beautiful, auburn-haired woman. Despite her slightly haughty manner, she was respected by patients and staff alike. She was a widow, although it was rumored that she had been involved with a Croatian U-Boat captain.

Lucky man, the doctor thought, before moving on to his next patient.

The Countess recognized the soldier on guard outside the door, a grizzled-looking man in his late 30s.

"Hello Sergeant Mayr. How is your family?"

"Very well, ma'am," the Sergeant replied in an Austrian accent. "My oldest boy is joining my old regiment, in fact."

The Countess nodded. "He will do the emperor proud, like his father."

She meant what she said, but was uneasy. Would the Sergeant's son end up like the poor boy she had just watched die earlier? The Empire's cause was just, but the cost had been high, and there was no end to it yet.

"Thank you, ma'am. I've heard of your good work here." She smiled appreciatively. "He's waiting. It's an urgent matter, he said."

"It must be for him to leave Vienna," she replied.

The Sergeant grinned and knocked on the door.

"Come," came a voice from the inside.

The Sergeant opened the door.

"The Countess has arrived," he announced to the occupants.

"She may enter," said the same voice. However, the Countess had already done so. She recognized both men who hastily stood up to greet her. Sitting behind the desk was Prince Wilhelm, the head of the section of the *Evidenzbureau* which dealt with threats to the Empire of an unusual nature. On the other side of the desk was Lieutenant Vuljanić, who had joined the section a year previously.

"Please, please, do sit down," said the Prince.

Since the Countess had saved the naval base of Pula from destruction by the lunatic British Lord Burydan, she had become a favorite of the Emperor. She certainly knew it, and the Prince, whilst effectively her superior, knew very well that she would not put up with too many airs from him.

The Countess took a seat. They exchanged some pleasantries regarding her children, who were in Vienna, where she felt they would be safe. The Prince then turned to the reason why he was here.

"We have received information that the Russians have developed some kind of mind-reading technique. They have sent a man equipped with this ability— apparently a drug addict—to spy on our forces here, and find out about our future plans."

Once, the Countess would have dismissed such a story as outlandish, the fantasy of a degenerate mind. However, experience had taught her otherwise.

"The creature I encountered on the Trans-Siberian express in 1906—the one that murdered my husband and many others—was able to absorb the minds of its victims. So, mind-reading certainly seems possible. However, are your sources impeccable?"

"Yes," the Prince replied. "The information came from more than one source. However, it is not just your experience with such matters that the Empire needs. Another target for this operative is to investigate the Polish Supreme National Committee. I understand you have contacts with them?"

The Countess nodded. "Of course. They're based in Kraków, where I grew up." She noticed an interested look from the Lieutenant. "Lieutenant, are you familiar with the politics of Galicia?" she asked.

"Not in any great depth, I'm afraid, ma'am," he replied

"The Supreme National Committee, of whom I am a supporter, wants to unify Galicia with Russian Poland, under the rule of our Emperor. It is past time my countrymen were liberated from the Tsar. My husband was from Russian Poland, and I moved there to be with him. However, I could not stand seeing my people become part of such a backward empire. I did like the Tsar and the Tsarina on a personal level, but they did not do enough for my people. They have come under the influence of that degenerate Rasputin. Take it from me, monks like him are just trouble." She realized she was digressing. "Yes, I certainly do have contact with the committee, and it's imperative the Russians do not interfere with them."

She knew she was well known as a Polish national-ist, but one working within—and for—the Habsburg Empire. She was also concerned about the part of Poland occupied by Germany. She hoped the Kaiser would be reasonable after they won the war.

"Excellent," said the Prince. "There is a third reason why we need you. The agent the Russians are sending has a bodyguard. It is Dr. Cornelius."

Dr. Cornelius! The Countess had encountered him before. His criminal activities in Sarajevo the previous year had been part of a successful plot to give the French and British a super-weapon that could have won them the war.

"I will appreciate the opportunity to meet him again," she said.

The Lieutenant piped up. "We believe that he has used his surgical skills to change the appearance of both himself and the Russian agent. You won't be able to recognize him."

The Countess nodded. It made sense. The Doctor's description had been circulated to all their agents throughout the Empire. And perhaps this telepath was known as well.

"As you know," aid the Prince, "I would much pre-fer you to have stayed in Vienna as a journalist rather than coming out here as nurse, but it seems to have turned out well in light of this assignment."

"I had to help my fellow countrymen more directly. This war has not gone so well. I can hardly sit around in Vienna whilst it rages here. Have you any idea of the suffering of our soldiers?"

"I get reports," said the Prince. "My son is on the front."

The Countess softened. "My apologies," she said.

"Accepted," said the Prince. He continued. "Your mission is to stop these two men. The implications of a mind-reader are devastating. Try and capture them alive, if possible. The Lieutenant and the Sergeant will work with you. You are in charge, but they are not to leave your side." He raised his hand. "Please, no protests."

"I had no intention of protesting," she replied. "I am delighted to have their assistance."

"You will have a liaison to the military here as well. General Borojević has been briefed and has agreed to give you whatever you need."

"Borojević has an excellent reputation, due to his actions against the Russians at Przemysl and in the Carpathians. I look forward to meeting him," said the Countess. "One of your countrymen, I believe?" she said to the Lieutenant, whom she knew to be Croatian.

"Yes, ma'am," he said. "It will be an honor to meet him."

"Let us get started without delay, then. The Empire is counting on us."

Kraków, Galicia, 16 April 1915, 8:45 p.m.

Dr. Cornelius and Yuri were in a back street ending with the back wall of the Hotel Central. Yuri had some earphones on, connected to some kind of sucker attached to the wall. Wires connected to the earphones on the sucker were linked to a small box in front him. Both men were dressed poorly. They looked like peasants from the countryside, or vagrants. That had been the Doctor's plan, and thus far, it had worked.

Cornelius looked at Yuri. He was unrecognizable from before. Previously, he had a full head of hair and a young face. Now, he was balding, with a rough, middle-aged face. The Doctor was satisfied with his work. For himself, he had decided to wear the face of an older man with a short beard, wearing cheap, slightly fractured spectacles. He had perfected the technique of face sculpting so much that he was able to change his own features with no assistance. He could also change teeth, but this was difficult, and he had not bothered to do so this time. It hardly mattered anyway; he had yet to hear of anyone being recognized solely by their teeth.

Cornelius' thoughts turned back to the street. It was quiet, no one was present. He idly wondered about the machine Klebb was using; he must take a discreet look at some point. Given that its owner was a drug addict, that might not be too difficult.

Earlier that morning, he had come across Klebb injecting something into his arm—some kind of pinkish fluid. "It helps keep me alert," The Russian had said. The Red Hand had once been involved in drug trafficking, so Cornelius knew their effect. Whatever Klebb used, it made him weak and unreliable, but that also meant that he may be able to manipulate him if he had to.

Klebb had caught the Doctor's thoughts and was pleased the surgeon had no idea of the true purpose of the serum. However, his main concern now was to listen to the thoughts of those inside the hotel. It was fortunate indeed that the Polish Supreme National Committee was meeting on the other side of this wall, meaning that there was a clear line of thought to their minds, with no interference from any others'. However, stray thoughts did occasionally come from hotel staff and clients, the nearby buildings and, of course, Dr. Cornelius.

The meeting inside was ending. At first, it had been difficult to identify who was who. When hearing thoughts, people did not often identify themselves. However, thoughts seemed to have a different "sound" to them when their owner was speaking. So Klebb would zoom in on those, and at the same time, scan the thoughts of those listening. They would identify the speaker. In a short time, he was able to ascertain the composition of the Committee and felt he knew more about their politics than they did themselves.

A stray thought came into his head, but not from the meeting. He jumped up. "Someone's coming," he said to Cornelius, but the Doctor saw no one. Then, out of a door halfway down the alley came an old man. They had both prepared for this eventuality and immediately had bottles to their mouths, looking convincingly like a pair of drunks.

The man who had come out of the doorway, turned, and saw them. He came down the street. He was wearing a flat cap and coat, holding a lamp. Cornelius quietly cursed; it looked like a night watchman. They started singing in a drunken manner in German. Since the Doctor knew no Polish, they were to pose as Austrian vagrants, traveling from place to place. The watchman came up to them.

"Go home!" he said in Polish. Then he looked at the box on the floor, with the headphones out. "What's that?" he asked.

"Distract him," Cornelius said in English.

Klebb complied, picking up the box and talking to the old man in German. "It's where we keep our food," he said.

Meanwhile, Cornelius had taken a small whisky bottle out of his pocket and opened it. The old man looked at him.

"I need a sip of the good stuff; do you want some?" the Doctor said.

Something feels wrong here, the old man thought.

Klebb knew exactly what the Doctor was going to do. "Look, let me open it for you," he said, drawing the old man's attention back to him.

The Doctor brought out a cloth, poured some of the bottle's contents onto it, then moved swiftly behind the watchman and placed the cloth firmly on the old man's mouth. The watchman dropped his lamp, but struggled ferociously. He was not going to his death meekly. Klebb grabbed hold of him, but the wily old man deliberately fell over, pulling both men to the ground.

Momentarily freed, the old man stood up. He then gave a horrendous gasp and collapsed.

Cornelius took his pulse. "He's dying. The poison has done its work. We must leave immediately. He will be found, but it will be assumed that he died of natural causes."

Klebb placed his equipment into the bag and then the two men disappeared into the night.

Later, they arrived at their lodgings. It was little more than a small, run-down room. Klebb looked at it distastefully.

"Could we not have a better place than this? We could have rented somewhere slightly more congenial and cheaper than your man's rent which you have on expenses."

"Renting elsewhere means we have to register," Cornelius explained patiently, "and that can be made available to the police, who are no doubt checking people's movements, given the war. Certainly, if we eliminate anyone in too obvious a fashion, they will immediately start checking hotels and so on. My contact rents us this room for a high fee, yes, but for this, there is no registration to be shown to the police or anyone else. He uses this building for certain, er, business operations, although it is currently empty, due to the war. Remember also, if we are discovered, he will likely have to abandon the property."

Klebb seemed satisfied. The Doctor continued:

"If anyone asks, we are here as night watchmen, just like, I suspect, that man was. We need to be more circumspect with your equipment. Once that had made him suspicious, we had to kill him. Incidentally, how did you know the man was going to come out of the door?"

"I head the door unlocking," Klebb said.

"I heard nothing," replied the Doctor.

"One of my talents is my excellent hearing. That is a requirement when using the listening equipment."

The Doctor looked satisfied. Klebb decided to move things along.

"I've heard enough information tonight. Your explosive device will be needed."

"The bomb is secreted in this very building," the Doctor said. "My contact has provided us with something that will destroy the entire hotel."

Klebb was reading Cornelius's mind. He was delighted that thoughts of the bomb-maker came into his mind. Now, he knew who he was and where he was based—Berlin of all places! *The remnants of the Red Hand must work very well indeed to be able to construct and smuggle a bomb all the way to Galicia*, he thought. The Okhrana must get hold of the bomb-maker and make use of his talents.

The effect of the serum was starting to wear off. He decided to try for more while he still could.

"It did cross our minds to use your talents to infiltrate someone into the Polish group, someone disguised as one of their members," he said. "However, it was assessed as being too risky. Such an infiltrator may not come across convincingly to those who know him well."

The Doctor simply nodded. His thoughts were in agreement with Klebb's words, and he wished to get some rest. However, there were some other thoughts in the background, but Klebb could not hear them. So he pressed on. He had been cautious up to now, but sensed that the surgeon's secrets were within his grasp.

"Your skills must have been hard to come by," he said, raising his hands, "Of course, I don't expect you to tell me how."

And there it was! At the forefront of the Doctor's mind was how he had come by his surgical skills in the first place. There were other thoughts of sinister experiments on humans that came later to help perfect them, but now Klebb knew the genesis of what had made Dr. Cornelius Kramm the sculptor of human flesh.

"I certainly will not," said Cornelius.

Klebb laughed. "Let us retire. Tomorrow, we have a long day ahead of us. I need to send a message to my superiors, but first, we must try and find some enemy officers we can eavesdrop on. Our effort came to nothing today. It is important that we find out about their military plans."

Kraków Gendarmerie Headquarters, 17 April 1915

The Countess was seated at a table with a man in an Austro-Hungarian General's uniform. He was balding, fit-looking, and wore a moustache. They had been introduced to each other and had sat down. She was well-dressed, as always, but her garments were all in gray. She felt it would not do to dress too fashionably in a town so close the front.

"It is good of you to come to Kraków and meet with us, General Borojević. Your time as commander of the Third Army must be precious."

"Countess", replied the General, "it is my pleasure. I am aware of your activities last year in Sarajevo and the debt our navy owes you. I must thank you myself for what you have done on behalf of my men, although, sadly, they can never know. I am delighted to be your liaison. Whatever I can do to help, I will. You need only to ask."

The Countess was always impressed by such proper chivalrous attitudes. She would often get negative attitudes due to her being a woman.

"Thank you, General. Of course, we have much to thank you for, given your distinguished efforts to defend us against the Russians. I am also pleased to say that the travel book you wrote, *Durch Bosnian*, when you were stationed in Sarajevo, was of great use in helping familiarize myself with that city."

The General smiled. "I am honored to hear it. Lieutenant Vuljanić? You sound like a fellow Croatian."

"I am sir, from Karlovac, now in the 96th Karlovac Infantry Regiment," the Lieutenant replied, a little nervous for being in the General's presence.

"A fine town. I'm from Banovina, myself. Now, I believe you both have a remarkable story for me?"

The Countess related what the Prince had told her.

"It is almost unbelievable—a mind-reader? And this Dr. Cornelius, he is able to shape faces at will? But I must believe this not only because of the high regard the Emperor has for you, Countess, but also because I am aware of some of the materials the Empire keeps in Sarajevo—the advanced technologies, artifacts from other worlds and so on. Mind-reading would be a powerful weapon, one that could change the fate of this war."

The Countess responded. "It is difficult to know how to counter it effectively. We chose to meet you here as it's less likely that these men would be watching this station. We assume that places where soldiers gather would be their first target. Nonetheless, all the rooms around this one are empty—although we do not know the range of the thought-reader, or telepath as such people are called."

"I will issue orders for my senior officers to limit their interactions with anyone they do not know—something which they should be doing anyway—and to immediately report anyone who may be acting strangely. That might help us in avoiding this thought-reader and also any infiltration by a lookalike. I could bury this town under troops, checking everyone to help you find these men, if you will?"

"No, General. The telepath is likely to able to sense troops around every corner. Furthermore, we need to catch him and Cornelius. They could elude your troops and head elsewhere. This threat must be dealt with here and now."

"At least, let me provide you with some troops. Some of my men are from this city; their local knowledge could prove useful to you."

The Countess pondered this. "We already have the local gendarmes' cooperation, but I suppose that a reserve of a few soldiers could be useful—but they would have to await our call."

There was a knock on the door. The Countess and the General simultaneously said "Enter," then both laughed.

A Sergeant entered, swiftly saluting the General. "Mr. Jaworski has called," he said to the Countess. "He is waiting for you at the Hotel Central."

"General, I am sorry but I must leave," said the Countess. "I think time is of the essence. Lieutenant, please liaise with the General's staff in order to arrange for his reserve."

They made their farewells, with the General bowing to the Countess. Then she and the Sergeant left the station.

Outside, there was an armored car. On closer inspection, it appeared to be an open-topped civilian roadster, but it had armor plating all around it. The Sergeant opened the back door, letting the Countess in, then went to sit in the driver's seat.

"How are you finding driving *Elizabeth*?" she asked.

"Not a problem, Countess," he answered. "It seems able to ride smoothly on any terrain, and at high speeds too."

"Excellent." She only let trusted people drive her *Elizabeth*.

It had been a gift to her from her British friends, Professor Saxton and Dr. Wells, before the war. It was given to her on the condition that she would never share its technology. The *Evidenzbureau* were keen to learn its secrets, but she had kept her word. The car remained a mystery; it was not clear who had built it, or indeed if there were others like it. Her friends had told her that they thought it would be best used in her hands. Certainly, a fleet of such vehicles had not been deployed by the

British, deepening the mystery. It had served her well, and she had allowed its use as an ambulance, saving many lives in the recent battles against the Russians.

"Proceed, Sergeant," she said.

The car drove off.

Klebb and Dr. Cornelius had changed into more respectable garb, and the surgeon had changed their faces slightly. That, coupled with a wash and shave, made them look like the salesmen from Salzburg they claimed to be.

They were seated at the Wierzynek restaurant on the main square, eating lunch, not far from several officers enjoying their lunch. The Doctor was puzzled by Klebb's tactics. How would they be able to use the listening equipment? And what did they expect to hear if they did? It was not a given that these officers would be discussing military plans. They had already visited three cafés that morning, and Klebb had been displeased by all of them. What was he up to?

Klebb looked at him and smiled. "I think we are done now here, but we can take our time. Our next engagement is not until the evening."

The Doctor wondered as to this change of mood.

Klebb was indeed very pleased. He had been scanning the minds of the officers and the soldiers they had passed or sat nearby all day. The cafés had provided scraps of information. However, the German colonel sitting at the next table had been thinking about an offensive by the Central Powers that was to take place on 5 May. This was vital information, which he had to get to Saint Petersburg at once.

Tonight, they would kill some Polish politicians and tomorrow, they would assassinate a top Habsburg officer. On top of that, he now had the secrets of Dr. Cornelius. He started thinking of his future. He would be well rewarded for this. His work may well ensure Russian victory here in Galicia. Perhaps he would become a favorite of the Tsar and Tsarina? He would certainly give better them advice than that damned monk of theirs. He started laughing.

Dr Cornelius looked at him. "What amuses you?" he asked. And Klebb simply laughed more. *An effect of his being a drug addict*, the sculptor of human flesh thought.

At the hotel, the Countess was meeting with Władysław Leopold Jaworski of the Polish Supreme National Committee. They were in the manager's office, with the door slightly ajar, and the Sergeant standing outside. They had made small talk at first, reminiscing about the past. They had known each other for several years.

"You say, Irina, that there is an espionage effort against us?" said Jaworski, a man who looked around fifty, balding with a beard. "I must say that we had assumed that already."

"I am glad to hear it," replied the Countess, "but there does seem to be a particular effort, of which I cannot say too much. It is very real."

"And you cannot tell me what this effort is?"

"I fear I cannot."

Jaworski looked affronted. "Am I not to be trusted?"

The Countess soothed him. "Of course, you are. You know that I hold you in the highest regard, but you must know that there can be no exceptions in security matters. However, as you can see, I have chosen to share

88

these concerns with you. I have little doubt that you can help us deal with it."

He looked placated. "Of course, I will do whatever I can to help," he said.

"Thank you. Tell me, have you noticed any strange behavior amongst your Committee? Anyone acting out of character?" The Countess was trying to determine if the Doctor had already infiltrated the Committee with a lookalike, having satisfied herself that Jaworski was not thanks to their initial small talk.

"No, not all. Are you suggesting that we have a traitor amongst us?" he asked, horrified.

"Not necessarily. Has there been any strange incidents? Anything out of the ordinary? Any incidents of any kind?"

Jaworski pondered for a moment. "Well, there was the death of a night watchman at the back of this hotel. He was starting his work early, and it seems he collapsed from a heart attack."

"That is unfortunate, but is there a connection with the Committee?"

Jaworski looked awkward. "Yes, we were having a meeting there at the time the gendarmes think he died. That's why I'm here today, preparing for another meeting tonight."

"What meeting? I was not aware of it."

"It was a meeting of some delicacy."

Now it was the Countess's turn to feel affronted. "I may not be a member of the Committee, but my work for the Polish people, I think, does entitle to me to the courtesy of being informed about such meetings. Kindly tell me what transpired."

"We are trying to set down the groundwork for the union of the Austrian Poland with Russian Poland, after our armies defeat the Russians, of course. As you know, Piłsudski's incursion was not the success we had all hoped for."

"I strongly supported that incursion myself. However, I have lived in the Russian Poland. I can assure you that the fear of the Tsar is strong. Hopefully, with imminent military success, that will change."

The previous year, the Polish activist Józef Piłsudski had led the First Company of Poles from Kraków into Russian Poland in the hope of starting an uprising there, but it had failed. The Countess had been disappointed, but not entirely surprised.

"Tell me more," she continued.

"We have managed to bring here, to Kraków, a couple of important Polish figures from Russian Poland. We hope they can help mobilize the population in our favor when our armies start to liberate them. Secrecy is paramount. We are also hoping they can cause dissent in the ranks of the Poles in the Russian army."

The Countess understood then why the Russians had selected this as a prime target for their telepath. "Whilst I am disappointed that I was not privy to all this, I am pleased at your initiative. The current situation, where our people are fighting each other on different sides, is truly horrendous. A united Poland under our Emperor would prevent this from happening again. You say there is another meeting tonight?"

"Indeed! We hope to finalize various matters before our compatriots return to Warsaw—they face a difficult journey. Then, we intend to inform the authorities of what our plans are, which will no doubt be of great help to Field Marshal von Hötzendorf."

"That previous meeting—where did it take place in the hotel?"

Jaworski stood up and pointed at a layout of the hotel on the wall. "Here," he said, pointing to a room at the back.

"Did the night watchman die on the alley behind the hotel?" she asked,

"Yes."

The Countess realized that this could be significant. This would be the perfect place for a mind-reader to operate, assuming the wall was no impediment. It was probable that the night watchman had disturbed the spies. Dr. Cornelius no doubt had found a way of murdering the poor man, making it look like natural causes. Poison most likely.

"Władysław, this is what you must do. Proceed with the meeting as planned. However, you must arrive thirty minutes late. Please do not ask me why. You are to tell no one that you have met me, or share anything of what I have told you."

Bemused, Jaworski nodded. The Countess knew that if he was there at the beginning of the meeting, the telepath may be tipped off immediately, and he and Cornelius would escape before being captured. And that would not do.

Having bade farewell to Jaworski, the Countess and the Sergeant returned to *Elizabeth*. She briefed the Sergeant on what had been said.

"We will have to observe that alley from a distance, and hope that our thoughts won't tip them off. We cannot have gendarmes or troops nearby; that, too, may tip them off. When they arrive, we must be sure it is them, and not anyone else who may have business in the adjoining properties."

"I have some ideas on that, Countess,"

"Excellent. Let's discuss them when we meet with the Lieutenant. Take me to the Royal Cathedral on Wawel Hill. I wish to pray for our success tonight."

The Sergeant nodded and drove her to the Cathedral. It was well known that the Countess was a devout Catholic. He often wondered about God's ways himself. He came from a poor background in the village of Kandersfeld in Austria. Yet, here he was, an army Sergeant having a conversation with a Countess and dealing with strange phenomena. God—and the *Evidenzbureau*—did indeed move in mysterious ways.

Dr. Cornelius was escorting Klebb to a bench by the river Vistula. They were back in their peasants' garb. After lunch, they had returned to their safe house, where Klebb had assembled a lengthy coded message for Saint Petersburg. Now, they were headed for a drop off point, a bench with a view of the river.

Klebb beckoned the Doctor who sat next to him. Klebb discreetly stuck a cigarette packet containing the message under the bench.

"That will be picked up later today," Klebb said. "As we are by ourselves, I think I can mention that, in addition to the chaos we shall cause tonight, I think we can do one final thing before we leave. Tomorrow, we shall assassinate General Borojević."

"Not Field Marshal von Hötzendorf?" asked the Doctor.

"Too difficult to get to him. I have the authority to choose another target. Borojević is a competent officer. Once he is dead, we can leave."

"It sounds a bit risky to me. What is your plan?"

Klebb could see that the Doctor was not keen on doing this at all. He could not be told that, in the process of reading the thoughts of the officers earlier, he had learned the details of Borojević's whereabouts. He had also discerned the high regard that his men had for him. Killing him would help when the Russians would launch their own offensive to counter the one the Central Powers were about to start.

"I need your expert opinion," Klebb replied. "After the General is dead, you will have earned your fee."

Klebb could see that this had worked. The Doctor was very keen to get the money that had been promised.

With binoculars, the Countess and Lieutenant Vuljanić were watching the alley behind the Hotel Central from the Sandomierska tower on Wawel Hill. Although it was dark, the street lighting would enable them to see if anyone showed up. The Sergeant was ready at the wheel of *Elizabeth* outside.

"Are you sure we can get there in time if we see them?" asked the Lieutenant.

"You know *Elizabeth*'s capabilities. We can be there in a couple of minutes after the Sergeant starts her up. Running down the stairs may take us longer than the actual journey by car. Meanwhile, we must stay at a distance so that the telepath cannot detect us. He may well sense us when we drive down the alley, but there will be nothing they can do at that point." She looked at her pocket watch. "It's now 8:55 p.m. The Committee will soon be starting their meeting. Cornelius and the telepath should turn up soon."

A couple of minutes later, they spotted two shabbily dressed men with a large bag turn the corner of the main road into the alley.

"This can't be them, surely? They're just vagrants," said the Lieutenant.

"That is precisely why it could be them, Lieutenant. Spies do not dress as gentlemen—at least most of the time."

They could see them standing by the wall, talking.

"Look! The way they move has changed. They're no longer acting like vagrants," said the Countess. "They think they can't be seen. Now, they are indeed talking like the gentlemen they no doubt think they are. We must move swiftly."

They ran down the stairs.

Klebb was perturbed. He could sense the minds on the other side of the wall. However, he heard the thoughts that Jaworski had not yet appeared. And he was keen to kill the chairman.

Cornelius was taking a box out of his sack. It was a simple-looking wooden box.

"And that will be enough to destroy the building?" asked Klebb.

"Not as such," answered the Doctor. "It's been designed so that the explosion will blow against the wall, affecting this building only. It will blast inwardly with great force, smashing most of the ground floor. It will likely bring the rest of the building down. These Poles you dislike so much will not stand much of a chance."

Was this Russian not listening when I told him this earlier? He was probably a peasant elevated to his position by his betters because of his linguistic gifts, Cornelius thought.

Klebb heard the thought. He would enjoy the moment when Russia had mastered the secret of changing people's faces and relish the fury he knew the Doctor would feel when he would discover that fact.

"Excellent," he said. "However, let us wait a few minutes, just in case there are latecomers."

Then, another thought hit his head. And another. It was a woman's thoughts, in Polish. It said:

They may detect us now! We are close. They may be reading my mind!

He turned to the Doctor. "Set it for two minutes! We've been discovered!"

Cornelius had no intention of setting the bomb for two minutes, discovered or not. There must always be time for any delays in escaping a bomb set to go off.

Suddenly, they were bathed in headlights. A car was roaring down the alley. Cornelius set the bomb for five minutes and affixed it to the wall, where it held. That was enough time to get away—or to bargain with if caught.

"Through that door," the Doctor shouted. Klebb was already heading towards it; it was the same door that the night watchman had come through the previous night. It opened. Klebb ducked as a bullet whizzed over his head. The two men went in, slammed the door shut behind them and bolted it. They were in what looked like a kitchen. No doubt the night watchman had come here to find something to eat before doing his rounds. Had he not instructed the staff here to bolt the door at night?

"Exit?" shouted Klebb in Polish at a startled cook.

Before the man had time to point, the Russian was already running off. Mystified, Cornelius followed, carrying Klebb's bag which the Russian had left behind in his hurry to escape.

Their pursuers clambered out of the vehicle. They tried to go in, but the door refused to budge.

"We must go round," the Countess said.

The Sergeant noticed the box on the wall.

"I am sure that is a focused bomb. It could destroy the hotel," he said. "Drive back down. I'll head into the hotel and get everyone out."

The Countess nodded. She had heard of such devices, used by elite criminals.

They drove back, with Sergeant hanging on the outside. She was going to admonish the lieutenant for shooting at the men, but there was no time, and anyway, it may be better to shoot them dead than let them get away.

The Sergeant got off at the end of the alleyway, whilst the Countess turned *Elizabeth* around the corner, driving down a small road that backed onto the alley.

Suddenly, she and the Lieutenant saw Cornelius and Klebb, who had managed to leave the Hotel, running down that same road.

"Split up!" shouted Klebb as he took one side of the road. The Doctor simply doubled back the way he came. He heard a woman's voice shout: "Stop or I'll shoot!", but he kept moving. Then he heard several shots— presumably at Klebb.

He found himself back in the alley where the bomb was. He knew it was going to explode away from him, but he had never run faster in his life. He crossed the alley and went down another street. He finally stopped when he was certain he was no longer being followed. He caught his breath and started walking again at a normal pace. He had to keep moving; he had run past some people who would report him to the gendarmes, perhaps thinking he was a thief. He knew who the woman in the car was—Countess Irina Petrovska. How was she involved? For now, he had to make his way back to their safe house, which was the plan if and Klebb were forced to split up. But first, he would a make a quick detour…

The Countess and Lieutenant Vuljanić had taken shots at the fleeing Klebb from the *Elizabeth*. However, the Russian ducked and weaved, eluding all the bullets.

The Countess stopped firing. She was concerned that she may inadvertently injure a passerby. She also realized the man they were chasing this had to be the telepath.

"Stop firing, Lieutenant," she said. "We will run him down."

Klebb listened around him. There were a number of voices he could hear, all talking about the shots they had heard. *Are the Russians here?* he heard. Some windows were opening. He took full advantage of the incipient panic and shouted out:

"The Russians are here! They are bombing the city; they are in the next street! Run, now!"

A few people began to leave their homes in a panic. Kraków had been briefly under siege by the Russians the previous year. Klebb saw someone exit a house and onto the street. He quickly ran into the now abandoned house just as *Elizabeth* was turning the corner.

"Where did he go?" a frustrated Countess said.

Then there was an explosion.

Dr. Cornelius had returned to the drop off point. He heard the explosion and was satisfied that the bomb had done its work.

He went to the bench and retrieved the cigarette packet. He took out the piece of paper and unfolded it. It was written in code on both sides. Clearly, Klebb had a lot to say. He took out a pencil, and some scraps of paper he had on his person. It was a simple code, and he could hardly believe the Russians were still using it. A nearby lamp provided some light, and he had to strain to see, but he started decoding the message.

Halfway through, his blood started running colder with every word. First, there were details about a Central Powers military offensive along the Gorlice-Tarnów line to be launched on 2 May. How on Earth did Klebb know this?

Briefly, it also mentioned their plan to assassinate Borojević beforehand. Then there was a mention of the Supreme National Committee of the Poles, and the bombing action to be taken. Both these actions would certainly help a Russian strike before 2 May, which was likely to happen when they read the message.

Finally, there were details about him. Cornelius became more disturbed with every word. It was revealed how he had become the sculptor of human flesh. As a young medical student, he had hired sailors to engage in some drug running, to help live more luxuriously. One of these men had had facial deformities which, as an aspiring surgeon, he had noted. This sailor had later journeyed to China, and returned with seemingly a new face, all his deformities removed. The young Cornelius Kramm could not believe it, but ascertained it was indeed the same man, not least due to the same tattoos.

The sailor told him that he had saved a Chinese from drowning. In return, the sailor had taken him to his home village where some kind of surgery was performed on him to change his face.

When he qualified as a doctor, Cornelius and his brother Fritz had journeyed to China, looking for opportunities for their fledgling Red Hand organization to smuggle opium. He had left his brother for a while to travel to the hidden Ling Valley, where the sailor said he had his face changed.

There, he found a village that was known for healing those with deformed or damaged faces. The villagers told him that, many years ago, two brothers had come from the West and had stayed in the village. Their names, translated from the local dialect, was Ténèbre, or Shade. They knew the secret of making flesh soft, pliant and malleable, and had used it on some locals, either to repair their damaged faces or to punish them by turning them into monsters. They had eventually left, forced to flee to escape the wrath of a man named Kronos, but some of their secrets had been left behind. It involved a mysterious serum used to loosen the flesh, which could then be molded in any shape one desired.

Cornelius had told the villagers that the process was evil; that those who it was used on should be watched carefully, and that it should never be used again. He generously offered to take all the serum left behind by the two brothers to be destroyed safely elsewhere. He never got to the bottom of who the brothers were, but he now had the means to become a sculptor of human flesh.

Klebb had spelled out a concise version of all this in his message, along with a suggestion that someone should be sent to the Ling Valley at once to obtain information, and if possible samples of the serum, from the villagers. Cornelius had always suspected that the villagers, should they overcome their fear, might be able to provide more samples of the serum—not all of them had cowed in terror when he had told them the process was evil. He had once considered sending a Red Hand force to wipe out the entire village, but it would have attracted attention, and the Tongs might have had something to say about it.

The Doctor looked at the message again. There were other details about him, such as the identity of the Red Hand contact who had provided the bomb.

How could Klebb know all this? He certainly had not told him. However, Klebb had asked him questions on these matters. He had thought about them... Could he then be a thought-reader? A telepath? He had read of research into these matters, usually concluding that the alleged mind-readers were frauds. However, could it be done? Perhaps the drug Klebb had injected into himself gave him these abilities? It would explain everything, including how the Russian seemed to know things in advance, such as the appearance of the night watchman, and even ducking in time to avoid a bullet.

Cornelius looked into his bag, to examine the so-called listening device. Opening it up, all he could see were a few wires and a stone taped inside to provide weight. It was nothing more than a prop—ideal to provide cover for a telepath!

He formulated a plan of action immediately. He would destroy the message, then kill Klebb, but not just yet. First, they would assassinate the Croat General; then he would eliminate him. He would return to Saint Petersburg with some plausible story about the man's death and point out that they had wiped out the Polish committee and killed an enemy general, which should be enough to claim his payment. It was a risky, but he needed the money.

As for now, he would try and think in Mandarin. Klebb's language skills were clearly European; he was not likely to know that Chinese language. And if he was proved wrong, or Klebb got too suspicious, then he would kill him at once and deal with Borojević himself, but it would be useful to have a telepath on hand for that job.

"I believe that's for me," a voice said.

It took Cornelius by surprise. He had been careless, getting wrapped up in his thoughts. The man had spoken in Polish, but the Doctor knew immediately that he was here for the message. He was a small man in an old suit.

The Doctor pulled out a knife and stabbed the man in the stomach. He staggered back in shock and Cornelius stabbed him again, right through the neck. The man toppled over and fell.

The Doctor realized that he had been angry. He was furious that his secret, which even his late brother had had limited knowledge of, was known.

He took the body and tipped it in the Vistula. He ripped up the message into bits and cast them into the river. No one saw him do any of this. He had blood all over his clothes. He headed back to the safe house, hoping that the dark would help disguise the stains.

The Countess surveyed the wreckage of the hotel with the Sergeant. She was still holding her firearm, a Doppelpistole M1912, effectively a double-barreled hand-held machine gun—a favorite of hers. She had used single shots, to prevent stray bullets from hitting civilians.

"You did well, Sergeant Mayr," she said. "It seems there were no casualties."

"There were few people in the hotel, essentially just the Poles and the hotel staff. Had the place been full, it might have been a different story," he replied.

"I miscalculated; I thought they would be spying tonight. Furthermore, we have lost them," said the Countess.

"We did save the Polish committee and the hotel staff. Had we not been here at all, then they would have succeeded in their aim," said the Sergeant.

"We must at least be thankful for that."

The Lieutenant came up to them. "The gendarmerie has already searched the buildings where we lost the telepath. The found no one, although they reported a man shouting. 'The Russians are coming.' That was probably our man, trying to cause a panic to cover his escape. I've told the gendarmes to make inquiries in the city, I have given them the descriptions of the two of them. The troops General Borojević promised are already helping. Some of them will patrol the city during the rest of the night, although I suspect the spies have gone to ground."

"Very well," said the Countess. "There is not much more we can do now. We should get some sleep and reconvene first thing in the morning."

When Cornelius arrived back at the safe house, Klebb was already there. The Doctor was already thinking in Mandarin.

"What happened to you?" Klebb asked, pointing at the blood stains.

"I had to deal with a gendarme," Cornelius replied. "There is an organized search. I must destroy these clothes at once. We must abandon the peasant disguise. How did you escape?"

"Someone left his house open. I took cover there and came out after out pursuers had moved off."

"They were led by Countess Irina Petrovska. She may be a woman but, believe me, she is a formidable foe. Someone in Russia must have leaked that we were here."

"Nonsense!" replied Klebb, outraged. "The Okhrana is the most secure organization in the world!"

Cornelius rolled his eyes. "Nevertheless, she did not appear out of nowhere. That will not disturb our plans, as she knows nothing about that. It is correct that you changed your plan from assassinating the Field Marshal to the General only yesterday?"

Klebb nodded.

"Excellent!" the Doctor said, clapping his hands. "You know, I am quite enjoying this. It reminds me of my younger days, back when I was in the opium trade in China. Those times certainly set the blood pumping!"

In fact, the sculptor of flesh could not stand being so close to the action; in the old days, his Red Hand operatives would have dealt with the more physical elements of the business. However, he thought that this story might help explain why he was suddenly thinking in Mandarin.

Klebb had certainly noticed it. In fact, he had done so before Cornelius had even opened the door. He could not understand what the Doctor was thinking. He was known as being mysterious; the Okhrana were unaware of his previous activities.

There were thought flashes of English, but nothing substantive, just disjointed words. Had he somehow found out about his thought-reading? Or perhaps he was merely reliving his glory days in China?

Klebb was uneasy. He wondered if it might not be safer to eliminate Cornelius at some point soon.

He had only enough of the Lynx serum for one more day.

18 April 1915

The morning came. Dr. Cornelius had not slept well. He had kept an eye on the door to his room all night, catching moments of sleep now and then, but always with his gun in hand.

He grabbed two large bags from underneath his bed and went into the front room. Klebb was already awake and refreshed, reading a newspaper.

No doubt he has taken the drug, thought the Doctor in Mandarin. He tossed a bag to the Russian.

"Put this on," he said.

Klebb took out the pike grey uniform of a Lieutenant in the Austro-Hungarian army.

"I thought we may need these, and had them prepared before our arrival here," the Doctor said, bringing out his own—a Captain's uniform. "It was made to your size," he added.

The Countess was also awake and breakfasting in the gendarmerie that served as her base of operations. Lieutenant Vuljanić came in.

"One of the gendarmes had a woman approach him. She said she saw a blood-stained vagrant heading into a neighboring house. They're looking into who the owner is. They also fished a dead man out of the river. It looks like he was stabbed to death. They are awaiting our orders."

The Countess got up. "Send the Sergeant to look at the body and see if he can find out more. That house may well be their hideout. We need to get there at once, in force."

Minutes later, she stood outside by the *Elizabeth* with the unit of soldiers that the General had detached to her.

"Lieutenant, take these men; we're going to search that house. The telepath may 'hear' us coming, but with so many men, their room for escape is limited.

The Lieutenant and the soldiers ran down the street, efficiently smashed the door and stormed in. The Countess drove down slowly after them. The Lieutenant came back out.

"There is no one here."

The Countess went in. The Lieutenant beckoned her up some stairs to the first floor.

"This looks like where they were staying," he said.

The Countess entered. The room was sparse, with two doors which led to the bedrooms, which were also empty. There was a table on which lay some discarded newspapers. She went over to them and looked. There were different papers dated from the last few days. One was folded to a page with an article on General Svetozar Borojević. Could they be planning to assassinate him? Would they be so stupid to leave such an obvious clue behind? Or was it a diversion? She had no choice but to follow this up.

Klebb and Cornelius approached a small barn on the outskirts of town. Their walk had been uneventful, gathering a few salutes on the way. They still had their vagrant faces, but cleanly shaved, and with their uniforms and caps, they now looked very different.

The Doctor entered the barn. In front of them was an armored car, with machine guns sticking out of the front over the engine and on the sides.

"My contact obtained this for me," the Doctor said. "It is a prototype called the Junovicz P.A.1 used by the Austro-Hungarian army. Money can obtain anything, especially these days."

Klebb looked astounded. "What are we to do with it?" he asked.

"It's very simple. We drive up to General Borojević's HQ and kill him," the Doctor said, pointing to the machine guns. "Then we drive away at great speed."

"You're insane! I thought perhaps we should use a sniper's rifle."

"Are you a sniper?" Cornelius asked, coldly.

Klebb shook his head.

"Neither am I. You're also assuming we could get a decent line of sight. This way, we're sure to get him, and the shock of his death will help us get away. I already have a route planned for escape. The criminal world can do things faster than the authorities. This is why I charge so much. Now, you say you know the General's movements. A morning walkabout at around 7 a.m.?"

"I also know the passwords the sentries use," Klebb said.

"I somehow knew you would. Your espionage skills have impressed me greatly. Be ready to use them. As it's a Sunday, let's hope some of the soldiers are sleeping in."

The Doctor did not ask for the passwords; he knew that Klebb would only know them when he read them in the sentries' minds.

"Let's waste no more time, then," he concluded.

They got into the armored car and started the engine.

It was at that moment that the Countess and the Lieutenant sped by in the *Elizabeth*, too fast for Klebb to pick up their thoughts or even hear them due to the armored car's noise.

Klebb went to open the barn door to let the armored car out. By the time their vehicle had come out of the barn, *Elizabeth* was already out of sight.

"Are you sure, Countess?" asked General Borojević.

The Countess had just arrived and asked to see him. His standing orders were always to let her through.

"Not really, but that article indicated that you were at least of interest to them. According to the investigation, that house was being used by two men who recently showed up, saying they were employed locally as night watchmen. Now, they're gone, leaving behind nothing but burnt clothes and the newspapers I mentioned. They may have simply escaped, or they may plan something more sinister yet. Dr. Cornelius has used infiltration doubles of officers before."

"After our meeting, I instituted extra security measures. Passwords may be useless against a thoughtreader, but anyone who wants to come near me must also be recognized by my staff."

"I think, General, that you should stay inside for a least a few hours more while we investigate further."

The General looked a little exasperated. He needed to focus on the coming offensive. "I cannot do that, Countess. However, I will ensure that there is always a guard with me today. The Captain here," he pointed to an officer next to him, "has been with me continually for the last few hours and, if he were a double, he could have easily killed me by now and made his escape. Now, I must do my rounds."

Outside, Dr. Cornelius's Junovicz P.A.1. had passed through a number of checkpoints. They knew the passwords and their reason for being here—they wished to show this new armored car prototype to the General--as plausible. They even let some soldiers look inside. They were coming to the last checkpoint.

"Damn!" exclaimed the Doctor.

"What's wrong?" asked Klebb.

"The Countess's vehicle is parked right there." The Doctor was beginning to think that the Countess had telepathic powers, too. It could not be coincidence that she was there.

"What should we do?" asked Klebb

"We proceed. Don't you want this assassination done? And while we're at it, we can dispose of that meddling Countess as the same time."

He drove the vehicle towards the next checkpoint. Klebb opened the door and gave the guard the password and told him they were there to see the General and demonstrate the Junovicz for him.

"Sorry, sir, but you have to wait," said the guard. "Before you can proceed, we need to ensure that you are both known by someone here. Do you know of an officer who could vouch for you?"

The guard peered inside at Cornelius, noting his rank. *These men are not expected* he thought, which Klebb heard.

"We have no time for this," Klebb insisted. "Please direct us to the General. This vehicle is top-secret, and we've not been able to send specifications to senior officers. They need to see it for themselves to see its capabilities."

At that moment, the Countess exited, followed by the Lieutenant, the General and his aide. She went over to her car, clearly about to leave. Cornelius saw a chance and started to mount the machine gun. The quick-witted guard saw what was happening and shouted "Stop!" at the Doctor.

He raised his rifle, only to be rewarded by a bullet in the head by Klebb. But his cry had had the effect it needed. Cornelius was still grappling to move the weapon into a better firing position, but was now too late. The Countess and the General had dived into *Elizabeth*, while the two officers with them had taken cover elsewhere.

Cornelius fired. His bullets hit *Elizabeth*, but only made small dents. Other troops started firing back. The Doctor was forced to return fire lest a stray bullet enter his vehicle.

He slid back into the driving seat and turned the vehicle away.

"Get behind the gun and fire at anything that moves," he told Klebb.

There was a sudden jolt and then they were spinning. Cornelius cursed. The Countess had rammed them with her own vehicle. It gave Borojević's men a chance to attack the Junovicz.

The Doctor completed the turn of his armored car. *It was time to retreat*, he thought. A sword stuck through the front observation port, missing his neck by inches. Outside, soldiers cheered. It was Borojević himself on the vehicle who had attacked with his ceremonial sword.

The Doctor swerved the vehicle and threw the General off. Then he drove off, heading away from the camp.

"Go back! We must kill Borojević!" shouted Klebb.

"You go back!" shouted the Doctor. "They will attack ups with grenades and all kinds of weapons now.

Why, that sword almost killed me! We do not have to go far to escape, and I don't intend to let them catch us!"

Klebb pointed his pistol at him. "Go back now," he ordered.

"Shoot me and we crash. At least, with my plan, we escape and can try again."

Klebb looked uncertain, but kept the gun aimed.

I will kill him the first chance I get, thought the Doctor. But he had slipped. He had thought in English, and Klebb had heard him.

"What is your escape plan?" the Russian demanded.

"We will stop at the next village. There, I have a house and a cart ready to take us to the next step in the escape route," Cornelius replied.

His thoughts, however, told a different story. He would shoot Klebb dead immediately. He would then see if the Countess was in pursuit and try to lure her out of her vehicle, or somehow disable it, before heading off toward the city where the real escape route started. Klebb also heard thoughts indicating that the Doctor had read, and destroyed, his coded message. He decided he would kill Cornelius as soon as they stopped. Then, he would deal with the Countess himself, and would some-how get back to Kraków and get word to Saint Peters-burg about the new offensive before it was too late.

"Very well, proceed," said the Russian.

Back at the camp, pursuit was being organized. General Borojević had been thrown off the vehicle, but his landing had not been too hard; he was already back giving orders. The Countess went up to him.

"I can catch up with them. My vehicle has certain, er, properties, including that of speed."

"Properties that also include somehow your not being injured when you rammed his car?"

"A certain shock absorption design, General. Now, I must go."

She climbed into *Elizabeth*, the Lieutenant jumping in on the other side. She closed the door and sped off. General Borojević wondered where that technology came from.

The Junovicz had come to a stop.

"After you," Klebb said to Dr. Cornelius, indicating he should get out. Then he would shoot him. Suddenly, new thoughts popped into his head.

"The Countess!" he said.

The speed of her arrival meant that her thoughts were suddenly becoming clear, so he was distracted momentarily. Cornelius leaped out of the car, ran around it to confuse Klebb, and headed into the village.

Klebb try to run after him, but the Doctor had already disappeared. And the Countess's car was rapidly approaching. The Russian decided he would eliminate her and the Lieutenant—a dangerous Polish aristocrat—first. Then Cornelius.

He moved towards them, preparing to shoot. He knew he would know ahead of time when they were about to fire. Indeed, the Lieutenant fired first, but Klebb had ducked and fired back at him, hitting him. He then read the Countess' mind a moment before she brought out her own firearm. Unfortunately, it was the Doppelpistole!

In panic, Klebb ran towards the village, hoping that the Countess would not fire that way. But he was too late. She fired, moving the gun left and right, bullets spraying forward. Klebb avoided the first few, but other bullets hit him, right in the chest.

He died instantly, his body crashing to the ground.

The Countess looked around for the Doctor, but could not see where he had gone. Behind her, Lieutenant Vuljanić was bleeding to death. She could not abandon him for the likes of Dr. Cornelius.

She went over to him and administered aid.

"Thank you," said Cornelius to a bemused villager as he took his horse.

The villager could not speak German, and simply assumed that this officer needed the horse for war purposes.

The Doctor rode off. Things had not gone well. However, he still needed his money. Perhaps his friend in Saint Petersburg might help.

Saint Petersburg, 10 May 1915

Spymaster A.V. Brune de St Hippolite was in attendance at a social function at the Alexander Palace. He hoped to meet with the Tsar soon, in order to ask for an increase in his budget. The mission with Klebb had been a disaster. No word had been heard from either Klebb or Dr. Cornelius. The hotel had been destroyed, but with no loss of life. That must have been a bungled attempt to kill those damn Poles. Nothing had been achieved, and the Central Powers were enjoying a successful offensive. Had the two men been captured? Had the Lynx serum fallen into Austrian hands?

He saw the Tsarina with that monk, Rasputin. And next to him was a balding man with gold rimmed spectacles—Dr. Cornelius.

Rasputin beckoned him over. Cautiously, the spymaster went over. He decided to try and get his side in first.

"Your majesty, this man is…"

"A valued agent of yours," interrupted Rasputin, "who has not been treated well by you, it seems."

The Tsarina spoke. "The Doctor has told us of his attempts to find out about our enemies in Galicia. It seems that the man whom you sent with him was... I cannot speak the words…" She looked distressed.

Rasputin patted her arm. "Fear not, your majesty. I shall speak on your behalf. This man, Klebb, we are told by Dr. Malbrough here…"

"A top agent," the spymaster interrupted, trying to control the conversation.

"A top agent?" exclaimed Rasputin, his voice rising. "He claimed to have unearthly powers, to read minds—powers that can only be obtained by consorting with satanic forces!"

The monk gesticulated wildly, with his eyes rolling upwards. Brune de St Hippolite saw that a few of the other guests looked their way, including General Boris Liatoukine, another dangerous character.

"And now," the monk said, "you refuse to pay this brave man what you promised. A payment that will barely feed him for a month!"

"I would like an explanation for all this," the Tsarina said.

The spymaster knew he was in trouble. Lying to the Tsarina could have serious consequences. What story had been concocted by the Doctor? And how did he know Rasputin?

The monk came to his rescue. "I suspect that our friend here was unaware of Klebb's true nature, and that he sent these men on their brave mission in good faith. He was not to know that Klebb would desert the Doctor, getting shot whilst fleeing the Austrian gendarmerie. However, we can fault him for not paying the Doctor. Russian honor can be restored by payment. Full payment," he added meaningfully. "Then, we will refer no more to this sordid affair."

Brune de St Hippolite saw his way out and took it.

"Of course, I shall see to it immediately."

"See that you do," said the Tsarina. "I wish to hear no more of this."

The spymaster sensed he was dismissed, thanked the Tsarina, and walked away. He hoped that their Vozduhoplavatel base would provide better projects soon.

Later, Rasputin and Dr. Cornelius spoke together.

"Is my debt settled, my friend?" asked Rasputin.

"It most certainly is," replied the Doctor.

He recalled how previously he had healed the face of a man Rasputin had disfigured in a brawl, an act the monk had later regretted for whatever reason. Dr. Cornelius had been contacted and repaired the injured man's face. He had asked Rasputin—who was already influential—for no payment, merely a favor to be repaid at some point. It had been a wise decision. The sculptor of human flesh now had something to celebrate.

"Let us drink more," he said to a delighted Rasputin.

Deuxième Bureau, Paris, 12 May 1915

Simon Hart read the report from their agent, Leo Saint-Clair, a.k.a. the Nyctalope. Saint-Clair had gone to

Vozduhoplavatel and located the lab where the Lynx serum was. He had scared Professor Ossipoff into revealing the secrets of how they had unlocked its power—the simple knowledge of this Meyral effect upon certain individuals with latent psychic powers.

Had their own department not halted their research into the Lynx, they may have noticed the correlation with the Meyral themselves, Hart thought.

The Nyctalope had then destroyed the Russian's serum supplies and the entire lab, although he had not killed the professor which would have been against his code of honor. He had even brought back some of the Russian produced Lynx serum. Only a man with such powers could have ventured out into Russia and back.

As for the other part of the plan, that had gone very well too. Their spies in the Okhrana had told them of the plans for the Lynx. They had no assets in Galicia, and so information was fed to the *Evidenzbureau* via certain channels. It included the idea the telepath was a drug addict, to mislead anyone who might have seen him injecting the serum. The *Evidenzbureau* was led to believe that it had found out these secrets from Russia, rather than being fed them by the French.

It had been decided that this was a separate matter to the war. Russia had committed an act of aggression against France with its theft of the Lynx. No other power could have the serum, although it did appear that the fading of the Meyral effect made it useless in any event.

Best of all, was the act that he had planned these operations. His hiring of the traitor Maréchal had been forgotten. It was now time to leave the office and relax.

Jacquemain saw Hart leave the building and cross the road to meet an attractive woman—one who was certainly not his wife, but the sister of one of the other officers.

Hart is a good Frenchman, he thought approvingly.

Austro-Hungarian army mobile field hospital, Galicia (Poland), Austro-Hungarian Empire, 14 May 1915

The Countess was back in her nursing uniform, albeit off-duty, sitting next to the hospital bed of the sleeping Lieutenant Vuljanić. He had been shot in the stomach and, despite an infection, would recover.

Sergeant Mayr had already been there to report on their hunt for Dr. Cornelius. It seems that the former lord of the Red Hand had commandeered a horse and disappeared. She doubted that this would be the last she would hear of him.

The Gorlice-Tarnów offensive of 2 May had been immensely successful, liberating much of occupied Galicia and Russian Poland. It was good news for the Polish people, who, like so many others, had suffered during the war, either as refugees fleeing from the Russians, or under Russian occupation. It looked like Poland may become unified as she had dreamed, but a cost no one had anticipated.

Her thoughts turned to the telepath. It was doubtful there were others like him. The Russians would have had advance warning of the offensive if there were.

But for now, her patients needed her.

The Deadly Projector Over Split

The Isonzo Front (The War between Italy and the Austro-Hungarian Empire), August 1916

The Slovenian soldiers were terrified. Before them, hovering over the trench, was Death itself. The horror of it was heightened by blazing sunshine of the day—one expects this sort of thing in the night, surely? Things were bad enough—the Italian invaders had almost taken the town of Gorizia—but now this?

Instinctively, they opened fire on the being. The bullets had no effect. They seemed to disappear through the specter, making it shimmer slightly. The soldiers stood their ground, fighting their fear. Death, garbed in cloak and hood, had his traditional scythe in his right hand. He raised the scythe and a bolt of black lightning flew from the tip of it.

Lance Corporal Frančišek Zupančič was from Radvanje. He was not only terrified, but regretful. He was never very keen on going to church. *I must apologize to Father Krajnc*, he thought. He was then hit by the lightning. He seemed to glow black and collapsed.

His fellow soldiers fled the trench. None wanted to be next to be claimed by Death. The Specter faded away. The Lance Corporal lay dead, his body unattended, his pike grey uniform blackened. Fear was etched on his burn face. Later, his parents would be told that he had died from a fire caused by shelling. The Habsburg Empire did not want the truth of things to get out, lest it cause panic.

Days later, a Captain Marić of the 25th Zagreb Home Guard Regiment was riding slowly through woods under Austro-Hungarian control. He cursed. It was early dusk, and he had an important briefing to get to. *Damn these Italians,* he thought. They had invaded in May of last year—taking advantage of the war—in order to annex his homeland.

The Italians had finally scored their first victory in taking Gorizia, although they had paid dearly for this advance. And now, there was a story that the Italians had enlisted Death to their cause—a story his superiors had told him to suppress. But was there something in it?

His mind went back to his journey. *There should be enough light to get to the regional HQ in time*, he thought. There was a path of sorts, with trees on either side. He stopped his and looked forward. *Was that a man I saw?* He rode very slowly forward, taking his side-arm out of its holster. He was well within his own lines, but this did not feel right. He could see something moving behind a tree. It looked like a man, with his hand on a tree. The thing revealed itself. The Captain shuddered. What stood just before him was a specter. A man with a skull rather than a head, garbed in some kind of foul-looking garment.

The Captain looked at the creature, fearful. He had heard of what had happened to Lance Corporal Zupančič. And yet—could it be merely a man in a mask?

Then, the thing started to levitate. *Not a man in a mask*, he thought. Captain Marić had no intention of ending up like the unfortunate Lance Corporal. "Back to Hell, you go!" he shouted, and fired at the specter. His

118

horse started momentarily but remained calm. The Captain was pleased at how well he had trained the beast, but less so as his bullets went through the specter, causing the shimmering he had heard about in the previous incident.

Fear gripped the Captain, as it would anyone in such a situation. He then noticed his horse was still calm. Surely, if this was Death in front of him, the horse would be reacting?

The specter started to raise its hand to point at the Captain. Although this thing had no scythe, the soldier reckoned that perhaps this thing did not need one to fire its black lightning. He dismounted fast—the woods here were a little dense around the path for the horse—and moved into the woods.

Black lightning flew from the finger of the specter, but missed the Captain completely. *Death appears to be a bad shot*, thought Marić. He then noticed a small thin line of light—barely perceptible—coming from the other side of the woods to the specter.

He fired at the source of the light beam. The specter suddenly turned sideways in mid-air and then fizzled out. There were shouts, but not in the Italian of the invaders, but in French. "Retreat!" he heard.

The Captain was an educated man. French was a language he had long mastered. He felt he had the advantage. He fired again and started moving towards the shouts.

He could see some figures moving off at speed. And then he saw an Italian soldier on the ground, struggling to get up. "Do not leave me!" the man shouted, in French, at his retreating fellows.

Marić did not give chase, lest these obvious Frenchmen decided to stand their ground. No one would know about this if he got killed. And he had a prisoner. He looked at the fake Italian soldier, trying to crawl away. He was bleeding from the shoulder. One of his bullets had hit home.

The soldier stopped crawling and turned around. "I surrender," he said in French.

"What is a Frenchman doing here in Italian uniform?" Marić asked.

An obscene gesture was the response he got. Marić groaned inwardly. *It was going to be quite something to get this man to HQ.*

Italian military facility, near the front

Simon Hart considered the base given to his team to be ramshackle. Did these Italians not realize how important their French allies were? It was little more than a large hut with a smaller one nearby to act as his team's sleeping quarters. Still, his men were happy about it; it meant they would be slightly more inconspicuous.

He had come here directly from Paris. Things here were not going as well as they should be. *Where is that damned Professor Marcus?*

He went outside and spoke to a nearby soldier. A few minutes later, the door opened and the Professor was shoved in by a soldier.

Ah, thought Hart, *Warrant Officer Duval had found him. Excellent man, that Duval.*

"How dare you treat me like this?" spluttered the Professor.

The two men made something of a contrast. Simon Hart was clean-shaven and well-dressed as befits a French intelligence officer; the Professor, who was balding with a goatee beard, wore a lab coat.

"I have been waiting long enough for you. Please be seated," said Hart brusquely.

The Professor muttered some obscure Italian oath and sat down.

Hart started with the reason why he was here. "I have heard the report from Warrant Officer Duval about what occurred. He says that, quite against his advice, you ventured with the projector too deeply into enemy lines. Consequently, one of my men is now in the hands of the enemy."

The Professor responded. "Your men failed to realize that the charred body of an enemy officer, killed by Death itself, would create tremendous fear in the enemy, especially so far behind their lines. This war must be prosecuted more fully. Italy must take the territory promised by the allies to her."

Hart knew that Professor Marcus an Italian irredentist, a follower of the crank Gabrielle D'Annunzio, was mostly concerned with laying claim to territories beyond their borders—specially the Slovene and Croat parts of the Habsburg Empire. The Professor did keep going on about it. Expansion was the reason why Italy had joined the war.

"And as I say, one of my men is now in the hands of the enemy. Who knows what he has been subjected to in order to make him talk. We are fortunate that you did not come across a whole group of Croat troops. Suppose the projector had fallen into their hands?"

"I would use the projector to its fullest ability to deal with them," said the Professor. "I would die before being captured. Furthermore, only I know how to work the projector."

"I am sure the *Evidenzbureau* would at some point be able to work it out. After all, you only know how to

121

work the projector because of our expertise and resources. You came to us, remember?"

Indeed, he did remember. Marcus well recalled that. Through his sources, he knew that the French had advanced research into esoteric technology. He also knew the Austro-Hungarians did as well, but he had considered them an enemy even before the war. The French, it had to be, as his homeland did not have the same level of facilities Paris had.

"And might I add," continued Hart, "that you manipulated the research so that only you could work the projector."

The Professor almost snorted, but didn't. That was certainly true. However, the French scientists he worked with would not take too long now to understand how to operate the projector fully. It concerned him that the French would use it for their own ends, rather than it being used to further the ambitions of Italy.

On thinking of that, the Professor snorted anyway. "It is not my fault that your scientists, useful though they were, were not able to master the projector completely."

"Regardless, you and the projector are to be moved to the Western front, where we shall use it to defend France and create fear amongst the German army. The military will direct its use, rather than you."

The Professor scoffed. "You will find, *mon ami*, that my government will not agree to that."

"They already have. Italy is keen not to upset us, given that the Allies have promised them Adriatic territories."

The Professor was furious, but he was no fool. He decided to be calm.

"I see any protest by me would be of no consequence—although you can be sure that I will protest.

Then, I will do as you ask. I will not disobey my government," the Professor said.

"I respect that. Make your protest swiftly. We leave tomorrow. In the meantime, can I see the projector?"

The Professor nodded and rose. He went over to a table with some maps on it and moved it aside, along with a mat underneath. There was a small hatch on the floor, padlocked. He unlocked it and there was what looked like a small grey box, about the size of a brick. He took it out and put it on the table. He put his hand on the top of it. The box started to glow in many different colors. And then an image of Death appeared before them.

If the Professor had intended to startle Hart, he failed. He was unmoved. "It works well," the Frenchman said.

"Yes, I have become more attuned to it. The controls seem to intuit what I want. It records paper images I show it and then projects them at my command. I now believe this has a dual purpose. First, communication over long distances by its beam, perhaps projecting the image of the user to another person. I also suspect it is a form of entertainment, projected to an audience in a similar fashion to our Kino, but in three dimensions. Further, it must have been used as a weapon, one that uses some form of light to destructive effect."

Hart had heard much of this before, he knew the Professor enjoyed talking about his theories. It was a useful way of finding out more from the Professor, as the scientist could not resist discussing his new theories.

"You said the craft from another world crashed near Genoa in 1911, near your observatory. Surely, it can't be that much of a threat if these pilots crash so easily?"

"I suspect there was something in our atmosphere that caused a problem," the Professor replied. "I had spotted it from my observatory, stationary high up in the atmosphere, directly above me. And then, something went wrong, and I saw it crash. I went to the crash site, much of the craft seemed to dissolve into the soil, except for the projector, which at that point seemed misshapen.

"My idiot superiors thought it to be a meteorite and suggested it be put on display in a geological museum. It is fortunate that, after further examination, I saw it change into the rectangular box shape we see here, and brought it to your department. When Italy is under firm leadership, I will command the observatory. Strength will be needed to deal with these Saturnians."

That last bit was new to Hart. "Deal with these Saturnians? What do you mean?"

The Professor looked at the box. "The projector... it connects with the mind. Your organization is aware of the potential of telepathy, and here we have a weapon that our minds can command. And yet, it seems to contain information. I have been able to sense--I would put it no more than that—that this was an unmanned reconnaissance mission, from the sixth planet, sending back information about our world. It seems to have wanted to know our level of scientific development, which explains their position above my observatory. I have a particular interest in Saturn. I believe the Saturnians seek empire. We must prepare for the future."

Hart looked unconvinced. "These Saturnians, why are they delaying? Surely, they would have invaded by now?"

"Who knows what their strategy is? However, a strong Italy will defend Europe and the world!"

Hart was dubious about that, but said nothing. However, the Professor's words simply meant that the projector had to remain under French supervision.

"Indeed," he said, humoring the Professor. "Very well, I have other matters to attend to. We start back to France tomorrow in the morning."

Both men bid each other a good day and Hart left.

"Keep an eye on him, Duval." Hart said to the Warrant Officer who was standing guard outside. "He seems cooperative, but you never know. I shall return in a few hours, I have to see an old friend."

The Sergeant nodded and smiled. It was well known that Hart had a number of mistresses—he would always claim to be seeing an 'old friend.' It was one of the reasons he was so popular with the soldiers attached to this branch of the Deuxième Bureau. Duval was also glad to be leaving. He was none too keen on having to wear an Italian uniform to conceal the French presence here from the enemy.

Inside the hut, Professor Marcus activated the box by simply placing his hand on it. In front of him an image of Hart appeared, exactly as he looked a few moments ago. Hart had no idea that the projector could perfect such a likeness, thinking it could only produce crude replicas from magazines of images of Death. Indeed, previous use could only project images of humans that were not that detailed and transparent. However, his work with the projector had gone a little further. It was able to study Hart for a few minutes, seeing him in three dimensions—there was only a slight transparency, which could be seen only from a couple of centimeters. He switched the image off and projected it outside—a small beam of light going through the wall door and outside.

It's still daylight, the Sergeant won't see it, thought the Professor.

Outside, the Sergeant noticed Hart coming back. "I almost forgot," said Hart, "Could you inform our liaison Captain Esposito of our intended departure times tomorrow? Best to do it now, to prevent any offence. I think the Professor can't get up to much mischief for a few minutes."

The Warrant Officer agreed, and moved off, happy to help Hart get to his rendezvous on time.

Professor Marcus swiftly left the hut, with the projector in his hand.

Later, Hart was furious. At first, he did not believe Duval's story. Then reports came of the Professor leaving the military area in the company of an Italian officer, who claimed he was elsewhere at time.

Hart let his fury abate. After all, the Sergeant could not have known that the Professor had improved the use of the projector. Further, he was incommunicado for a couple of hours due to his own assignation, which he didn't want too many people to know about.

A couple of days passed and then came a report of a Death sighting, in relation to a robbery. The report was in Slovenian newspaper.

What was the Professor doing in enemy territory? wondered Hart. Marcus was too much of an Italian irredentist to become a traitor. No, he was up to something. Whatever it was, there was a huge risk that the Habsburgs may capture him and the projector. And his assets in the Habsburg Empire were somewhat limited. However, he knew a man who could bring back the Professor from there—for a price.

Inverlair Lodge, Scotland.

A scarred wreck of a man was speaking to his wife. It was not going well. She was pleading with him.

"Astor, you must believe me! I am going to stand by you. You must believe me! I am not going to leave you. Have I not stood by you for the last two years? Have I not moved here from London to be with you?"

The wreck of a man responded, "You will betray me, Ellenor, like the weaklings in the government have. They have imprisoned me here," he said, waving his hand round the room, which was little more than a bedroom with a table and washing facilities.

"Astor, you are here for your own good, to be treated for your injuries."

"No! My injuries have been treated as much as they can. What can anyone do about this?" he waved his hand across his scarred face. "They cannot make me a proper man again."

She looked at his burnt face. Gone were the handsome features of the man she had married, replaced with a burnt face. Gone was the confidence of the adventurer Lord Astor Burydan, the man who, with his friends, had taken on the master criminal Dr. Cornelius Kramm. The Doctor had once imprisoned her, testing some foul drug on her, and was responsible for the death of her sister. Lord Burydan and his allies had crushed Dr. Cornelius, his brother Fritz, and their Red Hand criminal empire. She had married this man—her hero. Now he was just this paranoid, wounded man. However, she was his wife, and she took her vows very seriously.

"You are as great a man as any," she replied. "Few have had the adventures you have. We will return to

London soon, and you can plan the future. As soon as the doctors here say you are better, we can go."

"Doctors! This is a prison for the inconvenient, the building lent to the government for the war. They will never let me go."

"You are a free man, Astor, if you want to leave now, you could."

"They would stop me, have you not seen the guards here?"

"I can see we are going nowhere again today. I shall return tomorrow, when perhaps you are in a better mood." With that she strode out of the room.

As soon as she left the corridor, she turned around and saw an orderly leave the adjoining room and knock on her husband's room. She thought nothing of it—the orderlies sometimes went to check on him after her visits, to make sure he was not distressed.

The 'orderly' received no reply to his first knock. He tried again. "Go to hell!" came the reply. The orderly simply walked in.

Lord Burydan took in the thin, bespectacled bald man in front of him.

"Dr. Cornelius!" he hissed. He tried to leap at him, but he only got up from his chair and stumbled forward, his injuries preventing him from doing anything else. Cornelius took Lord Burydan's shoulder and firmly pushed him back into his chair.

"Criminal scum! I should kill you!"

"Why would you wish to harm me, Lord Burydan?" the master criminal asked. "We were, at least technically, on the same side the last time we met. Do you not want to know why I am here?"

"To kill me, no doubt." He then laughed strangely. "Look at me. I have no objection."

"Why would I wish to kill you? No, I am here to make you an offer."

Lord Burydan stared into the Doctor's eyes. "What kind of offer?" Burydan knew his tone gave himself away. He tried to suppress it, but hope was suddenly within him.

The Doctor knew immediately that he would be able to convince the man. "To restore you. Am I not, after all, the sculptor of human flesh? I can change men's faces," he gestured to Lord Burydan's body, "and their bodies."

"For a price," said Lord Burydan.

"Of course. The price is simple. You will accompany me to help capture a man and a special weapon in hostile territory, and perform a special task. And then you will be free, with your face and body restored."

"I am no criminal."

"Indeed not. This mission is for your ally, the French. You remember Simon Hart, from our last encounter? He is the one employing me. For you, this is a war mission."

"Does my government know of this?"

"I have no idea, Lord Burydan. Your involvement is my concern only. You are committing no crime, as far as I am aware. Furthermore, I understand you a legally a free man. If you disappear from this residence, again you will have committed no crime."

"How do you know that I won't walk away after you've restored me?"

Cornelius smiled. "The initial treatment will be temporary. Should you escape me, you will revert to your present form within 48 hours."

Lord Burydan responded angrily. "You could have a hold on me forever!"

"It would be bad for business if it got out that I re-neged on my agreements. You may even kill me in a fit of rage. And anyway, if I did do that, would it still not be better working for me than living out your days like this?"

Lord Burydan looked at the floor. Then he looked up again. "What is this special task?" he asked.

"Our mission is likely to be interfered with by the adventuress Countess Petrovska. Your job will be to kill her."

"Kill a woman!"

"Spare me your mock horror. Let us recall that, in the past, you cold-bloodedly killed two of my employees by throwing them to alligators."

Lord Burydan laughed, but this time it was more the laugh of his old self. "Yes, I recall," he said, with a certain relish. "The world was better off without them, but a woman?"

"A woman who is an enemy of your country..." *And now*, thought the Doctor, *the killer blow*. "...and also the woman who pushed you into the fire, creating your current predicament."

Lord Burydan froze. He recalled the events of two years previous, where he had possession of a super-weapon that could destroy whole cities. Who cared if the Hun were killed in their millions? The war would have been won. And then, on the ship carrying the weapon, the Habsburg agent, Countess Irina Petrovska, had inter-vened, destroying his plans. He suspected he had been pushed into the fire, but he could not quite remember. One moment, he was on deck, the next in the flames. And yet, he had heard her cry "Farewell, Lord Burydan." Yes, yes, it made sense now. It was the Countess!

Cornelius could sense he was near. Now to finish it. "You could be a whole again, be a man again for your wife. Do you wish to see her go off with another man?" Lord Burydan flashed a look of hate at him. Cornelius went on, "Everything can be yours again. Come with me now, and within hours, you will be restored. My equipment is not far. In the morning, you will enjoy the Sun on your unscarred face. This could be your last night spent like this."

"Let us go. I wish to settle with the Countess."

"Excellent," said Dr .Cornelius.

He was delighted. His former enemy now worked for him. And what's more, Lord Burydan thought the Countess responsible for his disfigurement. That was amusing to him, because it was he who had pushed Burydan into the fire, not the Countess.

The island of Brač, Dalmatia, Austro-Hungarian Empire

Countess Irina Petrovska looked out onto the Adriatic. She could see the city of Split in the distance, a few kilometers across the water, with the Dinaric mountains behind. She was in the village of Sutivan, seated at a café on the small Riva, near to the main village church. She looked to her right, and saw her friend Josip walking past the small castle *Marjanović* and towards her. She waved at him. He was pleased to see her. She looked striking, an auburn-haired beauty wearing the most fashionable Viennese clothes.

Josip sat down. "My dear Countess, you look as beautiful as ever."

"Ever the charmer," she replied.

He sat down. "Why are you here, Irina? I am aware you are kept busy with nursing duties and your journalism work. I hear that Vienna holds your work in high regard, including certain military circles."

The Countess knew that Josip was involved in politics—he was a member of the Croatian People's Peasant Party. Clearly, he had heard something about her exploits beyond nursing and the occasional piece in the fashionable Vienna Press.

"I do my duty to my people and the Empire, Josip."

Josip smiled. He knew that she was a Polish nationalist, deeply concerned with the fate of her people and politically wanting a united Poland, currently split between three powers within the Habsburg Empire.

"I know, Irina. And your interest in fair representation of the peoples of the Empire is well-known and appreciated by people like me. I do hope you can put in a good work with the Emperor, and his heir Karl regarding our cause. We believe some form of Croatian unit, within the Empire at least combining the lands of Dalmatia, Slavonia, Croatia…"

The Countess interrupted him. She was sympathetic, and loved discussing politics, but right now she needed information.

"Josip, forgive me. I do have some important questions for you. First, I would just like to thank you for looking after my property here for me..." *Which is why the* Evidenzbureau *assigned me this mission, my links here provide excellent cover,* she thought. "…But I also need your help, your knowledge of the area, here and on the mainland," she pointed towards Split.

"How can I be of service?" he replied, sensing immediately something important was going on. He had also noticed a couple of upright-looking gentlemen on another table who he noticed kept glancing at them.

They changed subjects when the waiter approached, speaking about her holiday home in the village, how her seafaring friends, the Lukšić family, were and so on.

After the waiter left, Josip leaned over to her across their table. He glanced with his eyes over to the table with the two gentlemen.

"Ah," said the Countess, "Captain Marić and Lieutenant Vuljanić" she said quietly. They are with me, part of my entourage, shall we say, along with my butler and maid."

Josip realized there was much truth in the rumors about the Countess.

"Josip," she said, "have you heard anything about these tales of a man dressed up as Death robbing people? And the incident in Supetar two days ago?"

Supetar was the island's administrative center, not far away from Sutivan, where Josip lived.

"I have. In fact, I have spoken to the man who was robbed. The press reported a man dressed up, but he insisted that it was real. That Death appeared before him and demanded money. He admitted to me that he was drunk and on his way home. He's a sensible enough fellow once sober, but when drunk, he is rather less so. I would not be surprised if he simply lost the money and invented this story to placate his wife, who would not be amused at the loss of his wages." Josip nodded towards the two officers. "Also, when he went to the police, he was then questioned by two mysterious men." He glanced again at the officers.

"I am sure they had their reasons," said the Countess, smiling. "After all, we are at war, and these robberies have taken place all the way from the Isonzo front down to Split, where there have been a cluster of such robberies. I am interested in writing about them for a

Vienna newspaper. Have there been any unusual happenings of late? Any strangers?"

"We are at war, everything is strange. However, there is something. There is an Austrian visitor in Supetar, a Gerhard Huber. He has been flashing money about and has been staying at the *Praha* hotel for the last week or so. He speaks German, but with a strange accent. He keeps saying that the Dalmatia will become part of his country, which is odd as we already come under Vienna, as the barmen keep telling him."

This interested the Countess. "Has he been spoken to?"

"Yes, his papers are in order. He claims to be here to look at the stars. He's been here a for a week or so, with a couple of trips to the mainland."

"The gendarmes have not informed me of this individual," the Countess said, thoughtfully.

"I am sure he is harmless. I met him myself. He's an accountant with an interest in astronomy. He rambled to me about Dalmatia being his and then bored me rigid with talking about the stars."

At the other table, the two officers were speaking to each other, whilst carefully looking around the area. They spoke of the war, both agreeing the recent Italian advance would be repelled; despite their numerical superiority, their enemy had not made much progress since entering the war.

For the Captain, this was all new. He had been swiftly seconded to the *Evidenzbureau* to work with the Countess on finding the fugitive. The soldier he had wounded had died from infection, but he was clearly French and could barely speak Italian. They also knew that the Italians were hunting a man with certain unspecified equipment, and that this person had disappeared.

The *Evidenzbureau* had put things together. It was likely that a French soldier had, for whatever reason, stolen the mysterious device and was now on the run, using it to get cash in robberies.

The *Evidenzbureau* further believed that a certain unit of French intelligence was behind the device, and now, they had to get it, before the French agents did.

At that moment, a rough-looking man dashed over to the café, collapsing in a chair.

"Rakija! Now!" he shouted at the waiter, banging his fist on his table.

The Countess looked disgusted at this uncouth person. "I've seen him around for the past few months," said Josip. "He moves around the island, looking for the odd job to pay for booze."

The waiter simply looked at him—they occasionally had to deal with his sort. "That ghost in the newspapers! He's in Ložišća, he was robbing people by the church! It's not a man in a mask, he's real! It's Death! Death!"

The Countess went over to him. "Describe what you saw," she ordered. Her tone brooked no dissent. The Captain and the Lieutenant stood by her, reinforcing her authority. She knew the village he mentioned –about six kilometers away.

"People were going to evening prayer, then Death appeared, demanding money for their sins! They refused to give it, holding their crosses against him. He pointed his scythe at one of them—and lightning of some kind hit the mayor, burning him to death."

The two officers exchanged a brief glance. That fitted with the first attack in the trenches, the details of which had not been publicly released.

"I ran all the way here, without looking back," the man said.

The Countess looked at him suspiciously. "Did no one come with you?"

"Every man for himself. The others no doubt ran to their homes. I wouldn't stay there. I'm off to Split on the first boat out."

"The Countess turned to the two officers. "If this man is telling the truth, we have to move fast." She then spoke to Josip, "Keep an eye on him. Send for my butler to assist you." She promptly left with the officers in tow.

Nearby was her vehicle, which she named *Elizabeth*, specially armored for the war, parked next to the castle *Marjanović*.

She and the officers got in. "I'll drive. I know the way."

The two officers piled onto the back seats.

"Hang on to your hat, sir" said the Lieutenant to the Captain.

The car headed off, picking up speed and running along a rough road out of the village.

"How is this possible," asked the Captain. "We must be going at 60 km an hour across this road."

"It was a present from my British friends from before the war. And its secrets defy our expert's knowledge—as it did my friends."

There were a number of mysteries regarding the vehicle. Professor Saxton and Professor Wells had given it to her as the only appropriate reward for helping saving London in 1912. They had not been in contact since the war began.

Within minutes, they were approaching a small bridge over a ravine.

"The *Franz Joseph* bridge is up ahead soon," said the Countess. "The original bridge was destroyed in a flood, the locals petitioned our Emperor for help and he paid for this new one, hence its name."

On the far side of the bridge, a square-jawed man leaned on one side of the stone bridge. He was on the external side, standing on a piece of ground just before the ravine. He held a rifle, an Enfield P14.

Dr Cornelius certainly knows how to get the best weapons, I'll certainly say that for him, he thought. He saw the car he was waiting for in the distance. He let it come closer, to get his shot right. *Perhaps it might fly off the bridge and into the ravine—that would be a fine spectacle!* he thought.

The man moved away from his position. *Why not let that Hun see have a glimpse of who did this, and thus why she is going to die.*

Lord Burydan moved to the middle of the bridge and raised his P14.

The Countess saw a man on the other side of the bridge and started to brake.

The British Lord took his shot.

A bullet hit the windscreen, but bounced off. The Countess halted the *Elizabeth* on the bridge.

Lord Burydan remained standing. He fired more shots at the Countess. The bullets bounced off the windscreen. The Countess stared at the man.

"Lord Burydan!" she exclaimed.

She picked up her Doppelpistole M1912 by the side of her seat. On the bottom of her windscreen, she moved a small slat, put the barrel off of the Doppelpistole through the revealed slot, and opened fire.

Lord Burydan dived aside, having seen what she was doing. He rolled back to lying behind the bridge wall, with the ravine just a few centimeters away, and out of the line of the Countess's fire. The occupants of the car then heard a noise.

"Is that… laughing?" the Lieutenant asked.

"Yes," said the Countess. She remembered the British Lord from their last encounter. He was quite unhinged then. What was he like now?

The British peer was exhilarated. What fun this was! *The Countess is keen to provide some sport!* He started to move down.

"We have to get out—take the fight to him," Captain Marić said. "If you cover me, I will go back and around the side—try and flush him out with a few shots. He must be pinned down right there."

Before the Countess could say anything, he leaped out of the car and ran back. He had his Rast & Gasser M1898 service revolver with him. Within seconds, he was back at the beginning of the bridge. He looked around the side and saw nothing. Where did the man go? It was certainly getting darker, but he should certainly be visible.

Someone shouted. The Captain whirled around—and took a shot in the arm.

Lord Burydan had somehow appeared on the other side of the bridge, right next to the car, rifle now slung on his back. The sides of the car had armored plating, but he saw an observation slot.

Lord Burydan had a pistol, a Webley, which he stuck into it, twisted the barrel to where he thought the Countess was, but it was forced up from the inside by the Lieutenant. Then the car moved backwards. The Briton was dragged along and was forced to let go of his pistol. He fell to the ground, his rifle coming off his shoulder.

Now he was almost in point blank range of the Countess's gun. He jumped over the wall of the bridge before she could fire again.

"I'm all right, it's a flesh wound, stay inside—he must still be here," the Captain said. He moved as fast as he could toward the car door and got it in swiftly.

At that moment, a number of men approached the bridge, from the direction of Ložišća. The Countess recognized one of them—Ložišća's priest. He approached the car, his hand shielding his eyes from the glare of the headlights.

He came nearer and recognized the driver. "Countess? Are you well? We heard shots"

"Until next time, Countess—which will be very soon" came a voice in English, preventing the Countess from replying.

She saw Lord Burydan in the nearby field, waving at her. He then ran off into the dark.

"See to the Captain," she ordered the Lieutenant and got out of the car. The priest and the other men were rather startled to see the Countess wielding a machine gun. She also had what seemed to be a pair of opera glasses. She looked across the field in the near dark with the glasses. The image she saw was largely green, but she could see no figures. Lord Burydan was out of the range of her optical instrument. Pursuit might be difficult, given it was unclear which direction he had headed off in. More importantly, there was another place to get to at once.

"I am sorry to have disturbed you all, Father. Has there been a major incident in Ložišća tonight?"

The mystified priest shook his head. "Nothing at all happened," he said.

"Thank you, I thought as much. I am sure someone will come to explain it to you shortly—and I shall return at some point to explain in person also," she added.

She looked at something on the bridge. She saw a rope attached to the side, hanging down. She spotted a couple more. She rolled her eyes and got back into *Elizabeth*, reversed off the bridge, turned and went back the way she came. She knew she had to drive more slowly due to night having fallen, which could cost her the mission.

"He's gotten away. We must head to Supetar. How is Captain Marić?," she asked the Lieutenant.

"I'm perfectly fine," the Captain said, keen to show he was not incapacitated. "A flesh wound."

She glanced at the Lieutenant who was bandaging him, who nodded.

"You mentioned something about a Lord Burydan… Is that the English adventurer?" asked the Captain.

"The English lunatic more like," the Countess replied. "Did you notice those ropes? He was swinging underneath the bridge, jumping from rope to rope. That's how he was confusing us."

"Is he an acrobat?" asked the Captain.

"An exhibitionist, certainly."

Lieutenant Vuljanić looked puzzled. "I've read the report on the Pula affair. How can be here? He was severely burned."

"Quite so," said the Countess. "They were burns no man could recover from. Surely, Lieutenant, you must know who we really face? It is Dr. Cornelius Kramm."

"The master criminal? The Lord of the Red Hand?" asked Marić. "I read in the papers that he was killed in

America. That would have been before the war. And wasn't Lord Burydan one of his arch-enemies?"

"He certainly is not dead," the Countess said. "He now operates in Europe. He sells his criminal services to the highest bidder. Perhaps the French have hired him. His surgical abilities are far beyond anything known to medical science. Only he could have restored Lord Burydan. And no doubt, he was now working for Dr. Cornelius in return. Given Burydan was unhinged in the first place, I daresay whatever enmity Lord Burydan felt for him has been very easily set aside in return for restoring him."

"What has this got to do with our mission?" asked Vuljanić.

"This was plainly a trap, no doubt to eliminate us. Dr. Cornelius is after the same man and weapon we are. He may have been hired by the French or the Italians, or even possibly operating on his own to get this weapon. It is likely that he is in Supetar right now, going after the man Josip told me about."

"Thanks for the warning shout, by the way, but I could not make it out," said the Captain to the Lieutenant.

"That was Lord Burydan," the Countess said. "I think he has some kind of warped sense of honor. I suspect he just did not want to shoot you in the back, although he was quite happy to try and destroy whole cities the last time I met him."

Elizabeth returned to Sutivan, by the Café where her butler and Josip were standing by the man whose information had led them to Lord Burydan's trap. She called the 'butler' over.

"Sergeant, that man led us into a trap. Find out what he knew about it. We have to get to Supetar." With that, she drove off.

The Sergeant, who was another of the Countess's group of operatives, went over to Josip. "Sir, do you have somewhere private where I could speak to our friend here in private?"

Josip nodded. The man jumped up, but the Sergeant shoved him by the shoulder back down. "Now, my friend, you don't want me to use this, do you?" The sergeant moved his jacket, revealing a pistol.

The Sergeant spoke in German, which the man could not speak, but he understood perfectly, promptly deciding that full cooperation was best.

In the dark, Lord Burydan was walking in the direction of the sea, where his boat was. He, too, had a pair of glasses that enabled him to see in the dark—another piece of the Doctor's equipment. He was exhilarated. He had never thought that he would do such things again. Dr. Cornelius would not be pleased with his failing to kill the Countess. However, the good news was that he would likely get another chance. And the other good news was that the Countess would be too late in getting to Supetar. He laughed out loud in the dark. *What entertainment this all was!*

In Supetar, Dr. Cornelius was waiting outside the *Praha* hotel.

"You are sure that's him?" he asked the rough-looking man next to him, showing him a photograph of Professor Marcus.

"That's him. First saw him in Split, now he's in there."

"He had best be, Darko, given how much I am paying you for this information."

"No more Red Hand to work for, Doctor. Got to pay my bills. And you can afford it."

The man was insolent. He was a former member of the once-feared Red Hand organization, which Dr. Cornelius and his late brother had run. In the old days, he would simply have had the man killed for his tone—or perhaps be subjected to his surgical experiments. Things were different now. To eliminate him would be to ensure others would not work for the sculptor of human flesh.

A few people left the hotel, heading for the nearby port area, where a boat to the mainland waited.

"That's him," Darko said, pointing a balding man in the group. "Name of Gerhard Huber. I'm told he has a ticket to the mainland tonight."

Dr. Cornelius was satisfied. This was Professor Marcus. What a fool the man was. No attempt at disguise and committing robberies within a small geographical space. He stood out here on the island of Brač in the last few days. The Doctor was surprised the police had not already picked him up.

"There are too many people around," the Doctor said. "Let's follow him."

Professor Marcus got on board the boat. His pursuers bought two tickets and got on board, keeping a discreet distance from their target. Shortly, the boat set off.

It was some minutes later that *Elizabeth* roared into the town. The Countess and the officers ran over to the hotel, with Captain Marić firmly banging on the door. He was determined to show that his wound was minor. The startled owner came out.

"I understand a Gerhard Huber is staying here. Is he present?" demanded the Countess. Her imperious tone brooked no dissent.

"No, he's left on the last boat to Split," replied the owner.

"My men must check. Check the hotel register and his room."

"This is my property…" started the owner.

"I am the Countess Irina Petrovska. I trust you have heard of me?"

The hotel owner indeed had and became more respectful. "Yes, of course. I have read some of your articles and I know you have property on our island, but why are you so interested in my guest and who are these men?"

"We are on important business for the Empire. Help us, keep quiet, and I shall give your establishment a mention in an article I am preparing." The owner was delighted and quickly showed the officers the man's room which was on the first floor—he indeed was not there.

They came back down to report to the Countess.

The hotel owner volunteered some information. "If it is of any help, the fellow did say he was going the *Hotel Bellevue* in Split."

"Likes to live well, this one," said the Countess. The Lieutenant suppressed a smile. Much the same could be said about the Countess.

She looked over to the harbor. There was a boat there that had brought over *Elizabeth*. Its captain was an intelligence agent, prepared to move at a moment's notice. She turned to Vuljanić.

"Get our boat ready, captain, we leave for Split at once. Then take *Elizabeth* and pick up the Sergeant. I'd like to know what he has found out from that man in the café. Make sure he is restrained until he can be taken into custody, his actions nearly got us killed." She looked around. "Just where is Dr. Cornelius? The sooner we get to Split, the better."

It took around 45 minutes to set off. The Countess wondered if that gap of time would see the man they were after snared by Dr. Cornelius.

Dr. Cornelius himself was not amused. First, he and his minion were not able to get to the Professor coming off the boat. There were far too many people about, despite it being night. There were also the odd gendarme. And people were suspicious—there was a war on, after all. They followed the Professor along the Riva from the harbor towards the *Hotel Bellevue*. They stayed outside, whilst he went in.

"What now?" asked Darko.

"We enter after him," said the Doctor. "Some improvisation may be required to get into his room and to persuade him to come with us. I have a spray to render him unconscious if need be. We will use it on staff if we have to—better someone finds a sleeping body than a corpse." The Doctor cared nothing for human life, but he did know that a corpse would create a much bigger commotion just when he did not need it.

Lord Burydan suddenly bounded up to them.

"Splendid boat, you've got there, Cornelius. It got me here quickly." he said in English.

"Silence, you idiot," replied the Doctor. "The English language is not one the locals will ignore if heard. How did you find us? You were supposed to return to our hideout."

Lord Burydan beamed at the Doctor, and then switched to German, and said in a lowered voice, "Well, old man, I got back here and parked the boat right there…" He pointed to a mooring area by the Riva. "…I wanted to have a quick look round this place you know, in case of trouble. Spotted you very easily, you stand out with that bald head of yours."

Dr. Cornelius was about to explode when Lord Burydan continued. "Didn't manage to kill the Countess—that car and bloody villagers appearing on the scene." He thought best not to mention the loss of his weapons and considered himself fortunate he had left a spare Webley on the boat he used.

"You failed!" the sculptor of flesh hissed.

"No, no, old boy," replied the Briton. "A temporary delay. You must admit she's not caught up with you, so the ruse worked to that extent. Er, she didn't capture the target?"

"We have not seen her, and the target is in there," the Doctor said, pointing to the hotel. He suppressed his rage. "We now have to get in and get him out. We must deceive the hotel receptionist, or perhaps bribe him, into giving us his room number."

"Leave it to me, I can act Kraut," said Lord Burydan.

With that, he strode into the hotel lobby and straight up to the reception desk. As it was night, there was only one person on duty, a young man, sitting in a chair. He stood bolt upright when he saw the Briton marching towards him. Lord Burydan slammed his hand on the desk. "Gerhard Huber. Get him down here at once, Pig-Dog![9]"

Dr. Cornelius and Darko rushed in behind him.

---

[9] German: *Schweinhund.*

"Mein Herr," said the young receptionist, "we do not simply call down the guests". He turned to ring a bell behind him, which would summon other staff. The man was clearly a drunk.

"Don't you 'Mein Herr' me!" shouted Lord Burydan.

He leaned over the desk, turning the young man round and lifted him up by his lapels. "What number room is he in?" the Briton menacingly asked.

"204!" the terrified young man said.

Dr. Cornelius sprayed something on the man, and he immediately lost consciousness.

"Put him down into the chair—gently" the Doctor said.

Lord Burydan did so.

"No one appears to have heard you," Cornelius said. "We are fortunate."

"That's due to not dilly-dallying and taking action instead."

Cornelius stared at him. He had had enough. "Your luck ran out once. And it's thanks to me that you stand here so arrogantly. Do not make me reconsider our arrangements. Enough of your rash actions."

Lord Burydan suddenly looked concerned. Then he gave a theatrical bow. "My apologies. Let us get the man we are here for."

The three men swiftly went upstairs.

In room 204, Professor Marcus lay down on his bed. Things were going well. His room even overlooked the Prokurative square next door, its Venetian style stirring his irredentist feelings. He thought of how he had gotten to this position where greatness was within his grasp.

The war had not gone so well, despite Italian numerical superiority and the recent victory. This had enraged the Professor. How dare these Slovenes, Croats and the rest defy the Italian invasion of their lands? Further, how was it that the Italian military leadership bowed to the French on the use of the projector? *If only Gabriele d'Annunzio was in charge!*

Shortly after his escape from Hart's group, he had made contact with irredentist sympathizers. After demonstrating what he could do, he informed them that he wanted to do something to smash the Austro-Hungarians. He proposed he go to Vienna and assassinate their Emperor, which, he thought, would hasten Italian victory and deliver annexation of lands promised through the Treaty of London.

Time was of the essence—not only the French, but officially the Italians were seeking to recapture him. The irredentists were none too keen on assassinating Franz Joseph—it was too risky, they felt. However, they suggested another target that would soon arrive in Spalato—the Italian name for Split—on the Dalmatian coast. They had good information leaked to them by intelligence sources. And this target may be more politically useful.

The Professor was not so sure, but he was persuaded by one of the irredentists, who pointed out the target's potential threat. The Professor was both convinced and impressed by this man, who already had a reputation and was now an NCO in the Italian army. *Along with D'Annunzio, this Benito Mussolini was one of the men needed to lead Italy!* the Professor thought.

His train of thought was interrupted by a knock on the door. "There is a fire, we must evacuate" came a voice from outside.

Fire? The Professor was suspicious. He kept quiet.

Another knock. "Mr. Huber, please! You must come out immediately!"

The Professor could hear nothing. Surely, there would be commotion throughout the building? He looked out of the window onto the square. A few people were idling about. No sense of alarm there. He quickly took the projector out of the bed and activated it.

Outside, Dr. Cornelius had hoped the Professor would simply open the door. He nodded at Darko. The man took a sharp tool from his pocket and stuck it into the lock. After a few seconds, he stood back and gestured at the lock to indicate it was now unlocked. Lord Burydan prepared for action.

"Open it," commanded Dr. Cornelius.

Darko opened the door and was struck by the visage of Death within the room. This version floated towards the men. Darko looked terrified.

"It's just an image, idiot!" said Lord Burydan.

The Briton grabbed Darko and shoved him in, following. Darko unwillingly flew at the specter—and went through it. The creature flickered and the unfortunate Darko seemed to burn, twisting in the room, making a gasping sound. He collapsed, a blackened corpse.

"Slight miscalculation!" said Lord Burydan.

The Professor pushed his hand deeper on the projector, and another Death image appeared.

"Off," said Dr. Cornelius to the Professor. He had used the moment of Darko's burning to get to the Italian and hold a pistol directly to his head.

The image disappeared. Dr. Cornelius took the projector from the Professor. He noticed it tingled his hand slightly.

"Who are you?" asked the unnerved Italian.

"I am Dr, Malbrough. and this is…"

"Lord Astor Burydan," exclaimed the Professor. "And you are in fact Dr. Cornelius Kramm, the so-called sculptor of human flesh. I recognize both of you from the newspapers. I followed the whole Red Hand affair very closely. You are supposed to be dead, but clearly you are not. However, I thought the both of you were mortal enemies?"

"The war makes unlikely allies, Professor."

"It certainly does," said Lord Burydan, beaming. The Professor thought that there was something not quite right about that man.

"Let us leave," said the Doctor. "I will have my gun on you at all times, Professor. My instructions are to bring you in alive, but the retrieval of the projector is paramount. I will kill you if need be."

"Nonsense. Only I know how to operate it."

"I have my instructions, and it's not open to debate. Move."

"One moment," said Lord Burydan, who was looking out of the window. "Looks like a gendarme or some such out in the square. Looks bored. My sense is that he's not on alert. Let's wait a few minutes until he clears off."

Dr. Cornelius nodded. He spoke to the Professor. "I am curious, Professor. What is the origin of this projector?" he asked, holding it up in his other hand.

"Hart has not told you?" asked the Professor.

"He told me what it does, not its origins. I don't think you invented it, it seems a little advanced, plus your field is astronomy. My pardon if I am wrong."

The Professor looked a little ruffled. "Well, I do have an interested in other sciences. However, you are correct. Hart did not tell you—very well, I will. Just to spite him."

He told him about the alien craft and the crash.

Still keeping an eye on the gendarme, Lord Burydan laughed. "From space? What tosh!"

"I suspect he's telling the truth, Lord Burydan," said the Doctor. "Censorship, bribes and disbelief keeps such matters out of the newspapers. Your government have specialists to deal with these things, including old friends of the Countess, incidentally. In Sarajevo, the Austro-Hungarians have a repository of mysterious technologies and strange relics, including some of otherworldly origin.

"By Jove!" exclaimed Lord Burydan.

The Professor became animated. "When Italy wins, you can be assured that I will be given full access to what is held in Sarajevo. I will find out all their secrets."

"The gendarme has gone—seemed to leave the square heading away from us," said Lord Burydan.

"Wait!" said the Professor. "Do you not want to know why I am here?"

"No doubt some scheme to attack the Dalmatian locals. It matters not. We have caught you and it's time to go," replied the Doctor.

The Professor remained where he was. "Hear me out," he said. "I am here to use this projector to assassinate Archduke Karl, the heir to the throne. He is due here for a meeting. I will use the projector to kill him in front of many witnesses. Death itself will be seen to have intervened in the war. It will be a terrible omen for the Austro-Hungarians, and will demoralize them. Let me do this, and then I will leave with you quite willingly. We will be heroes to Hart!"

"Could we get a bonus for this?" asked Lord Burydan of the Doctor.

Dr. Cornelius considered this, whilst noting the Briton's unheroic interest in money. "What meeting is he here for?" he asked.

"It will be secret, held in the cellars right under Diocletian's Palace tomorrow evening. It's just a few minutes from here. Archduke Karl will be meeting with the Croatian politician Stjepan Radić, to discuss reform in the Empire including a unified, autonomous Croatian unit. There is talk it would encompass even Bosnia-Hercegovina. Your allies the Serbs would not like that, and of course, we Italians would be concerned."

Lord Burydan scoffed. "Concerned? No doubt, given the limited gains of your army. Have to give it these Habsburg Hun types—they certainly have your measure!"

"How dare you! Our gains have been glorious!" said the Professor, despite knowing the truth of the Briton's words.

Lord Burydan continued laughing.

Dr. Cornelius cut in. "I have no idea how Hart, or his government might react to such an assassination. No, we will do only what we are contracted to do."

The Professor spat. "Money—is that all that motivates you?"

"Very much so," replied the Doctor.

Lord Burydan simply grinned and said, "Let's be off then!"

"What about him?" the Professor asked, pointing at Darko on the floor. He was still twitching.

"He will be dead soon enough," said Cornelius. He was happy to let the man die slowly for his insolence. He would pay the man's family his fee with a bonus—which would leave his reputation intact.

The three men left the room and went down the stairs. The Professor doubted he could escape these two men, at least not at the moment, with their guard up. They exited the hotel.

At this point, Fate decided to give the Professor a chance. They were surrounded by a group—three men and a woman, all pointing guns at them. Dr. Cornelius groaned inwardly. The Countess and her friends. That idiot Burydan's failure to kill her meant they were about to fail in their mission. *Where was the Englishman, anyway? He was with us only a moment ago*, he thought.

Cornelius swiftly aimed his own weapon at the Professor's head, grabbing hold of him and twisting him so that the gun was clearly aimed at the man's head. "Countess, I will kill this man if you do not move out of the way," he shouted.

"Don't be ridiculous," the Countess replied. "Hand him over, and you will be fairly treated."

Meanwhile, Lord Burydan had bounded upstairs to the first floor, revolver in hand. He had spotted the group an instant before leaving the hotel. *The Doctor lacks my experience in combat. I saw them a mile off*, he thought.

He stuck his head out of the window on the first floor and looked down. His line of fire to the Countess was obscured by one of the men –so he aimed at him.

"Good night, servant of the Boche!" he shouted, and fired.

All of the Countess's group had turned upon hearing him. The shot hit the Captain, knocking him into the Countess. The Lieutenant and the Sergeant fired back, but Lord Burydan was already gone.

The Professor took the chance that was offered by the chaos. Lord Burydan's surprise attack had momentarily distracted the Doctor, and his gun had moved away from his head.

The Professor grabbed the Doctor's arm and twisted it. The gun fell out of Cornelius's hand. With presence of mind, the astronomer shoved him away, grabbed the gun from the ground and aimed it at Dr. Cornelius.

Without a word, the Doctor gave him the bag containing the projector. He was not going to die for it. The Professor grabbed the bag, took out the projector, and then disappeared.

All present were non-plussed, not helped by people coming from all over, to see what the commotion was. The Countess aimed her weapon at Cornelius. Vuljanić went over to the Captain, who lay on the floor.

"He's dead," said the Lieutenant.

"Cover that window," said Vuljanić to the Sergeant. "I am going in to get that Englishman."

"I think not," said a voice.

They turned around. Lord Burydan had come from behind them, and had his Webley aimed at the gendarme he had seen earlier, now taken hostage by the Briton.

"Drop the weapon, Countess," ordered the Englishman. "Doctor, come to me."

The Countess did not comply. "He can go, but we are not dropping our weapons," she said.

"Very well. I will kill you some other time, Countess."

The sculptor of human flesh went over to him. "We are going back into the hotel, now," said the Briton.

The three of them backed into the hotel with their hostage, and slowly went up the stairs. The Countess and the Lieutenant followed.

"Stay back, Countess," Lord Burydan warned.

They turned the corner of the stairway and were out of sight.

The Countess and Vuljanić slowly moved up the stairs when the gendarme ran down and said: "They jumped out of a window!"

The two men ran away from the hotel, with Dr. Cornelius limping as he ran. His landing onto the Prokurative had not been a very controlled one. They ran down the Split Riva and, within moments, had boarded the boat Lord Burydan had moored nearby.

Burydan activated the motor and the boat moved off at speed. "You know Doctor," Lord Burydan said, "jumping out of windows is a specialty of mine, very useful in the adventurer business. I must teach you how to do it!"

Dr. Cornelius cursed.

A passer-by informed the Countess of men who had jumped into a boat. She and the Lieutenant looked out to sea. It was dark; all that could be seen were one or two lights on the islands opposite.

They headed back to the hotel. The Countess was angry and upset, but maintained her composure. The lunatic Englishman had killed a good man.

The Professor was streets away. He was pleased. The projector had intuited that he wanted an image in front of him of what was behind him. It was lucky it was getting so dark; otherwise all present would have seen some movement in the air, the drawback with that tactic.

He felt now that the projector was understanding him more, linking more with his mind. *This projector must have had some kind of symbiotic relationship with its Saturnian creators, and now its relationship with me is growing stronger* he thought. Tomorrow, he would unleash its full potential.

Dr. Cornelius and Lord Burydan traveled not far along the coast and docked the boat just outside of Split. They left the boat and headed into a dilapidated house by the sea. They took the engine of the boat. Both men had night goggles on, enabling them to see where they were going. Lord Burydan had asked Cornelius where he had obtained such equipment, but the sculptor of human flesh merely said he had a good supplier of advanced items in Berlin.

They entered and walked over to a wall, against which there was a cabinet. They moved the cabinet revealing a trapdoor. "Go down and wait for me," said Cornelius. "I have to make contact with Hart. It is not a straightforward process. It will have to be a few hours. Get some sleep. Use the escape tunnel if you need to."

The Briton nodded and Cornelius left.

The Countess entered room 204. The crowd been swiftly cleared by the gendarmes, and the lieutenant stood guard over the Captain.

"Have you found anything?" she asked Sergeant Mayr, who had been searching the room.

"No," he replied.

The Countess looked over to the blackened body of the minion. "A lesson there for those who consort with the likes of Dr. Cornelius. Let us hope we can help provide a similar fate for Lord Burydan."

The Sergeant nodded his approval.

The body suddenly groaned. "Help me," he croaked.

The Doctor returned to the house in the early hours of the morning. Lord Burydan was already awake, and in the house, rather than the cellar.

"Good morning, Doctor!" said the Briton. "What have our employers told us?"

The Doctor replied "We have a new task. We must capture the Professor, but prior to his attempting at assassinating Karl, even if that means killing him. Hart is concerned that such an assassination could eventually implicate France, blackening their name, but would also see French leaders become targets in the future."

"Are we going to get a bonus for this?"

"No," lied the sculptor of human flesh. "Hart thinks we should have captured the man and his projector by now. He expects results today. And we shall deliver."

"Indeed!" cried the Briton.

Cornelius looked at him. He was intrigued by this interest in money, not that he was paying the man anything bar his treatment. The Doctor could exploit that.

"Have you looked at yourself today?" he asked Lord Burydan.

Concerned, the Briton took out a small mirror from his pocket. He looked at his face. He could see some greyness on the skin. "I need my treatment," he said.

"Yes," said Cornelius. "However, this is an excellent time to again mention that I am less than amused by some of your behavior. You failed to kill the Countess, letting her interfere later on. Further, your blundering into the hotel could have raised the alarm."

"Hang on, I did manage to get us out of there. We were outnumbered and outgunned."

"Yes, but from now on, you must control yourself more. If we fail, I will not be paid. And if you have contributed to any failure through your behavior, then I will discontinue your treatment."

Lord Burydan could feel his mind suddenly under strain. He had been given a new life. He could not let that go.

"I apologize, Doctor," said the Briton, in a tone of voice less exuberant than usual. "You must understand, the way I operate is much different to yours. However, I will adjust."

"Excellent," said the Doctor. "I have been considering what happened earlier. It is my guess that the Professor's disappearance was not due to his actually becoming invisible, but rather his usage of the projector. I suspect he did something that projected the street behind him, in front of him."

"Damned clever, these spacemen," said Lord Burydan. "Pity that Italian has the projector. We could make a lot of money from it."

"We could. However, it would not be long before the French found us. It is best to take the money. However, there is no harm in taking a look at the projector when we have it. But that is for later. Tonight, we will head to Diocletian's Palace. Unlike the Countess, we know where the Professor will turn up. We must be cautious until then. I shall provide a new face for myself, but not for you. The underlying damage to your face and body could complicate the permanent setting of your face. You may dye your hair... No, shave it all off. It may cause a momentary failure in recognition at some point—a moment you can exploit."

Lord Burydan looked appalled, then laughed, "Yes, I think I can manage that."

"Good. Let me give you your treatment for your face, and then we shall prepare in earnest."

Later in the day, in Split's Civic Hospital, Darko was on the verge of death. A priest entered the room where he had received treatment.

"I understand I am needed?" he asked the Countess, who was standing by the bed, along with the Lieutenant.

"Thank you for coming, Father," said the Countess. "This man is a criminal. His way of life has led to this." she pointed at the man, his face and arms visible above the sheets, but blackened with burns. "His only words were to ask for the last rites. There can be no question of denying him."

The Priest nodded and performed the rites. Darko turned his blackened head to the Countess and in a rasping voice said, "The Doctor abandoned me... To hell with him. The Italian who was with him spoke of killing Archduke Karl and the politician Radić..."

He then fell silent. The Countess went over to him. "He is dead." She turned to the priest. "Thank you, Father. We must take our leave of you. Please do not repeat what you have heard – we will deal with this."

The priest nodded his assent. The two Habsburg agents left the room and exited the building.

Outside the hospital, the Countess turned to the lieutenant. "It seems we were wrong. We are not looking for a Frenchman using a weapon to rob members of the public, but an Italian wishing to assassinate the heir to the throne and the Croatian politician, Stjepan Radić."

"I saw Radić earlier on, he's here in Split," said Vuljanić. "He spotted me and called me over; he knows my father. He is here in Split for a meeting. He mentioned he's staying at friend's residence. It was just a few meters away."

"We must go there, at once; you must lead the way," said the Countess.

They got into *Elizabeth*, where the Sergeant was at the wheel. Vuljanić gave him the directions, and the vehicle moved off. They briefed the Sergeant on what they had to find out.

"Who is this Radić, and what has he got to do with the Archduke?" asked the Sergeant.

"He's head of the Croatian People's Peasant Party. He wants more rights for Croatia within the Empire. I can see why an Italian would want him dead, but the main target must be Archduke Karl, who of course may have the power to help Radić," responded the Countess. "I can only assume he must be meeting the heir here somewhere—information it seems that was not given to us, neither by our superiors or the authorities." She would have words with people about that, she thought.

Vuljanić spoke. He knew a lot about the Croat politician. "Radić has popular support, not like the Yugoslav committee in London, the capital of one of our enemies, a group which wants union with Serbia, a country that will accommodate Italian demands to our land along with their own territorial ambitions," he said angrily. "At least, the Empire fights the invader."

The Countess nodded. She sympathized with politicians such as Radić, whom she felt had had similar goals as herself—autonomy for a united Poland within the Empire. There was talk of some kind of Slavic unit within the Empire, under the Emperor, but no longer split under between the separate rule of Hungary and Austria as now; it would invariably be run in Zagreb. Such talk had displeased not only Belgrade, resulting in the assassination of Archduke Ferdinand, but no doubt Italy too.

The Countess was concerned. Emperor Franz Joseph was elderly, his time would be soon. She had expectations that the heir to the throne would be sympathetic to Polish autonomy. Whatever this Italian had planned, it must be stopped. She wondered what Dr. Cornelius was up to at that moment.

It was early evening. Dr. Cornelius and Lord Burydan were nearly on the seafront by the south entrance to the Diocletian's Palace. It had been built by the Roman Emperor as retirement home for himself in the last years of the third century with him moving into it in 305 AD. Since then, the city of Split had grown in and around it. However, some parts of the original remained.

Not that either Dr. Cornelius or Lord Burydan knew or cared about any of this history. Their concern was the gate to the lower level of the palace at the South wall. It had been closed off, and a couple of gendarmes stood nearby. Both Cornelius and Burydan had been observing it during the day, at a distance. Currently, they were talking as if they were locals merely stopping for a chat. They had passed the entrance a number of times that day.

"These gendarmes are not very good, are they? They've not spotted us lurking about all day," said Lord Burydan.

"Indeed not," replied the Doctor, now sporting a full head of hair, beard and mustache. He disliked changing his face—he was concerned that frequent use may do damage—but if Professor Marcus had recognized him, so could others. "Be alert, it's almost 8 p.m. The meeting begins in half an hour. The Archduke and Radić will soon be here."

The Countess and her party arrived at the place where Radić was staying. He was just leaving the house when he was startled by the *Elizabeth*.

"Of course, I know of you, Countess. And yes, I know that you are a wartime agent of the Empire."

"Mr. Radić," said the Countess, "you must believe me. Your life is in danger, and so is that of the heir to throne."

"It's very secret. Only tomorrow will it be announced he is in Spilt, but only in regard to his duties as a Field Marshal. We are meeting to discuss the position of Croats in the Empire."

"Where?"

"Below Diocletian's palace. I am due to be picked up..."

"Get in," the Countess ordered, and the Sergeant bundled the protesting politician into the back of *Elizabeth*.

By the entrance to the Palace, Dr. Cornelius momentarily turned to the sea. Before him, a specter of Death appeared, different to the one in the hotel. Dressed in a dark cloak, its skeletal hand beckoned at him—the skull seemed to be grinning.

"He's here!" Cornelius hissed at the Briton.

Lord Burydan turned around. "Where?" he asked.

The Doctor looked back to sea. The specter had gone.

"I saw one of those projections. Look around, he cannot be far. He must have somehow recognized us."

They walked around but could see only a few passers-by.

"He will need to have sight of the Archduke. You walk a few meters that way, I shall go in the opposite direction."

Lord Burydan took a few steps. He could see a man approaching.

Behind him, Dr. Cornelius headed the other way, and spotted a car approaching. *This can only be the Archduke*, he thought, as a gendarme told him to move away.

Lord Burydan turned around, hearing the car in the distance and turned back the way he was headed—and suddenly realized the man in front of him was Professor Marcus.

He did not dare take out his gun—there suddenly seemed to be a number of gendarmes milling about and, given what had happened in Sarajevo two years back, they would shoot at him if they saw him with a gun.

He intended to get near to the Professor and see if he could surreptitiously point a gun at him. That was the plan agreed to with the Doctor, but liable to go wrong. He quickened his pace, and nearing the Professor, he moved across the road towards him.

"Excuse me…" he said in his best German, moving his hand to his hidden revolver.

But Professor Marcus had seen him and reached into his bag.

Suddenly, there were shouts and screams. Specters of death had started appearing all around, including right in-between the Briton and the Professor. Lord Burydan backed away. A specter aimed its scythe at him and a bolt of black lightning fired from it, missing him by inches as he ducked out of the way.

"Too slow, old man!" said the Briton pulling out his Webley and firing at the specter. The thing shimmered as the bullets flew through it.

Dr. Cornelius had heard the shouts and saw the Archduke's car still approaching. He noticed some of the specters moving his way. And he felt fear, but was not sure why. It must be from the projector. He ran into the way of the vehicle.

"Stop! Go back! There is an assassination attempt!" he shouted, making sure he was not too close to the vehicle, lest he be mistaken for the assassin.

The driver looked in horror at the creatures behind the Doctor and reversed.

The specters were firing at the car, but the bolts fizzled out after a few yards, and then they seemed to slow to a stop.

Limited power. Yet, clearly there are more of the creatures than on previous occasions, the Doctor noted.

The Professor could see the Emperor's vehicle reversing, and was furious. More specters were appearing around him, producing a kind of wall and firing at Lord Burydan, who was able to duck and dive from the bolts of the slowly-aimed scythes and fingers, laughing whilst doing so.

The Countess arrived in *Elizabeth*. She jumped out, followed by the Lieutenant, Sergeant Mayr and Radić. The heir to the throne, appeared to be arguing with a bearded man. The driver stood by the heir, warily pointing his revolver at the Doctor.

"Never mind what those creatures are! Go!" shouted the bearded man.

The Countess recognized the voice—Dr. Cornelius!

She ran to the Archduke. He recognized her immediately.

"Countess?" he said.

She pointed at the Doctor. "This man is an enemy of the Empire, and those creatures are here to kill you."

"But he saved my life", the Archduke protested.

"Yes, but for his own ends, no doubt." She turned to the driver. "Get in the car! You are to take His Majesty out of the city and far away to safety."

"No! I am not going anywhere, Countess! I am not leaving any of my subjects to the mercy of these demons."

Lord Burydan dashed up to them. He was going to shoot the Countess, but noting her weapon, and those of her colleagues, he thought better of it. The Countess looked at her operatives and shook her head slightly, effectively telling them to stay their hand against the killer of their colleague.

"What news?" the Doctor asked nonchalantly.

"The projector has melded itself to Marcus's chest. It's like they have joined together."

The Doctor was irritated at Lord Burydan's blurting out of the Italian's name. However, at this point, he was more concerned over his fee. Whatever else happened, if he had saved the Archduke, he might get at least the bonus from Hart.

"I must go now, Archduke. My work here is done. And may I remind you that I am not subject to your authority."

"Such impertinence!" shouted the heir to the throne at the Doctor. "But yes, you may go. I am not ungrateful. Countess, let them go."

The Countess aimed her gun at the Doctor. "The Emperor says he will stay and you can go—and as his subject, I must obey his orders. So you and this British madman can leave, but first, what do you know of this Professor Marcus?"

The Doctor could see he had little choice, it was best to give her the information she needed. "Professor Marcus is an Italian astronomer and irredentist. His machine is an off-world projector of some kind. Its powers grow stronger by the minute. It now seems to have taken to emitting waves of terror. Destroy the projector, or the man, or both, and you will stop this. Can I leave this to you now?"

Further conversation was curtailed by the appearance of a Death specter above the Palace, some three hundred feet-tall, scythe in hand. In the dark, it seemed like a floating skull, with the metal of the scythe next to it, creating if anything an even more terrifying image.

Across the channel, in Sutivan, Josip stared at the specter on the mainland.

"By Jingo!" exclaimed Lord Burydan.

And then waves of terror assaulted them, and the whole city.

A voice came from the creature. It spoke in Italian. "Come to the Peristyle, Karl. Come and face execution. This war shall be over, and Italy will reign in these lands. Fail to comply, and I will start killing the citizens of this city. Follow my minion!"

Professor Marcus stood exultant. The Peristyle was an open-air square within Diocletian's Palace, with columns on three sides. He was on the south side, where four columns held a triangular gable above a semicircular arch. On his left, there was an ancient sphinx; to his right, he could see the Church of St. Dominus, with its tower and belfry. The historical setting pleased him enormously, but the location was also strategic. He stood on a stone platform under which was the exit from the cellars to the square. It amused him that his foes would not spot him immediately.

Symbiosis with the projector was not a surprise to him, but its increasing power was. Indeed, there were no more beams of light projecting the images. Perhaps the energy was always there, untapped due to not being properly integrated with the operator? The Professor laughed. There would be much time later to contemplate the projector's mysteries.

The heir to the throne walked towards the entrance of the palace, beckoned by a death specter.

"No!" cried the Countess.

The Archduke turned to her. "I must... I will not see my subjects killed. Whatever, happens Countess, I order you sure to ensure this man fails in his ambition."

With that, he strode off.

The Countess could barely move out of fright, and had dropped her weapon without realizing it. What had Dr. Cornelius said? The terror came from the projector? That meant it was not real, merely an addition to actual fear. She drew from deep within herself, from her faith, her belief in God to resist this fear. She slowly started walking after the Archduke. Behind her, Dr. Cornelius and Lord Burydan had also started moving, drawing on different reserves.

Dr. Cornelius could fight back the fear with his rationality. He saw the Countess' discarded weapon. He picked it up and slowly walked forward. He saw Lord Burydan alongside him—smiling!

"You provide such entertainment, Doctor!" said the Briton.

Clearly, his madness was helping him deal with the terror. Behind them came the Lieutenant, the Sergeant and Radić, all drawing on some reserves to fight the terror, but they were knocked back by fleeing people seemingly coming out of all directions, some in their night clothes.

The Archduke walked up the stairs from the lower level to the Peristyle. A number of people were there, paralyzed with fear. The heir to the throne turned around. The Italian Professor stood there, a little above him, with the projector attached to his chest.

"What you are doing," shouted the Archduke at the Professor, "is against all norms of war! Stop terrorizing these civilians! The civilized world will not accept what is happening here!"

The Professor scoffed. "A new way of thinking is coming, Karl. The future will be decided by the strong, and the weak will be washed away. Men of vision— Italian men!—will lead the way. Sooner than you think, with the help of this device," he pointed to the projector, now melded to his chest.

"Now, Karl. In front of all your subjects, renounce your claims to Dalmatia and the other lands we covet! Accept they must be given to Italy."

Professor Marcus noticed the Countess emerging on the square from the stairs.

"And you must be Countess Irina Petrovska. Yes, Hart told me all about you. An aristocrat? Look at you crawl."

He turned his attention back to the heir to the throne. The Countess did not know what to do—she had no weapon. She cursed herself for not picking it up, but the fear was making it difficult to think. She could barely get up off the ground.

"Countess!" came a hissed whisper from behind her.

She looked around. Dr. Cornelius was on the stairs, just outside of the Professor's sight—with her projector gun. The fear was paralyzing him. He did not have the Countess's strength. But he had her Doppelpistol. He managed to shove it across to the floor to her.

She grabbed it and pulled herself up to her knees. *God must have a sense of humor to send me such a helper*, she thought.

She aimed at the Professor, who was just a couple of meters in front of her, and fired.

A volley of bullets smashed into the projector on the Professor's chest. It seemed to explode into light, blinding everyone there.

The Professor fell to his knees, screaming, cuts all over him. Remnants of the projector were melting off him, flailing onto the floor, with parts of his burnt flesh. He felt a hand over his mouth, and then a whisper in his ear.

"Do keep the noise down, old man."

After a couple of minutes, the Countess's vision started to recover. She looked around to see Dr. Cornelius. He raised a hand to her in farewell and disappeared back down the stairs. There was no time to pursue him; she had to see to the heir to the throne.

Dr. Cornelius dashed out of the entrance, easily eluding the Sergeant and the Lieutenant amongst the dazed crowd. Where was Lord Burydan? *To hell with him*, he thought. *Let him revert to his scarred state.* He went over to *Elizabeth*. The vehicle was locked. The Emperor's vehicle had gone. No doubt the driver had used it to flee. Unless Lord Burydan had taken it?

No projector, no professor. At least, he would get the bonus for his role in saving the Emperor. Such an irony—French money paying for saving one of their enemies.

The Doctor started his journey back to the hideout.

In the palace, the Countess went to the Archduke.

"Where is our foe?" he asked.

"Probably dead," she said. "That sludge and blood over there," she pointed to the remains of the projector on the stone platform, dripping onto the stairs, along with some blood. "That appears to be what remains of him. Given his screams, I doubt he escaped."

The Archduke looked at her. "Countess, once again the Empire is in your debt, and more so myself. Ah, Mr. Radić..."

The Croatian politician had appeared, with Vuljanić and Sergeant Mayr as well.

"I am pleased that Your Majesty is well," said Radić.

"Thanks to the Countess. Our meeting must proceed tomorrow, in the morning. We will not let tonight's events prevent that."

"Your Majesty, what are the public to be told?" asked Radić.

"Traditionally, information on such science, whether from Earth or the Heavens, has been kept from the public in order to prevent panic. Is that not so, Countess?"

The Countess nodded. "It is a wise policy, especially in this time of war. No one knows how people may react."

"From the Heavens?" asked Radić. "I have heard stories about what is kept in Sarajevo, but is this true?"

The heir to the throne looked a bit sheepish. The Countess swiftly rescued him. "A turn of phrase used in incidents such as this. The *Evidenzbureau* will prepare some form of story. Indeed, I will likely contribute. You need say nothing on the matter. Specialists will be summoned to deal with all this. It is best His Majesty takes his leave now."

Dr. Cornelius entered the hideout and opened the trapdoor. He could see that no one had been here in his absence, due to the precautions he took.

As he climbed down, a voice took him by surprise.

"There you are, old chap! Beginning to think you would never arrive."

A lamp came on. Sitting on a chair was Lord Burydan.

"Present for you," the Briton said, pointing to his side. On the floor, bound and gagged was the Professor.

"He's in a bit of state. Seems to have passed out. Lots of burns to his chest. Grabbed him whilst you all seem blinded, went round the back with him, appropriated the bloody Hun's car and here we are. Thought it best not to grab you as well—just got him out damn fast before anyone could see. I knew you would find your way out."

"You did well," said Dr. Cornelius. He went over to the Professor. "I will be able to treat him." He looked over at the Briton. "What did you do with the car?"

"In the sea, old man. Along with that complaining driver. Didn't seem to appreciate my gun to his head."

Dr. Cornelius nodded, looking impressed by the Briton's actions—and his spotting the various clues that would have alerted him to intruders. "I will deal with the Professor's wounds, but first..." he went over to his equipment and flipped a switch.

"A bomb, set to detonate and destroy my equipment if I failed to return," he explained. "It would have gone off in about 30 minutes time."

Now, it was Lord Burydan's turn to look impressed.

A few days later, the Countess was back in her property in Sutivan, sitting by her window, looking out to sea. She looked at one of the Vienna newspapers she had ordered. A story by her had appeared, relating her witnessing a propaganda action by Italian agents. They had used cinema projectors stolen from Germany to project an image of Death over Split. They had been foiled by local people, but had escaped.

There was, of course, no mention of the Archduke or Radić, let alone her role and that of Dr. Cornelius. There were rumors of sightings of the Archduke Karl and Radić, but miliary intelligence had ensured these had not seen print.

Despite foiling the plans of Professor Marcus, she felt uneasy. The war grew ever more terrible. She still hoped for the Empire to prevail, and for Poland to be united and autonomous within it, but she was now concerned over the designs of their ally, Germany.

Her maid, Kata—another *Evidenzbureau* agent—came in. "We are ready to leave, Countess."

The Countess got up. She was going to return to her nursing duties, but first, she would journey to Zagreb to visit the wife and family of Captain Marić, to tell them what a brave man he was, who had died defending his homeland.

At the same time, Dr. Cornelius and Lord Burydan were on a motorboat approaching the French Riviera.

Their escape from Split had been circuitous. Smugglers of the Doctor's acquaintance were piloting the vessel.

Dr. Cornelius and Lord Burydan were discussing recent events. Cornelius had reverted to his own face. The Professor was sitting sullenly nearby. His chest wounds had been bandaged up.

"You know, we've done rather well," said Lord Burydan. He drew closer to Cornelius. "Now, I think we have worked well together, yes?"

The Doctor agreed. Despite some of his behavior, Lord Burydan's retrieval of the Professor had ensured the fee and the bonus from Hart would be paid. The Doctor intended to restore the man's face permanently. Lord Burydan was a more resourceful man than he had given him credit for. Best to simply conclude their business and let him go.

"Now, old chap, back home, I had certain… financial difficulties shall we say—adventuring did cost money, you know, and I was unable to earn whilst being stuck in Inverlair. I'd be interested in further collaboration."

"You wish to work for me?" asked the startled Doctor.

"Not for you, old boy, with you. Just so long as we do nothing against my government. They retired me and virtually imprisoned me, so I owe them nothing, but I'd rather they did not come after me for any reason."

"And your wife? She will guess who restored your face, and she will not forget who was responsible of her imprisonment and the death of her sister."

Lord Burydan recalled these incidents from before the war. It now seemed so long ago. The war had changed everything.

"My wife was looking to leave me. We will remain married of course, but I will certainly be going my own way. What do you say?"

"I accept your proposition, Lord Burydan." The sculptor of human flesh took great pleasure in this. The great adventurer Lord Burydan now reduced to working for a criminal mastermind. Not that the man seemed to mind too much, it seemed. The Doctor also was none too keen on the physical aspects of his work these days. This Briton could come in useful there.

"One thing," said the Doctor. "I have been instructed by Hart that the Countess is to be left alone. Again, he seems to fear that any harm that might come to her may trigger retaliatory assassinations on the likes of him. However, should she interfere with any future operations, that would be a different matter."

This was a lie, but he did not want the Briton to go after her and somehow find out who really pushed him into the fire.

Lord Burydan shrugged. "It will keep."

The men fell silent for a while. Then Lord Burydan looked over at the Professor. "What a miserable git you are, just sitting there."

The Professor said nothing.

Lord Burydan laughed. "You should have seen the look on your face when you spotted me at the gate. You weren't expecting us, were you?"

The sculptor of human flesh wearily joined in. "He had spotted us, Lord Burydan. He projected one of his Death images on me, just prior to your approaching him."

The Professor perked up. "I certainly did not. How would I have recognized you?"

"Not only was he surprised," Lord Burydan said, "but the projector was in the bag, not already in his hand, He brought it out, and let me tell you, he must have wet himself when he recognized me!"

"I certainly did not!" protested the Professor, with Lord Burydan laughing loudly at the Italian.

A dark chill went up the sculptor of human flesh's spine, a sensation he was not familiar with. What they said made sense. And that specter was different from the other ones. What had he seen *really*? And why was it beckoning to him?

Surely, it was all the projector, somehow? Surely?

The Prisoner of Budapest

Military Barracks, Buda Castle District, Budapest,
15 May 1917

"My preferred name is Bela Lugosi."

Sitting opposite the debonair actor, his companion, a man in his 50s, was slightly puzzled by this revelation. "Preferred name?" he asked. "I thought your name was Arisztid Olt?"

"In my business, we sometimes use what we call a 'stage name,' Mr. Grantaigle. "However, I have a couple of such names. Although I wish to keep my real name private, I will say Lugosi is named after my hometown of Lugoj. You will be hearing more of me as Bela Lugosi in future."

"Yes," said Grantaigle. "It has an excellent ring to it,"

The two men were seated in an ornate room, on comfortable armchairs.

"I agree," Lugosi responded. He looked around the room. "I understand that you are a prisoner here. That you are a French scientist captured by the Germans?"

"That is so. The Germans sent me to their allies, the Habsburgs, who have deposited me here. I find the scientists here quite knowledgeable. I worked with them to advance science and mankind. I cannot be concerned with the petty quarrels of the great powers."

Lugosi pressed. "Surely, as a Frenchman, you must feel loyalty to your homeland. Many of your countrymen would take a dim view of your cooperation with the enemy."

"I consider all mankind to be my countrymen," the scientist exclaimed. "Although I am certainly not any kind of socialist," he hurriedly added. "But enough politics. Please, Mr. Lugosi, tell me about your next film?"

Lugosi smiled and with great pleasure started to relay information about his next role.

Deuxième Bureau, Paris, The Same Day

"Do you believe this report, Hart?" asked General Dupont, the head of the Deuxième Bureau.

On the other side of the head's desk, Simon Hart responded, "I believe it's credible." He had called this meeting as soon as the name "Grantaigle" had been mentioned to him,

"As you know," Hart continued, "Grantaigle had been using alien technology to create a duplication process of living matter. Only his genius could interpret it. He insisted on staying in his castle, which the Germans destroyed, complete with all the equipment. We found his body in the remains. This report we have received from one of our agents however suggests that a scientist with that name is being held at a barracks building in Budapest's Castle District. I firmly believe that this is indeed the same Grantaigle, due to our autopsy."

"Autopsy?" asked Dupont.

"Yes. it occurred to me that Grantaigle may have duplicated himself. This would explain the reports of his presence in Budapest. A side effect of the duplication process is that when something is duplicated, both versions have their weight reduced by half. I had the body of the Grantaigle we do have exhumed. The remains weigh less than they should. As you know, a soldier was found nearby—two versions of the same man. Both weighed the same—exactly half the weight of what was recorded for the single version. They carried the same memories as well. They had no idea what transpired, but I surmise that when the Germans attacked, there was chaos. Grantaigle duplicated himself, perhaps to double his chances of survival, and the private somehow also got involved. It's also reasonable to assume that perhaps the Germans know something of this, if only because the scientist weighs half what a man of his age and build should."

Dupont nodded. "You want to mount some kind of operation to assassinate Grantaigle or retrieve him. If he is indeed being held at that building, he is near the Royal Palace. It's not as if our army is marching on Budapest. Further, such a move may thwart any future negotiations. Remember, Emperor Karl attempted talks earlier this year. The duplication process would be useful, but I cannot see how I can authorize an operation that is likely to fail and cause us embarrassment."

Hart had anticipated this response. "It's not just one duplication," he said. "Grantaigle had told us that the potential was to create many duplicates that could even be conditioned to obey without question. He spoke of creating armies and believed the mass issue could also be overcome in some way. If Vienna finds out these secrets and create such armies, we will lose this war, and Berlin and Vienna will be the unchallenged masters of Europe, and possibly the World."

Dupont's face betrayed no emotion. "Why did the Germans hand him over to Vienna?" he asked.

"The Kaiser is the senior partner in the war, with the Habsburgs very much the junior partner. We have always simply assumed this was the case in matter of the fantastic, the supernatural and alien technologies. Over the years, and during this war, I have always suspected, however, that in this area, the reverse is true. Only Vienna has the expertise to even remotely be able to work with Grantaigle. Our own personnel could not keep up with him. Why else would the Germans hand him over?"

Dupont nodded. "Very well. Assuming I authorize you to conduct such an operation in Budapest, how do you propose to do it?" But he already had a good idea as to what Hart's answer would be.

"I would hire Dr. Cornelius Kramm," Hart replied.

Schönbrunn Palace, Vienna, 16 May 1917

Countess Irina Petrovska had been summoned for an audience with Emperor Karl. It was an urgent request. She had been operating as a nurse near the Eastern front. As a journalist, she would often write of her experiences for the Vienna press. Ostensibly, the summons was explained as the Emperor wishing to thank her in person for her informing the Empires' multi-national citizens of the work of doctors and nurses on the front. However, she knew there would be more to it than that.

Indeed, that was the case.

"This duplication process, I cannot see much good coming out of it," said the Countess. "It seems we are playing at God in trying to create human beings."

The Emperor nodded. "We are then of the same mind. However, many in my government, and certainly in Berlin, firmly believe this can be used to win the war."

"Is it worth the price?" asked the Countess. "Wouldn't we be creating some kind of slave class?"

"No," said the Emperor. "I will not permit the process to get that far. I have been told, however, that the process may have medical benefits—not for the duplications of human beings but for that of limbs and organs specifically designed for the individual. Word from Budapest is that a breakthrough is imminent. This would help our maimed soldiers and our citizens. It is something we would have to give to the world. And I strongly believe we can outlaw human duplication. However, it is also troubling that our own scientists can barely understand what this Antoine de Grantaigle is doing."

The Countess nodded cautiously. "I can see that. It would help so many."

There was a pause. The Countess was wondering what her role in this affair was to be.

The Emperor picked up on this. "The matter is delicate. Berlin, who provided us with the prisoner, has fewer qualms about the duplication process, although officially they say otherwise. Another complication is the Hungarian Prime Minister István Tisza. He is generally loyal, but my relations with him are poor as he opposes my planned reforms. Although the *Evidenzbureau* is in charge, he has taken a great interest in the matter, which, under covert terms of the Dual Monarchy[10] he has some authority over such activities in the Hungarian side of the Empire, although the *Evidenzbureau* has usually kept the politicians in the dark. This he knows about, and he has used his authority to let Grantaigle have materials from our secret repository within the General Philippovich barracks in Sarajevo, more than the *Evidenzbureau* had wanted to hand over. This concerns me a little. I

[10] The 1867 Austro-Hungarian Compromise allowed Hungarian autonomy within the Empire, on a footing with Austria.

think he is trying to use the situation to take credit for whatever comes out of this, perhaps to strengthen Hungary's position."

"That would not necessarily be welcomed by a number of our nationalities. It is possible this Grantaigle could be manipulating the situation, given his advanced knowledge," The Countess said.

"Quite," replied the Emperor. "That is why I wish you to go to Budapest as my representative, to oversee matters, in particular this imminent breakthrough. Be cautious in your dealings with the Prime Minister. Furthermore, there is another complication: the Kaiser has his representative there, one Leopold von Reinhardt. He will need to be treated very carefully indeed. Should you consider things are going too far, you are to make it known to the Prime Minister and inform me with immediate effect, as he will not take orders from you."

"I will leave for Budapest immediately, along with some of my trusted *Evidenzbureau* colleagues," she replied.

Swiss military facility, near Geneva, 17 May 1917

"I thought the Swiss were neutral, old boy?"

The master criminal Dr. Cornelius Kramm turned to the man who had spoken. "They are, Lord Burydan. However, they have something we want."

"What is it, old man?"

The Doctor inwardly winced. He had long since given up trying to stop the Englishman from referring to him as "old man," "old chap," and so on. It seemed like Lord Burydan could not stop himself from calling people that. He still found it a little irritating, but Lord Burydan appeared wholly incapable of not speaking to people in that manner.

"It is a flying vehicle of probable alien manufacture," said the Doctor. "The Empires are not the only ones who have such secrets. How do you think we are going to Budapest? This machine flies silently. The Swiss use it to spy on their neighbor's military movements. They used it quite a lot during this war. Their security is lax, however. One of my former Red Hand employees sold me the information recently," he pointed to another man with them in Swiss military uniform. "He's in their hastily created air corps now. Once we are in, we take it, and we are away."

"Do you know how to fly it?" asked the Briton.

The Doctor pointed to the soldier. "Corporal Baumann here does."

"It is simple to fly," said Baumann. "I have seen the officers do it many times and I myself have done so, only on non-spying flights. The officers reserve the interesting things for themselves."

Lord Burydan simply nodded. Whilst in London, he had been summoned by Dr. Cornelius and was expected in Switzerland the next day. The peer of the realm responded immediately, using a regular route to get to Dr. Cornelius. The Doctor had a hold over him. Without the specialist drugs the Doctor administered, his face would revert to a scared ruin—the result of burns. Of late, the drugs lasted longer, allowing Lord Burydan more time away from the Doctor. However, the Doctor's grip remained strong—although the substantial sums he paid also helped ensure Burydan's loyalty.

All three men were lying flat, about 70 feet away from the building. They had backpacks and rifles with them.

"Proceed," the Doctor said.

Burydan got up, ran to the doors of the building and threw a grenade, then dived to the ground. The explosion blew down the front door, killing the guard on duty behind it. Burydan followed it up with another grenade, throwing it into the building, but this one was different. Soon smoke started coming out of the building.

The three men swiftly put on gas masks. They picked up their backpacks and rifles, approached the building and entered. There were a few Swiss soldiers lying on the floor. The men made their way through a short corridor, with the soldier in the lead. They came out into a hangar. In the middle, was an oval-shaped craft, about 20 feet across. It had a doorway in front, with steps leading to the ground. The doorway also opened to a short platform around the craft with a barrier about half the height of the doorway—possibly some form of observation deck, the Doctor thought. The craft was grey, with a few panels seemingly missing, creating patches of bronze appearance.

Lord Burydan gestured to one of the soldiers lying on the ground.

"Are they dead?" he asked Dr. Cornelius.

"No. Merely unconscious," the sculptor of human flesh replied. "The Swiss will be enraged that their vehicle has been stolen, but will keep it quiet. The more corpses around, the more fuss. It will teach them to improve their security."

The men went up to the craft to where there was a door. There was a large circular handle on it, which the Doctor twisted around. The door moved open, and the three men moved inside.

Once inside, it seemed clear that most of the hull, including the floor, was transparent. They could see the hangar outside. In the middle, there was a ladder which was built to extend downwards through a hatch. There were seats in front of some controls. On the controls, a number of labels had been affixed indicating in German what their functions were. Around the rest of the cabin, there were seats against the hull. Scattered around were binoculars and even a telescope.

"Impressive," said the Doctor. "We can see outside, but the outside cannot see us. I see its use as a spy vehicle. Can the outer hull change to provide camouflage?"

"Only in a limited way," answered the soldier. "A number of panels no longer work when the function is activated, and no one knows why or how to replace them. They have had it for ten years, but the scientists have made little headway into how it works. They have dismantled it in the past, but with no real results."

A common problem, thought Dr. Cornelius. Human science had yet to progress to be able to properly analyze the alien technology that occasionally fell from the skies.

Baumann pressed a button by the observation hatch door. The steps retracted, and the platform railings appeared in front. "We use this top pop out for a bit of fresh air," the soldier said indicating the platform. "At the right altitudes, of course." He twisted a lever and the door closed.

"All very impressive," said Lord Burydan. "However, I think we should be leaving."

"Take it up," said the Doctor.

"Strap in," said the Corporal. They did so, while the soldier sat at the controls. The Doctor noticed that the seat belts and controls appeared designed for the human form. He wondered as to the nature of the makers of this craft. The machine went up silently through the open roof.

"Demonstrate its capabilities," said the Doctor.

The pilot brought it to a standstill, hovering over the Swiss countryside. "First, let us talk business," said the Corporal. "I think my fee for helping you steal this craft is too low. After all, you need me to fly this machine now. I could have stolen it myself, you know,"

"You are being paid very well," said the Doctor, a hint of menace in his voice. "And if you were capable of stealing it by yourself, you would have done so."

Lord Burydan got out of his seat and pointed a pistol at the soldier.

"Yours, my dear chap," indicating the pistol with his head.

The Corporal suddenly realized that his holster was empty.

"I thought you looked a bit untrustworthy," said Lord Burydan. "Get up."

Baumann did as instructed. Dr. Cornelus covered him with a pistol.

The Briton sat at the controls. Starting to manipulate them, he started moving the craft in various directions, with Baumann being unsteady on his feet until Lord Burydan had mastered the controls. He then brought the craft to a hover.

"Did I mention I can fly biplanes?" asked Lord Burydan of the Corporal. "No? Not perhaps that I need to. The controls are really very simple, which is no doubt why you can fly this thing. Why don't you sit down now." He indicated the seat opposite the Doctor, by the door to the platform.

Lord Burydan indicated with his eyes the door to the Doctor, who nodded imperceptibly. Neither gesture was noticed by Baumann.

As the man went to sit down, Lord Burydan got up and opened the door. He grabbed the Corporal. "That's Lake Geneva down there. I think you could do with a swim. Only a few hundred feet down."

Baumann tried to resist, but Burydan's superior physique was too powerful. He shoved him onto the platform and over the safety barrier.

"Enjoy your dip!" he shouted at the man falling down in the dark towards the water. An anguished scream fading away fast was the reply.

The Briton went back inside.

"Excellent work, Lord Burydan," the Doctor said.

"Thank you. Budapest, you say?" the peer replied.

"Yes, I have some particular coordinates for you," he handed them over. "I have some familiarity with that city. I had some business there just prior to the war."

Lord Burydan noted a control titled 'Night Vision' and pressed it. The landscape below was illuminated through the hull, with features distinctly now visible with a hue of green.

"On we go!" said Lord Burydan and started to move the craft towards central Europe.

Dr. Cornelius looked below him at the Swiss landscape, now rapidly moving away. He was considerably pleased. *This machine will be of the greatest use*, he thought. The fee the Frenchman Hart was offering was substantial, and it was worth acquiring the machine to enable the mission's success. However, he was most curious about this Grantaigle. Hart had simply told him to capture and return him, or, if that was not possible for any reason, to kill him. The fee would be 50% more if he was brought back alive, however. Hart wanted Dr. Cornlius to move at once. There was no time for the Doctor to make his own personal inquiries as to who this

186

Grantaigle was and why he was so important. When he met the man, he would ascertain what his importance was, and then consider whether to use him for his own ends or simply collect Hart's reward.

The Banks of the Danube, Budapest, 18 May 1917

The Countess walked with her companion along the path on the Danube towards the neo-Gothic Hungarian parliament which had been built directly onto the riverbank a few years earlier. She wanted to talk to the man, Prime Minister István Tisza, away from his office and his aides. A number of *Evidenzbureau* operatives maintained a discreet distance. The balding, mustachioed politician was seen as linked to the Empire's war policy—there had already been attempts on his life.

"I hardly understand why the King has sent you as his representative. Am I not answerable to him, as his Prime Minister here?" said Tisza, somewhat irately.

The Countess attempted to soothe him. "The King has sent me not so much as a representative but also for my experience in such matters as this. He has full confidence in you." She was careful to refer to Karl as the King. In Austria, Karl was Emperor, but in Hungary his main title was King.

"Does he?" the Prime Minister responded. "I oppose his reforms; I hardly think he has much confidence in me. And as for his sending you, Countess, you are well known for your advocacy of Polish autonomy within the Empire, and other groups as well."

The Countess knew she had to play this very diplomatically indeed. "My views are known," she cautiously replied, "but firstly, Galicia is within the Austrian half of the Empire, not the Hungarian, and thus of no real concern to you. Secondly, given your position, you will be aware of the nature of the work that I do for the *Evidenzbureau*. There are few with my experience in such matters—and that is the only reason I have been sent here."

For a moment, it appeared that he was going to argue further, but then he said, "Whilst I have little doubt there is a political motivation for your being here, I accept that your knowledge of certain matters could prove useful."

"Then I am at least glad for that," she replied. "Of course," she continued, "I will be at tomorrow's demonstration."

The Prime Minister looked surprised but swiftly recovered. "My office was going to inform you," he quickly said. "Grantaigle has apparently made some kind of breakthrough. The Kaiser's representative, Leopold von Reinhardt, will also be there."

"It should be an interesting event," the Countess said.

Military Barracks, Buda Castle, Budapest, The Same Day

The Countess entered the room being used as the *Evidenzbureau*'s office.

"How did the meeting go?" asked a young officer.

"As well as could be expected, Lieutenant Vuljanić," she replied. "The Prime Minister is tolerating my presence, not that he has much choice. I don't think he will directly obstruct us."

"That is something. "

A Croatian officer, Lieutenant Vuljanić was a trusted ally of the Countess's within the *Evidenzbureau*.

"How goes our preventative operations?" she inquired.

"The local gendarmes have been very cooperative. Four addresses in Budapest are already under surveillance. Sergeant Mayr is commanding the most likely location. He is there right now."

The Countess nodded. The Sergeant was another trusted friend. "I may join him later."

A telephone on the desk rang. The lieutenant answered it. "Mr. Lugosi has arrived," he said.

"Excellent," said the Countess. "I will meet with him at once. Would you like to attend?"

The lieutenant nodded. He enjoyed films.

They both left the office and walked to the officer's mess, placed at the Countess's disposal for the meeting. The lieutenant opened the door for her. Bela Lugosi was seated in a comfortable chair. He stood up immediately.

Introductions were made, and the suave Lugosi took the Countess's proffered hand and kissed it.

"You are even more beautiful than your newspaper pictures suggest," the actor said.

"Thank you, Mr. Lugosi."

"Bela, please."

They all sat down.

"I must say," said Lugosi, "I am both surprised and not surprised that you do work for the *Evidenzbureau*."

"How so?" asked the Countess.

"One would not associate a Countess with working with a military intelligence organization, and, I understand, with such influence with them. However, your journalism covers many political matters and, in particular, what you have seen on the Galician front as a nurse. I have rarely read such intelligent and, when it comes to our injured, moving writing. It is then no surprise that a person with such insight would be utilized by the *Evidenzbureau*."

"Thank you again, Mr. Lugosi. It must be said also that you, too, have given great service to the King."

Lugosi nodded, "I was of some minor assistance," he replied.

Vuljanić spoke, "You volunteered for the war effort and served bravely with the 43rd Royal Hungarian Infantry Regiment on the Eastern Front against the Russians, rising to the rank of lieutenant. It was more than minor help."

"You are very kind," the actor replied.

The Countess could see that the actor did not wish to talk too much of the war. She was aware that he had been wounded and then discharged. As a nurse, she had already seen injured men who did not wish to speak of their experience. She decided to change the subject.

"Bela, I must thank you on behalf of the King for agreeing to speak to Mr. Grantaigle for the *Evidenzbureau*. I've read the report of your impressions of the conversation with him. As you know, my colleagues were eager to keep him happy, and given his love of Kino, you were sent to meet him. Of course, he was not informed that the *Evidenzbureau* were also interested in what you could glean from him."

Lugosi smiled. "Yes, your colleagues do not entirely seem to trust him. With reason, I suspect."

"That is why I wanted to speak to you," the Countess said. "You told my colleagues that you sensed he was not being entirely honest? Why was that?"

Lugosi took a moment to consider his response, then spoke. "In most of the conversation I had with him, it was apparent that he was genuine in talking about his love of the Kino. However, I was not so sure when he discussed with me his reasons for his scientific cooperation with our scientists. In my profession, some of my fellow actors are prone to, shall we say, exaggerate their performance when in the theater? When Grantaigle spoke of 'wishing to work for the good of mankind' and so on, I recognized the same over-the-top style. Of course, I cannot know what was in his mind, but it appeared to me that he was, if not lying, then certainly acting a part."

"Your observations are of great help, Bela," the Countess said. "I am aware that we can count on your discretion. I do feel we should help you in return. Would you be interested in doing an interview with me for a Vienna newspaper? I must confess it would be good for me as well, not least for helping explain my presence in Budapest."

Lugosi was delighted. "It would be my great pleasure," he said, clapping his hands together. "I would ask that a small part of the interview be devoted to the working conditions of the acting profession. It is an area of some concern to me."

"Of course," replied the Countess. "We shall conduct the interview within the next few days. My assistant, Kata, will make the arrangements and will be in touch. I will detain you no longer."

"It was my great pleasure to meet you, and I so look forward to doing so, again," Lugosi replied.

They made their farewells, and the actor left the building.

"Do you think Lugosi was correct in his assessment?" Vuljanić asked the Countess.

"I think it likely. Grantaigle's sudden wish to help us is obviously suspicious, although I fear that the Germans and, to an extent, the Hungarians are only too keen to believe him. Tomorrow's demonstration may reveal more. In the meantime, I shall join Sergeant Mayr."

Jókai Street, Budapest, That Evening

Dr. Cornelius and Lord Burydan walked down Jókai Street. "Do we need local knowledge, old boy?" Burydan asked his companion. "We could simply use our craft and a bit of brute force to get our man. I must say, I am feeling a little exposed here."

"We need as much information as we can get on the layout of the building," the Doctor replied. "Further, we need someone who can speak Hungarian. Our German may only go so far. My contact here is reliable; he worked well for me in the old days."

Lord Burydan nodded. "The old days" referred to when the Doctor was one of the Lords of the Red Hand, a criminal organization that Burydan, along with others, were instrumental in bringing down. The peer had found it best not to mention that in his current association with the Doctor.

"Turn off the street now," Burydan said as they passed a junction.

The Doctor looked surprised.

"We are being followed," hissed Burydan.

They both turned the corner and saw two gendarmes coming towards them on the road. A voice cried out from behind them, "Stay where you are!"

They both turned and saw the familiar form of Sergeant Mayr whom they had both encountered previously. The soldier was aiming a firearm at them. And walking next to him, armed with her usual Doppelpistole, was another familiar figure.

"Countess Petrovska," groaned Dr. Cornelius. "Again."

"Hands up!" shouted the Sergeant.

Both men complied. The two gendarmes behind them caught up and grabbed them both, having holstered their rifles. Lord Burydan immediately grabbed the gendarme nearest to him and swiftly took him in a hold by the neck with one arm, while the other pointed a pistol to the man's throat.

"Release him," the Briton said to the Countess, indicating Dr. Cornelius. Before she could reply, the other gendarme released the Doctor. Freed, he promptly stood next to Lord Burydan, wielding his own pistol.

The Countess was annoyed. Burydan was an expert in hand-to-hand combat. The gendarmes had been too swift in trying to grab him. Compounding things, the other gendarme had already released the Doctor, losing whatever leverage she had had.

Other gendarmes and *Evidenzbureau* personnel appeared, surrounding the men.

"Let us go," Lord Burydan said, "or this fellow gets it in the head, and believe me, we will get some of you as well. I will be aiming for you first, Countess." The Briton was still under the belief that the Countess had caused the disfigurement of his face.

A senior gendarme hurried to the Countess's side. "I can't let these men kill my officer. He has a family to support."

The Countess was also disinclined to let the man die, but was torn by the fact that to release her foes would cause much trouble later on.

"Quickly, Countess," said Burydan, shoving his prisoner's head with the firearm to press matters. Dr. Cornelius said nothing. He remained calm, letting the

Brition take the lead. *He seems to know what he is doing*, he thought.

"Let him go, and I will let you leave," the Countess said.

Lord Burydan sighed. "You might, but your lackeys here certainly won't. No, Countess. You will all stay exactly where you are, whilst we move away. I will release this chap when we are well clear."

Without waiting for a response, the Briton started moving away with his hostage, with Dr. Cornelius following.

The Countess indicated to all present to do nothing.

Burydan and the Doctor started to run, with their prisoner in front of them, Lord Burydan's pistol resolutely aimed at the unfortunate gendarme's head. They ran past some startled members of the public, eventually reaching the vehicle they had used to drive into Budapest from where they had landed. Dr. Cormelius took the wheel and Lord Burydan bundled the gendarme in the back. They drove off.

Lord Burydan could see the Doctor was going the wrong way and immediately understood. He leaned forward and opened the door on the gendarme's side.

"Farewell, constable!" the Briton exclaimed as he shoved the gendarme out. The man hit the road, breaking his wrist in the process. In his pain, he was still able to note the direction the car was heading. A number of passers-by rushed to his assistance. Despite his injury, he was extremely relieved. *Those madmen could just as easily have killed me as thrown me out*, he thought.

"I do so enjoy throwing people out of vehicles," Lord Burydan said, laughing.

Dr. Cornelius started to take a different route. "My little detour will hopefully put the Countess and her friends looking in the wrong direction. I have to assume that the *Evidenzbureau* and the Budapest authorities were monitoring our contact. I was wrong in my thinking their intelligence was poor; they never troubled us in the past."

"That's not good news, old boy," replied the Briton.

"Indeed. Our contact did tell us not to approach his house by car, as that might have attracted attention. Perhaps he was compromised and instructed to tell us that? Or he may simply have been under observation? Not that he would know where we landed, but clearly the *Evidenzbureau* has been prepared for our arrival here. The sooner we are in the air, the better."

The contact had indeed been simply under observation. *Evidenzbureau* soldiers had already dragged him out of the house and were taking him to their facility.

The Sergeant came over to the Countess, who was on the sidewalk talking to members of the public. "Yes, I am Countess Petrovska. I am here reporting on how our police and army capture potential traitors. I was armed only for my own protection. I must go now."

She went over to the Sergeant. "It can be tricky accounting for what I am up to. Anything from the Red Hand man?"

"He's refusing to cooperate. We'll see what we can get out of him when we interrogate him. We'll begin as soon as we get back. I doubt we will find those two tonight. The gendarme saw the direction they were going in, but I suspect they have gone to ground for now. You were right that Dr. Cornelius would likely be involved in this Grantaigle business."

"Given his nationality and value," she replied, "it would be logical to assume the French would want him back—or eliminated. And given the levels of security here, it was equally likely that they would hire Dr. Cornelius. It is unfortunate that we've only just been told about this Grantaigle, and even more unfortunate that no one thought to monitor old Red Hand operatives. The situation becomes more complex... I will see if the demonstration tomorrow can be cancelled. I have little doubt that Dr. Cornelius will be attempting something."

Dr. Cornelius and Lord Burydan were back in their craft, parked in an old barn just outside Budapest. It belonged to the Doctor, and had once been purchased as part of a failed narcotics smuggling operation—the business he had mentioned earlier to Lord Burydan. His partners had double-crossed him, and soon found themselves, not quite intact, floating down the Danube. He had considered it wise to keep the property and was pleased it had come in useful.

"What now?" asked Lord Briton.

The Doctor was reading a message from Simon Hart. The two men had brought certain equipment on board the craft, mostly weapons, but also some form of communications device. Lord Burydan observed the paper coming out of it. It looked like gobbledygook to him—clearly a code.

The Doctor relayed what the message said, "Hart informs us that his sources suggest this Grantaigle will be conducting some form of demonstration tomorrow at 14:00. He wants us to act well before then. But we will not."

"Why, old boy?"

"Not only is Hart more concerned about this mission than any other he has ever hired me for, but I also suspect he may not wish me to know too much about this Grantaigle. Using the facilities of this craft, we can, to an extent, eavesdrop on this demonstration, which presumably will tell us what is going on. We could get there much earlier, but there is no guarantee that whatever conversations are taking place will explain matters. The demonstration will be as useful to me as to the audience present."

"You are a cunning devil," the Briton said.

Dr. Cornelius nodded. "Merely one of my talents," he said. He looked over at a gauge on the control panel, marked "power." "From what the soldier told us, the craft needs time to recharge its power levels. The Swiss were unsure how it did so. The level is still a little low, however, it should be better charged for tomorrow."

Military Barracks, Buda Castle District, Budapest, 2 p.m., 19 May 1917

The Countess surveyed the laboratory. There was a great deal of what looked like machinery and tubing, as if it were from the engine room of a warship, although some of it was distinctly alien. *No doubt parts of the Saturnian technology from Sarajevo were fused with more earthly engineering,* she thought. There was an instrument that looked like a lens from a Kino projector perched on a stand, pointing at a chair with leads connected to the machinery. By the stand was a container with a cylindrical indentation, also with connected leads. In front of this were two rows of chairs, no doubt for the assembled guests.

Also present was Prime Minister Tisza and a number of his aides, including a man with only one arm. Grantaigle was surrounded by the scientists the *Evidenzbureau* had provided him with. He looked like he was putting the final touches on his machinery. Despite being a prisoner, he appeared to the Countess to be a little too much in control—something that troubled her.

The Prime Minister came over to her. "This should be fascinating. We could be on the cusp of a scientific breakthrough which could win us the war."

"My advice was that the demonstration be postponed until we have dealt with the threat from Dr. Cornelius," the Countess said.

"I hardly think he is capable of getting past all the security we already have, including the system your lieutenant has established to deal with any attempts at the facial disguises this Cornelius apparently specializes in."

"He does not always rely on that. He has a formidable intelligence and is capable of other strategies."

A man in German military uniform came over. "Ah!" said the Prime Minister. "Countess Irina Petrovska, may I present Leopold von Reinhardt, representative of Kaiser Wilhelm."

"At your service," said the German. Like Bela Lugosi before him, he stooped to kiss her hand. "I have heard much about you, and the Kaiser himself should like to meet you,"

"And I, he" she replied. She indeed wished to do so, to discuss German policy toward the Poles under Berlin's rule.

"I could not but overhear what you were saying, Countess," said von Reinhardt. "I am sure security is enough to keep out Dr. Cornelius. Furthermore, I do think there should be no delays on the matter."

"I accept that I am outvoted," she said. She had considered contacting the Emperor to overrule the Prime Minister, but she considered it likely he would not agree.

Such an act might have put an intolerable strain on an already difficult political relationship.

The conversation was interrupted by Grantaigle

"If I may have your attention," he said to the assembled group. "I have been working with my Habsburg Empire colleagues for a little while now, and I can inform you that we have made such progress that we can now present a demonstration. Today, I intend to replicate a human arm. The benefits of this should be clear. Those who are missing a limb due to reasons such as illness or war could have it replaced. Of course, we need to greatly improve our medical knowledge in the mechanics of re-attaching a limb. It will not be a simple process. However, I am confident that will be overcome. Now, Mr. Dénes, could you please step forward?"

The one-armed man did as he was asked.

"Mr. Dénes," Grantaigle continued, "works at a senior level in the government as I am sure you are all aware. This did not stop him from volunteering when war broke out. The Russians took his arm in an artillery strike, but his disability has not stopped him from returning to work in government, directly for the Prime Minister. Please, show your appreciation for him."

All present duly applauded. The scientist indicated the seat by the stand. "Please, Mr. Dénes, sit here," he instructed.

Dénes did so.

"We do not fully understand this technology," Grantaigle continued. "We know that it comes from the planet Saturn. We know they visited France, Italy and the Habsburg Empire, their vehicles crashing many years ago, possibly due to our different atmosphere. I suspect the machinery was used for either repairing injuries or duplicating people. Perhaps that is how the Saturnians reproduce?"

The Countess knew that Saturnian technology had already proved problematic in the hands of an Italian irredentist. This did not help her unease.

"However," said the Frenchman, "reproducing human beings in their entirety is of course prohibited. For now, I support this decision by your Emperor," said the scientist looking at the Prime Minister.

"King," the Prime Minister said, a little irritably.

"Of course, King. My apologies. What I will do now is aim this projector at Mr. Dénes. I have already, by the method of typing information," he pointed to what appeared to be typewriter keys on part of the machinery behind him, "instructed the apparatus to duplicate the arm."

The Countess interrupted. "My understanding is that Saturnian technology has a strong telepathic element?"

"It does, but this machinery, for whatever reason, does not have that facility, nor did the version I had in France, although the parts here are more advanced than what I had before—a compensation for the German bombardment that destroyed my chateau."

Von Reinhardt shifted uncomfortably in his seat. The Countess considered his explanation plausible, confirming what she had already been told.

"I shall now begin," Grantaigle announced. "The light from this instrument will focus on Mr. Dénes. However, you will notice shards of light will beam across the room. Do not fear, it is harmless, although it may make some of you dizzy for a few moments. I am now immune to such effects myself."

The scientist aimed the instrument on the stand at Dénes and pressed a button on it. A strange white light emanated from its end. It was not bright, yet seemed to fill the room in some way. After a few seconds, the light was cut out.

The Prime Minster spoke, "I feel a little dizzy." Murmurs of agreement came from Dénes and a couple of the *Evidenzbureau* scientists.

"As I said, it will pass shortly," Grantaigle reiterated. He walked over to a white screen at the back of the laboratory, part of which appeared to be a metal wall with large pipes on either side.

"Observe," he said, pointing to it.

Slowly, an image of a man appeared, with limbs outstated. The image materialized into that of Dénes, complete with clothes—and right arm. Grantaigle waved his hand over its image.

In the container, something started to materialize. First, bones, then muscles, skin, and then a shirt and jacket sleeve—matching those on Dénes's left arm.

High above, Dr Cornelius and Lord Burydan were listening to every word, albeit with a degree of static.

"I find it hard to believe that the Swiss made such poor use of this craft," Doctor Cornelius said. "We simply aim this 'eavesdropping' beam below…" he indicated to an instrument on the control panel, "…and we can hear conversations through roofs, walls and windows."

"Damn decent of them to have a skylight," said Lord Burydan.

Dr. Cornelius laughed. "Indeed! Especially as this Castle District is on a hill, no obstacle when you are flying above."

Grantaigle's voice came over the loudspeaker. "We now have a human arm. Bloodless, but ready to be attached once we have the skill. Furthermore, I believe we may even be able to replicate this technology ourselves, once your scientists have come up to my level of understanding."

Dr. Cornelius decided it was now time to proceed with their plan. "Take us down," he ordered.

"About time, old chap. I was getting a bit worried we may be spotted up here. The faulty camouflage gives us a bit of a glint."

Lord Burydan took the control stick and moved it down.

Within the laboratory, von Reinhardt addressed Grantaigle. "When can we start using this device?"

"Soon," replied the Frenchman. "I believe we can produce other machines—perhaps even mass-producing them."

He was interrupted by loud explosions from outside the building. The whole laboratory shook.

Outside, Lord Burydan stood laughing on the craft's platform. Below him, troops were scattering, and some aimed their rifles at him. He ducked below the platform's safety barrier and bullets bounced off it harmlessly.

"Another for good measure!" he shouted and threw a grenade over the side in the direction of the Royal Castle. He crawled back inside the cabin. He got to his feet and moved to an open hatch on the floor, whilst Dr. Cornelius held the craft steady. The thump of his last grenade went off. The Brition grabbed and pulled a lever next to the hatch. The ladder extended downwards, towards the skylight of the laboratory.

A soldier burst into the laboratory. "The castle is being attacked by an airship!" he exclaimed.

At that moment, the steel ladder smashed through the skylight, extending downwards, glass flying everywhere. A shard hit Dénes in the face, creating a huge gash with blood pouring out.

On the descending ladder was a laughing Lord Burydan, sporting a rifle.

"Greetings!" he shouted. And fired his weapon at the bewildered soldier, killing him. "Everyone back," he shouted.

Then he saw the Countess. *I may as well settle this score*, he thought. But suddenly, he noticed Grantaigle trying to move away towards the exit. "Get over here, Grantaigle," he said, aiming the weapon at him.

Grantaigle complied, but in doing so, came between the Brition and the Countess. Knowing this was but a short reprieve, Lieutenant Vuljanić grabbed her and shoved her out of the exit, the others hurriedly following.

Lord Burydan ignored them. He grabbed Grantaigle and handcuffed him to the ladder. He got onto to the other side and the ladder headed up. They were pulled into the craft and Dr. Cornelius closed the hatch. The craft shuddered and lurched.

Lord Burydan sat back at the controls. The craft lurched again, smashing into the barracks wall. The Briton struggled with the controls.

Dr. Cornelius looked out of the windows. Bullets bounced off the window, but he could see the soldiers were aiming at something else.

"They are aiming where the missing panels are!" the Doctor exclaimed. The craft gained height and moved away, eventually out of the range of the soldiers.

"It's sluggish!" cried Lord Burydan, "and the power level has dropped."

The Doctor ran over to the control panel. "The areas with the camouflage panels missing appear to have poor shielding underneath. They must have hit those parts and caused damage."

"Release me," shouted Grantaigle. He was ignored.

"Get us out of the city! Head west. We will land if we have to and let the ship recharge as much as possible before taking off again," the Doctor ordered Lord Burydan.

Back at the barracks, the Countess could see the craft moving slowly away. She dashed towards her vehicle, *Elizabeth*, parked nearby, with the lieutenant in tow. They got in and drove off down the hill and then through the street, following the craft westwards, occasionally losing sight of it, but still managing to follow.

However, the craft steadily moved out of their sight, appearing to descend.

"Is there an airfield nearby?" the Countess asked the Lieutenant, "We need something up in the air to see where they have landed. Their craft looked clearly in trouble."

The lieutenant took a look at the map he was holding. "Yes," he said. "*Elizabeth* should get us there in a few minutes." He started to give directions.

At speed, *Elizabeth* headed towards the airfield.

Dr Cornelius' craft landed in an empty field.

"We will stay here as long as possible to recharge. If we are discovered, we can at least take off with what power remains," said the Doctor to Lord Burydan.

"Who are you?" asked Grantaigle, still handcuffed to the ladder.

"I am Dr. Cornelius Kramm."

"The sculptor of human flesh? Yes, there were press reports you were alive. What do you want with me?"

"I am interested in your work. Working with me, we can create whole armies of men. I am sure your process can be modified to condition them to serve. And does your duplication copy brain wave patterns as well? No more need for brutal interrogations, simply make a conditioned copy who will reveal whatever one needs to know."

"I will not be a party to such a thing!" exclaimed Grantaigle.

"Oh, but you will. I have certain techniques that will ensure your cooperation."

Grantaigle looked appalled.

Lord Burydan motioned the Doctor away and spoke quietly to him. "I don't mean to be difficult, old man, but I thought we were being paid to take him to the French or to kill him?"

"Why do that when, with his knowledge, combined with my expertise, we could create a force to rule the world?" the Doctor replied.

"Er, yes, but I would not want to get on the wrong side of London. All very well helping you against the Hun and their friends, but not quite sure how this would be received in my club."

Dr. Cornelius looked at him. "Well, I will need someone to run Britain. Don't you want the job? I understand that, as a Lord, there would be no constitutional bar to your becoming Prime Minister as part of your

205

country's eventual surrender to me. I am sure you could run it well enough."

The Briton clapped his hands. "By jingo, I hadn't thought of it like that. Well, I see no problem then! Do tell me if you need assistance persuading this Frenchman to help out."

"That won't be necessary," said the Doctor. "He will cooperate soon enough."

Grantaigle looked even more fearful.

It was an unusual day for Hauptmann Heinrich Kostrba. He had landed just outside Budapest on official business when none other than the famous journalist Countess Irina Petrovska drove onto the airfield, requesting air reconnaissance to find some kind of flying vehicle that may have landed nearby.

He offered his services, and to his great surprise, she put on a pair of goggles and sat in the gunner seat behind him on his Hansa Brandenburg CI biplane. They had been in the air for a few minutes when he spotted a strange circular object in a field and indicated to the Countess what he had seen. She nodded and pointed downwards. Kostrba started circling, descending to take a closer look.

Dr Cornelius was outside the cabin, inspecting the damage to the craft, when he saw the plane. As soon as it started to circle, he knew they had been spotted. He ran inside.

"Take off! That plane has spotted us!"

Lord Burydan looked at the power gauge—it was still low. However, staying on the ground would likely result in capture. In the air, at least they had a chance. He took the craft up.

"I will give our visitors some good wishes while we are at this altitude," Dr Cornelius said.

He took a rifle and went out onto the platform.

The craft was around 60 feet in the air. Lord Burydan realized the power seemed to fight against rising higher. Outside, the biplane buzzed the craft. Dr. Cornelius tried to fire his rifle at it, but could not get a decent shot—the plane was moving too fast.

The Countess looked at the craft. It was a blur in the sky, but with some holes which looked like torn metal. It was not surrendering, but she could not let them get away with Grantaigle. She was suspicious of the scientist, but he was still a civilian. However, she could not let him be taken. His being in the hands of Dr Cornelius, let alone the French, could only lead to many more lives being lost in pointless battles.

She indicated to Kostrba to dive towards it again. She took hold of the machine gun and fired at the craft, trying to hit the already damaged parts—its weak point.

The Czech pilot was impressed by the Countess's actions. He silently resolved never to cross a Pole.

Dr. Cornelius tried one more shot, missed, and then jumped back inside, closing the door. The Countess's bullets had hit their mark, further damaging the internal machinery. The craft started to wobble dramatically. Taking a pistol, he rushed to release Grantaigle. He forced him onto the seating area and strapped him in at gunpoint. *I may as well try to preserve my asset*, he thought.

The craft started to veer wildly in the air, its camouflage fully disengaging and acrid smoke billowing out. It then headed downwards.

The craft hit the ground and skidded along until it stopped. Inside, all three men seemed surprised.

"At the speed we hit the ground, we should be dead," said Lord Burydan. "Yet, all that happened was that we were shaken around a bit."

"Some kind of inertia manipulation in case of emergencies," the Doctor explained. He wondered again as to who had created this vehicle.

The craft had landed at an angle. The door was now on the bottom. Dr Cornelius pressed a button. It opened slightly, and then stopped. All the power went out, and they were in darkness.

The Doctor grabbed his rifle and wedged it in the door gap, forcing it open. He could see the ground, three-foot way, due to the platform. He could hear engine noise outside. Awkwardly, he climbed out, rifle in hand, and dropped onto the ground. Then he froze. The biplane that had attacked them was right outside, its propellor powering down. And in the gunner's seat, he saw the Countess, machine gun firmly aimed at him. The Doctor calculated that he would be cut down well before he could use his rifle.

The Countess ordered the Doctor to drop his weapon and to stand up.

"Where's Lord Burydan?" she asked.

"Inside, injured," lied the Doctor.

They stayed there like that until local troops arrived. Having already been alerted by Lieutenant Vuljanić to look for the craft, they had seen the air battle in the distance and headed this way.

Lord Burydan considered taking Grantaigle hostage. He already had a gun on him.

"You had better just surrender," Grantaigle told him. "Kill me, and they will assuredly kill you. And they would rather see me dead than any possibility of your walking off with me."

"Impeccable logic for a Frenchman," Burydan said. He indicated to Grantaigle to go first and then followed.

The Countess, out of the aircraft now, shot Dr. Cornelius a withering look when Lord Burydan emerged, uninjured. The Doctor merely shrugged.

A couple of hours later, back at the barracks, the Countess entered the laboratory with Lieutenant Vuljanić, having personally seen both Dr. Cornelius and Lord Burydan placed in the cells, safely secured by Sergeant Mayr. The soldier also reported that it seemed the ex-Red Hand operative in their custody knew very little of use. Von Reinhardt was also present, having greeted the Countess on her arrival.

"I'd like to check on Grantaigle. He wanted to return to the laboratory immediately to check for damage," said the Countess.

"Perhaps he is up to some questions about the demonstration? We can't let these criminals, no doubt acting for the French, disrupt us," said von Reinhardt.

"I agree," said the Countess. In truth, she was exhausted. However, she could not forget Bela Lugosi's comments about Grantaigle.

They started to make their way to the laboratory.

"One moment," said the Countess. She headed back to the cells and returned. "I just wanted to check something with Sergeant Mayr."

They passed an army Colonel leaving the laboratory.

Inside, Grantaigle was looking around for damage. All three were taken aback to see the Prime Minister present.

"Prime Minister?" the Countess said. "I thought that you had gone to Parliament?"

"I did," replied the Prime Minister, "but I have returned to congratulate you on your capture of those French agents—a great service to the Hungarian Kingdom and the Empire."

"I am glad to see that you have returned, Prime Minister," von Reinhardt said. "Perhaps we can ask questions about the demonstration?"

"Of course," said Grantaigle.

"Splendid!" the German replied. "I am interested in how long it will take to mass produce these machines. We have had many men wounded during the war."

"It will not take long," Grantaigle replied. "A few weeks only."

The doors opened, and in came the Colonel the three had passed on the way in. Behind him, flanked by guards, were a handcuffed Dr. Cornelius and Lord Burydan.

"What are they doing here?" demanded the Countess.

"I ordered them here, so they could see the failure of what they tried to do," said the Prime Minister, "Colonel, you may stay here. You, other men, may take your leave."

The Colonel already had his pistol drawn and covered his prisoners with them.

"Do sit down," said Grantaigle.

Bemused, both the Doctor and Lord Burydan did as they were told.

"You will be duplicated," he told them. "Your copies will be conditioned to obey." He turned to the others. "Dr. Cornelius's mind will be at my disposal and this one…" he pointed to Lord Burydan, "…it will be interesting to see if his insanity can be cured in his duplicate."

"Steady on!" said Lord Burydan.

"This cannot proceed," said the Countess. "It is expressly forbidden by the Emperor,"

"King," said the Prime Minister.

Von Reinhardt intervened. "Whilst having access to these men's memories would be useful, I must bow to the Countess's judgement, and also point out that you are in no position to disobey the Emperor's ruling."

"King," said the Prime Minister, emotionlessly.

The Countess looked at the Prime Minister.

Dr. Cornelius immediately understood what had happened. *It was something I would have done*, he thought ruefully.

Standing by the projector, Grantaigle switched it on. Beams of light spread around the room. The Countess, Dr. Cornelius, Lord Burydan, Vuljanić and von Reinhardt collapsed, falling off chairs or collapsing to the ground. They were hit with dizziness they had not encountered in their lives before.

"Disobey the Emperor?" said Grantaigle angrily,

"King," said the Prime Minister.

Grantaigle stood over von Reinhardt. "Your soldiers attacked and destroyed my chateau! My home! They killed my other self, whom I had created using the technology my government had entrusted me to examine. I felt his death—it was agony. The attack on my chateau also resulted in the inadvertent copying of a French soldier who was with me. I can only hope both escaped. To hell with all Germans! When I get back to France, I will create legions of soldiers to crush Germany and her allies!"

Angrily, the scientist took the gun of the Colonel and shot the German in the heart. Then he realized he had made an error. He told the officer, "Go outside and explain what that shot was, and then wait until I send you the duplicates of these two..." pointing at Dr Cornelius and Lord Burydan, "...I want them taken to French lines," he said

The Colonel swiftly exited to carry out his instructions.

Grantaigle then addressed his captives. "It will be over soon. You will black out shortly. In the meantime, let me answer the questions that you are all no doubt all wanting to ask..."

He looked at the writhing Countess, one arm forcing itself behind her back. "You were right. The Saturnians did use telepathy in their machines. The equipment the French had did have that facility, which I finally learned to use, just before the German attack. The equipment from Sarajevo was so damaged that it had no telepathic function. However, my experience with the French-retrieved apparatus gave me the knowledge to be able to do something with the junk brought to me here.

"It was easy to duplicate one of the scientists assigned to me. I even solved the mass problem. I was now able to use other materials to create the required mass for duplicates—ones conditioned to obey me. Eventually, I copied most of the staff . What about the originals, you ask? I eliminated them by an injection of poison, and I used their bodies to help produce the mass required to create more duplicates. Unfortunately, none of the men I copied had the authority to get me my freedom. I then planned everything to get to someone who could—the Prime Minister, copied without anyone's knowledge, hidden in the machinery behind me.

"The intervention of these two…" he pointed at Dr. Cornelius and Lord Burydan, "…meant that the real Prime Minister did indeed go to Parliament. However, my version here is needed only to clear my departure. And with the Countess and the Lieutenant here, as top *Evidenzbureau* operatives, they can escort me safely, separately from Dr. Cornelius and Lord Burydan so as not to arouse any suspicions on our journey back to France."

Dr. Cornelius could see a way out of this predicament for both himself and Lord Burydan. In fact, he could see himself still gaining. There was, however, one problem to solve, and he did not know how to do it. He played for time. "Why," the Doctor gasped, "did you not copy everyone earlier?"

"You will have noticed this process is taking longer and with more side-effects than when I surreptitiously copied the Prime Minister, with a couple of my copied scientists also pretending to be dizzy. My machine can copy six persons at a time, but it takes longer for your biodata, as the Saturnians call it, to be duplicated. There were more than six guests here earlier. It was much safer to copy only one arm and one Prime Minister with minimal effects and no suspicions being aroused."

Meanwhile, the Countess was struggling. Her right arm was trying to reach the nape of her back. There, in a disguised fold of her dress, was a small pistol. She had obtained it from Sergeant Mayr earlier when she had gone back to the cell. The rule was that no weapons were permitted in the laboratory. Given the day's events, she had decided that this precaution was necessary. She pulled out the pistol. But her consciousness was fading. Everything was swirling. She could not afford to simply shoot Grantaigle, distracted as he was by Dr. Cornelius, and perhaps only wound him. The machine had to be her priority.

She aimed at the projector and fired. Her bullet hit the machine and it exploded. The beams of light disappeared. Grantaigle aimed his gun at the Countess. But then, fast as lightning, Lord Burydan had his hands, still handcuffed, around Grantaigle's head.

"Insane, am I?" the Brition asked.

Using his great strength, he twisted the scientist's head, breaking his neck. Grantaigle's body fell to the floor, dead.

The Countess, pistol still in hand, groggily got to her feet, slowly raising her gun.

Lord Burydan decided not to tackle her. He picked up Dr. Cornelius and headed out of the door at great speed. The Colonel was standing outside, a few feet in front of them.

Dr. Cornelius spoke. "Your instructions are to get us to French lines. Take us away at once. I will direct your route."

The Colonel nodded and took them to a nearby car. The Doctor noted that no one was in the immediate vicinity. No doubt the Colonel—or rather his copy—had ordered people away. The Colonel drove them off in a military car. "Be so good as to give us the keys to these handcuffs," the Doctor ordered. The Colonel threw the keys back.

"You are quite a clever chap," Lord Burydan said.

The Doctor nodded.

Back at the laboratory, The copy of the Prime Minister operated a switch by a large pipe on the wall. It opened, and the Countess glimpsed what looked like a slab with a human shape indented into it, much like the small container Grantaigle had used earlier to produce Denes's arm. Something was forming into it and the Countess could see the corners of other slabs behind it. Lieutenant Vuljanić tried to restrain him, but the duplicate shoved him into the Countess, who dropped her gun.

Then, the duplicated man pulled a switch above the slab and said "*Vive la France!*"

Suddenly, whatever was forming seemed to glow and burn. The duplicate Prime Minister collapsed, as did the two *Evidenzbureau* scientists.

The Countess and Vuljanić looked on, astonished.

Schönbrunn Palace, Vienna, 21 May 1917

"Dr. Cornelius and Lord Burydan got away," the Countess said. "The duplicated Colonel must have had some route planned already. No trace of them was found. As for the machinery, all the intricate parts were burnt or melted. Whatever things were growing in those slabs, of which there were six, were turned to ashes—mercifully"

"And all the duplicates are dead?" asked the Emperor

"Yes. Grantaigle must have programmed them to die when he did, and to destroy all the technology— some form of self-destruct with the '*Vive la France*' command somehow activating it after a switch was thrown. The scientists the *Evidenzbureau* had recruited to help on the project all died within 48 hours after Grantaigle's passing. It was no doubt a safeguard. The duplicate of the Colonel is likely also dead."

"Thank you, Countess. You have done well. This business has worsened my relations with the Prime Minister. Given he is partly to blame for this debacle, he has agreed to a change in the secret protocols of the Dual Monarchy. Budapest will have no further say in *Evidenzbureau* matters concerning extraterrestrial technology. However, I am not sure how much longer I can work with the man."

The Countess nodded. She hoped that relations would be resolved. The war could yet be won, and with that victory, a re-organization of the Empire, which needed Hungarian cooperation, could be achieved, one which would benefit the Poles, Croats, Slovaks, Czechs and others, and take it firmly into the future.

Dr Cornelius' residence, Berne, Switzerland, 27 May 1917

Dr. Cornelius looked at his newspaper. "It appears that Prime Minister Tisza resigned in the last few days," he said to his British guest.

"I find politics boring," said Lord Burydan, sitting on a nearby chair, whisky in hand. "Has the money come through?"

"It has," the Doctor replied. "Mr. Hart seems to believe Grantaigle is indeed dead. No doubt whoever told him the scientist was in Budapest also told him that. The duplicate Colonel we provided also helped, even his simply dying for no reason helped convince Hart, I daresay. The money I received was substantial. I have already given instructions for your cut to be transferred to your account."

The Doctor was pleased overall. Yes, his craft had been lost—no doubt, it was now in that damn Sarajevo repository—and he had failed to get Grantaigle for his own ends. However, he was 200,000 francs or so richer than when this operation had started. He now had to attend to a minor, but important, chore.

"Let me now give you the serum to keep your face intact. We don't want it deteriorating into the scarred state it was in before I repaired that," the Doctor said.

"About that," Lord Burydan replied. "Is there any need for this? You can give me a serum to permanently fix my face, without having to come back every month."

"I would then lose my hold on you," the Doctor replied.

"Yes, but I think I have served you very well these last three years or so. In this latest escapade, I got you out of that laboratory."

"And I had the wherewithal to pretend to the Colonel we were the duplicates he was expecting."

"Yes, but..."

The Doctor held up his hand to silence the Briton. A decision had to be made. It was true Lord Burydan had done well. If this man started to become too resentful, that could create problems in the future. Should he kill him now? No, that would only deprive him of a useful occasional employee However, would he still wish to work for him?

The Doctor put his hand down. "And if I were to do as you ask, would you still be willing to work for me, given I would have no hold on you?"

"Yes, of course! "said the Briton a little too enthusiastically. "You pay well, and I have a lifestyle to maintain! And I think the only way to get even with the Countess is to work with you. You do seem to run into her a lot."

The response saved his life. Had he said "no," the injection would have been poison.

"Very well," said the sculptor of human flesh. "Dr. Cornelius Kramm always rewards good work. You shall have the permanent serum."

Lord Burydan beamed. "You are a splendid fellow, Dr Cornelius."

The Doctor thought of the Countess. Yes, he did run into her a lot, as Burydan had said. This war was not yet over. There would no doubt be another encounter with her.

The Secret Archive of Vienna

General Phillipovich barracks, Sarajevo,
6 November 1918

Captain Nemec aimed his rifle and fired on the approaching French troops. The Frenchmen scattered and retreated. The Captain stopped firing. He was at the gate of the barracks. These Frenchmen—how were they here so far from their lines?—seemed well armed, but his own men, lined up along the walls of the barracks could hold them back. They had the measure of the French.

A man from the French side came forward, waving a white flag. He wore the uniform of a Colonel, and Captain Nemec held his fire. The Frenchman spoke in German. As an officer in the Austro-Hungarian Empire, the Captain knew the language.

"My friend, the war is virtually over. Let us through—we only wish to take what was agreed between your emperor and my government. You know of the materials we mean."

"What agreement?" the Captain said. "The war isn't even over yet."

What agreement indeed, Hart thought. There was no agreement; they were here to take certain materials before France's other allies did. The British and Americans already had their people on the way. And he heard that the Russian Bolsheviks were up to something as well.

"Your emperor has agreed to let us take certain items here away for inspection part of the coming cease-fire," Hart said. He had no compunction about lying. In reality he was a senior officer in the *Deuxième Bureau*.

The Captain, and some of his men knew very well what Hart meant by "certain items." The barracks had another purpose—they contained a repository of certain artefacts, items from other worlds and from this one. Weapons and objects of such advanced technology that they could not understand them.

Could the Captain let the French have them?

One of his men shouted something in French to Hart.

Hart responded. "Your man knows French obscenities, I do hope you bring him in line and surrender."

The Captain turned to his Sergeant, "Tell that man to keep quiet!"

"Shut yer trap!" the Sergeant shouted at the private.

The Captain was not amused by the soldier's inter-vention. It demonstrated a certain breakdown in disci-pline in the wake of the Austro-Hungarian Empire's de-feat in the war. At least, however, the man seemed will-ing to fight.

And so could he.

"Colonel Hart, I fear I must decline to surrender to you. I have had no instructions to surrender anything to anyone."

"I would urge you to reconsider, Captain," said Hart. He had hoped that he would not have to use his advantage. And now he did. He waved to one of men.

Captain Nemec and his men looked stunned as be-hind the French troops, the air seemed to shimmer. And then appeared what the Captain recognized as French 75 mm artillery field guns, along with some vehicles.

The Captain knew that artillery would destroy them. It would be suicidal to resist. The French could kill them all and take what they wanted anyway. Perhaps they could destroy the items before surrendering to the French?

As if he could read the Captain's mind, Hart said: "Any movement now from your troops and my artillery start firing directly at you all."

The Captain did not relish sacrificing himself and his men for nothing. That is, assuming that his men would obey such instructions. They were loyal, but even that loyalty would be strained, given their side's defeat and the political situation which was seeing the Empire dissolve. He felt privileged to have served with his men. In whatever came next for the peoples of the Empire, they would be needed at their homes. This war had created so many widows and fatherless children—why create even more for no gain?

"Very well," said the Captain. "You may proceed."

Matters were swiftly dealt with. Hart and his men took the artifacts. Things labeled coming as belonging to "far and distant things" and metallic body parts from "Planet 10" and various other strange weapons and objects. Hart was delighted. However, there was no documentation. Hart knew that such files existed in Vienna. However, he did not have the resources to take them. Coming to Sarajevo with an invisible convoy from the Dalmatian coast was one thing, but to get to the heart of the Habsburg empire in such a way? No, that was not feasible, and his superiors had forbidden it in any event, fearing it might jeopardize the German surrender negotiations. Further the invisibility device was already starting to wear out—based on the remnants of Saturnian machinery constructed by one his more difficult employees. Once it burned out, that would be the end of it for that technology. However, now Hart had much more to play with—as soon as his scientists could work it all out.[11]

Dr. Cornelius Kramm looked around him. He was in a locked room. He sat on one chair, and a couple of feet away was a desk with another chair. US Marshals stood outside. He sighed. He had become complacent. He, the legendary "sculptor of human flesh, had become complacent. He had fled the United States, careful to ensure that the authorities thought him dead. From being one of the Lords—the leading one—of the notorious Red Hand criminal empire, he had eventually come to Europe with a new identity and set himself up as a criminal for hire based in Berne. His cover of Dr. Malbrough had been blown in 1914, but he'd found Berne too congenial to leave and simply changed his name again. That had been a grave mistake.

A man entered. The Doctor would have considered a possible attempt at getting hold of the man and holding him hostage. However, given that he was manacled to his chair, this would not be feasible.

The slightly stocky man sat down on the chair behind the table. He was dressed in civilian clothing, but Dr. Cornelius noted a military bearing.

---

[11] The captured hoard would add to France's already impressive knowledge and use of such esoteric science. The effects on French society and the world are documented in many books published by Black Coat Press.

"My name is Hamilton. Dr. Cornelius Kramm, I am here to inform you that you are to be returned to the United States to face trial for a number of charges in relation to your leadership of the Red Hand criminal organization. Murder, racketeering, torture and much more, including causing a rail crash."

The sculptor of human flesh replied in his best innocent manner, "I am but a simple surgeon. My name is Cerral, I am not this Cornelus Kramm you are after."

"Your attitude will change once you are strapped into the electric chair," Hamilton said.

Dr. Cornelius considered the man for a moment. He could sense something was going on. "I find it odd that I was not simply arrested and handed over to you. Instead, I was kidnapped from my apartment by mysterious Swiss agents and dumped here. Perhaps it would be less embarrassing to the Swiss authorities? However, I have been held here for three days. If I were indeed Dr. Cornelius Kramm, surely, I would already be on my way to the United States?"

The military man started impassively at his prisoner. "You are a man of unique talents and knowledge," he said.

Dr. Cornelius tensed. He could see that there was a way out of his predicament somewhere here and replied. "I am indeed—and my talents are for hire. I am not cheap, however."

Hamilton decided to take things forward. "Dr. Cornelius, we have a proposition for you."

"I like propositions, but who am I dealing with?"

"The Military Intelligence Division of the United States Department of War."

"I see. And your proposition?"

Hamilton leaned back in his chair. "We can easily take you to the United States, ensure a swift trial and execute you shortly after—the public would demand it. However, we think you can serve your country."

Dr. Cornelius smiled. He had more or less forgotten he was a US citizen. "How might I do that? And what would be my reward?" he asked.

"We would like you to confiscate the Vienna Archive."

"The documents, papers and history of esoteric items? All the Austro-Hungarian secrets of an unusual nature. I can do that. However, I have to go immediately—others will no doubt have eyes on it. My reward?"

"You avoid a trial. You work for us as an agent in these matters. The Swiss have frozen your accounts and we have found your other accounts in other countries— we have used various means to discreetly take control of those; indeed we intend to use those funds in the service of our country. We will give you a salary. If you escape us, we will track you down, as we just have, and kill you. No trial."

"You must be desperate," said Dr. Cornelius. "However, you are right to offer me this deal. The old empires have had a near monopoly on alien technologies and strange science. The United States, despite its growing power, has none of this. I, on the other hand, am one of the few Americans who has experience of such matters. Have you considered appropriating the actual artifacts, held in Sarajevo?"

Hamilton looked rueful. "The French got there first."

"Ah, Simon Hart," the sculptor of flesh replied. "He hired me during this war; it does not surprise me he has moved so fast and so brazenly. I have to assume that diplomatic considerations prevent him from doing something similar in Vienna. A few days ago, I received a communication from him—then your Swiss friends swooped. Perhaps he was going to hire me go to Vienna, on some kind of deniable basis, of course, unknown to his superiors, but it seems that perhaps you somehow intercepted that message whilst looking for me."

Hamilton said nothing.

Dr. Cornelius continued. "The Habsburgs also have a facility in Transylvania, a castle that once belonged to one Count Dracula. There they stored their supernatural materials. Are you not interested in that?"

"No," said Hamilton. "Superstitious nonsense. In any event, we understand that Russian Bolsheviks led by the former German spy Von Bork has taken everything. They killed most of the people there to do it."

Dr. Cornelius considered this man to be ignorant—the Bolsheviks knew what they were doing. Still, his own experience of the supernatural was limited, and he much preferred dealing with largely scientific matters. He did not think that the Military Intelligence Division had found all his assets; but very likely they had left some alone in order to catch him should he renege on the deal and try to access them. He had become complacent and had been found. Now, he would make the best of the situation. He would work for Washington for now and bide his time.

"Your terms are acceptable. You have re-awakened my patriotism," he said, beaming. "We of the New World will surpass the Old World in these esoteric matters. Now, if you would release me, I have work to do to secure the archive—unless the likes of the Russians or British have gotten there first."

Warily, the military man called the Marshals to free his newest agent.

Restaurant Nervosa, Berne, 8 November 1918, evening

Hamilton was seated at the usual table of the US ambassador to Switzerland, which was in a discreet corner, out of earshot of the other diners.

"You trust this Dr. Cornelius?" asked the Ambassador, taking a drop of some fine wine.

"No, I do not," answered Hamilton. "However, he knows we are likely to simply kill him should he in some way double-cross us or flee."

"I must admit, Major Hamilton, that I am uncomfortable with all this. Dr. Cornelius Kramm should be tried and executed for his crimes, yet we are employing him instead."

The military man sighed inwardly. This diplomat was naïve. "I appreciate the moral concerns. However, our country is far behind our knowledge of the world of the fantastic. We entered this war and now our President is taking a leading role in constructing how world affairs are to be conducted. We cannot let our growing power be undone by some old empire suddenly understanding the secret sciences and knowledge they have locked away. Conceivably, the Germans or the Habsburgs could turn everything around tomorrow if they utilized some alien weapon they have—and our allies, the British and French, may could also pose a problem. And then, there are the Bolsheviks…"

The diplomat nodded his head. He had only recently been told of such things. Alien beings and so on. He was not even sure he believed it.

"I bow to your judgement," he replied. "I am glad that my contacts with the Swiss were of use. When will Dr. Corneilus leave the country?"

"He has already left—we needed to move fast. And your contacts proved invaluable—many thanks."

"Invaluable indeed!" a man said to himself not too far away.

Percy Phelps of the British Directorate of Military Intelligence had to restrain himself from bursting out laughing. One of those contacts was in fact his contact, who had told him of the strange requests from the Americans.

He was at a table in a small room discreetly behind the restaurant's kitchen listening to the two Americans. The table had been bugged for some time given that the US ambassador always liked to sit there. This was facilitated in an arrangement with the restaurant owner involving certain information regarding a mistress not getting to his wife. The information gleaned this evening would be of great interest to his superiors. He doubted anything would be made public—the American were their war allies, after all. However, something useful could be done with the information. He looked at the machine he was using. It was a Detectifone listening device, made and purchased from a company based in New York City.

The Americans have much to learn about espionage Phelps thought.

Castle Schoenbrunn, Vienna, 11 November 1918

The Countess Irina Petrovska had been summoned to see the Emperor Karl. An armistice had been signed.

Germany and her ally, Vienna, had lost the war. The Austro-Hungarian Empire was collapsing—the nationalities were asserting themselves, emboldened by President Wilson's fourteen points. She herself was preparing to leave for her homeland of Poland. Nonetheless, she was still technically a citizen of the Austro-Hungarian Empire and felt that she should answer the summons.

The Emperor was in the Blue Chinese Salon part of the building, known to be particularly sumptuous. She was shown to the Emperor, without any formalities. *A very obvious sign of the times*, she thought.

"Thank you, Countess, for coming at such short notice," the Emperor said. He was standing, dressed in military uniform. He gestured to her to sit, which she did, and he took a seat opposite her. An aide sat a short distance away.

"I believe you are heading for Poland?" he asked.

"That was my plan, given the apparent collapse of everything" she replied. "My efforts for a united Poland under your guidance has come to nothing with our defeat. However, I believe that General Józef Piłsudski will play a strong part in the future of Poland. I intend to help him."

"I am concerned for the fate of all our peoples. I wish your countrymen would consider remaining within the Empire," replied the Emperor.

"My countrymen are happy to have independence without being part of an Empire. I am afraid the simple fact of defeat has not contributed to the credibility of Vienna. And further, your former foreign minister Count von Czernin's deal with Ukraine—and your own unfavorable comments about Poles—have not impressed any Pole, including me."

The aide looked appalled. "You cannot speak to the Emperor like that!" he exclaimed, standing up.

The Emperor waved him back down. "If anyone has earned the right to speak frankly to me," the Emperor said, "it is the Countess."

The Emperor looked awkward. He knew very well of the Countess's strong Polish patriotism. "You must understand that I have had to balance the interests of all my peoples. As you know, I have made efforts to federalize the Empire in recent months. However, I do accept that an independent Poland would be just."

The Countess softened, "I do fear for the future without the Empire. Whatever faults it may have had, it was in a position to protect its peoples. And that included defending them from threats from beyond."

"You have guessed why I have summoned you," the Emperor replied.

"Yes. The raid on our facilities in Sarajevo of our scientific materials, and in Transylvania of our supernatural ones. The French and the Bolsheviks being respectively responsible.

The Emperor nodded. "Yes, and now all that we have left is our archive here in Vienna. The documents contained would be invaluable to the French and the Russians. It would give them a degree of insight into what they have. It is bad enough the French having all that information—but the Bolsheviks!"

"I quite agree," said the Countess. "The Romanovs were our enemy during the war, it is true. However, I knew them personally and they did not deserve their fate. The thought of such unholy things being in their hands disturbs me. I must say that days ago, I approached the *Evidenzbureau.* It was half-deserted. Prince

Wilhelm[12] was not even there. Nobody seemed to be in charge, and I had to leave. Later, I heard about the raids."

The Emperor responded to the mention of the Bohemian prince. "I am told he left to return to Bohemia; he believes he will now be crowned King, despite the public believing he is dead."

"I am sure Mr. Masaryk[13] will inform him otherwise," said the Countess. "Had he stayed at his post, perhaps we could have organized something to at least save the Sarajevo artefacts. I am aware the supernatural did not come under his authority. With him gone, that was when I started to make plans to return to Poland."

"Countess, I would ask you to put off your journey for one final assignment for the Empire."

"Of course."

"The Secret Archive here in Vienna is being guarded by soldiers. However, reports suggest that their loyalties to the monarchy may not be solid. It is only a matter of time before other forces intervene. Further, I do not trust the new authorities that are emerging either here or in Budapest. I was thinking that you could see to it that the archive is transferred to Germany?"

"Your highness, Germany has been defeated. It is now unstable. The archive could be stolen from them— or misused by whoever takes power—as much as here."

"Where else is there?" asked the Habsburg ruler.

---

[12] Prince Wilhelm, a pretender to the throne of Bohemia, had been given a senior post in the *Evidenzbureau* to keep him content.

[13] Tomáš Garrigue Masaryk, who a few days later became the first President of Czechoslovakia.

"The archive must go to those who will use it appropriately to protect humanity. The French cannot be trusted, as their raids shows. Their man, Simon Hart, is not someone who would use these things responsibly, only for furtherance of French goals. The Bolsheviks, of course, must not have them. Whoever takes possession must be strong enough to keep the information away from Von Bork. I believe my own country has too much to deal with already to take this on. The Americans are too young a country. There is only one realistic option: The British."

"The British!" exclaimed the Emperor. His aide looked as if he was about to faint.

The Emperor continued, "You cannot be serious, Countess! They are the ones most responsible for our defeat! Further, have you forgotten their attempts with the French to destroy the city of Pula—which you prevented?"

"Of course not," the Countess responded. "I was not thinking of those responsible for that. I was thinking of my old friends, Professor Saxton and Dr. Wells."

"I know of them—you were involved with them in that... 'Horror Express' incident in Siberia."

"Yes. they were responsible for ensuring the destruction of alien creature that posed a threat to life on this planet. A creature that had murdered my husband, Count Petrovski. That incident convinced me to take a role in combating such evil. In the years afterwards, they have defeated a number of unearthly threats, and I have helped them on occasion. They informally run an independent department for the British government. Working with them, we saved a large part of London from destruction in 1906—at the very time the great Austrian exhibition took place. Many of our fellow citizens were saved."

The Emperor nodded. "Yes, I recall."

The Countess continued, "Let us not be naïve—they will likely use the information for the protection of the British Empire. However, they do have a sense of responsibility—they will help outside of their Empire, as demonstrated in the Prague incident of 1910 where we asked for their expertise against the Jovian incursion. And we do know they have an antipathy towards Simon Hart and his department. Hart worked with other Britons in the Pula incident—primarily the lunatic Lord Burydan, but that had nothing to do with my friends. And we can be sure that once in their hands, they will be secure from Von Bork."

"It seems I have little choice," said the Emperor. "Very well. It will not surprise you to know that later today I announce that I will renounce all participation in the affairs of state. Thus, this will be the last covert order I give as Emperor. Countess Irina Petrovska, I task you with ensuring the Vienna Archive is entrusted to the care of the British."

"I will carry it out."

The Emperor opened an ornate box on the table. He brought out what looked like a key, made of something resembling white marble. "The Vienna Archive facility is not only guarded by loyal troops, but the most sensitive area is defended by what I understand is termed a force-field."

"Ah, yes," said the Countess. "It was left behind by the Jovian incursion. The *Evidenzbureau* could not fathom how it worked. However, I am glad it has been put to good use."

The Countess took the key from the Emperor's hand. "I know how to use this," she said. "I will move immediately. I will need a letter of authority from you. I will also contact Professor Saxton and Dr. Wells—we have not been in touch since the war began, but I have a method of communication.

Soon, she left the building. She went to her vehicle *Elizabeth*—a gift to her from her British. The car had served her well during the war, being resistant to bullets and capable of moving over any terrain. They were coy about its origins—it was something they could not quite work out, like so much fantastic technology that fell into the hands of the Empires. And the experts she allowed to look at the vehicle were also non-plussed. It had a communication device, letting her speak to her friends in London, who had a receiver. It had not been used since 1914. She had much to tell them now, including about Lord Burydan. She switched the device on and could hear the ringing tone to London.

The Vienna Archive, Nottendorfer Gasse

Dr. Cornelius stood at a short distance from the archive. The evening was drawing in. He had no disguise; he was limiting his face-changing skills at the moment, claiming—falsely—to his new masters that materials were short. He was observing the archive building. It was an *Evidenzbureau* building, but one that did not reflect the splendor of Vienna, and thus did not bring much attention to itself.

Cleary, someone was thinking sensibly by placing the archive here, thought Dr. Cornelius. There were a number of soldiers parked around the building. A frontal assault would likely end in failure. He had only a few

233

men in any event, remnants of his old Red Hand organization in Austria, whom he had to hire for this job, and they were not cheap either. *How good of the United States Department of War to provide their wages*, he thought.

A number of guards left the building, ending their shift. Dr. Cornelius observed them—one split off from the others. He nodded in his direction. As if out of nowhere, three men appeared from different directions, all following the guard. They looked as if they were locals, and started singing with bottles in their hand, playing drunk. The guard looked around at them, and then ignored them. They caught up with him.

"Drink! Drink!" they said to the guard and held the bottle under his nose. The soldier looked angry, but then the vapor from the bottle hit. He suddenly looked delirious and grabbed the bottle from the hand of one of the men, pulled away from then and took a swig.

Dr. Cornelius caught up with them, exasperated. "Get the drug away from him!" One of the men took the bottle away from the guard. They took the guard arm in arm, and then singing an Austrian drinking song, they all walked away.

A couple of streets away, they all entered a fashionable-looking house, which was in fact one of the Red Hand organization's old European safe houses. A man in his sixties let him them in. He looked harmless, but in fact he was Dr. Cornelius's former employee, one Tamas Varga, who looked after the house and simply took it over when the Red Hand collapsed. He hired it out to wealthy types who wished to conduct illicit affairs or to have meetings away from prying eyes. It amused him to charge an outraged Dr. Cornelius extra. After all, the criminal mastermind would be conducting rather strange criminal during his stay.

Dr. Cornelius and his men bundled their captive into what was a living room, with opulent furniture. Their captive immediately started dancing in the middle of the room, singing *Gott erhalte Franz den Kaiser*.[14]

"Get him into a chair!" snapped Dr. Cornelius. His men did as they were told and slung the unfortunate guard into a chair.

The Doctor noted that the guard—a soldier—appeared to have taken off some of his K&K[15] insignia related to the Habsburgs. He grabbed a chair and sat next to him. The drug he had taken was a special one, a recent concoction by the sculptor of human flesh. It made the subject highly intoxicated and also rendered very suggestible.

"My man," said the Doctor in fluent German, "you appear to have got yourself a bit drunk. We are going to look after you, and we will take you home. First, please, do tell us your name and rank. "

"I am drunk? I don't remember drinking?" replied the guard.

"We found you singing in the street, in these times we can hardly blame you. Now, tell us your name and rank and where you live?"

"I am Corporal Simon Fischer, I'm not bothering with the barracks anymore, I was heading back to my father's house in Favoritenstrasse."

"Please tell us the full address so we can take you there," replied Dr. Cornelius.

---

[14] *God save Francis the Emperor*, the Imperial anthem of the Habsburg Empire.
[15] Imperial and Royal.

The soldier did so, and one of the henchmen wrote it down.

"Excellent!" exclaimed the Doctor. "Whilst we await a carriage to take you home, I am curious about your role. I was in the army myself you know," he lied.

"I was an *Evidenzbureau* soldier. We guard the Vienna archive on Nottendorfer Gasse"

"Really? What is kept there?"

The soldier looked a little scared. "Documents describing terrible things, it is said. The worst is kept on the ground floor, in an invisible safe.

The Doctor looked non-plussed. "Invisible safe?" he asked.

"Yes," the Corporal said. "You can see the cabinets, but you cannot get to them. They're protected by invisible walls. The key was kept by Prince Wilhelm, but he has fled Vienna, and my part of the *Evidenzbureau* has simply disintegrated. We work for Renner now."

Dr. Cornelius nodded. He was aware that the Social Democrats, under the leadership of Karl Renner, had effectively taken over the governance of Austria. What of this invisible safe? It must be a force-field of some alien manufacture. It would present a problem.

"Who has the key now?" asked the Doctor.

"It is rumored the Emperor has it."

The Doctor asked a few more questions about the guards and the layout of the archive building. He then told the young man to sleep, which he did.

"Now, we must take a copy of his face," the Doctor said. "And then, one of you will see that he gets safely home. We cannot have his father go out looking for him and bring unwanted attention. He will sleep, intoxicated, for hours."

Felix Lechner was none too sure about having his face transformed into that of Fischer, if only for a short time. Dr. Cornelius told him that his physique was closer to that of the young guard, and he only had the resources to change his face, not his body. Lechner was uncertain as if that was meant to help persuade him. However, the Doctor offered him a special bonus—in US dollars—that swiftly pushed away his doubts.

Now, he approached the *Evidenzbureau* facility. His cover story was that he had lost the keys to his father's home and wanted to see if they were inside. He was surprised that the guards on the door simply smiled at him and let him just walk through. Discipline was clearly breaking down. Lechner wandered down the main corridor—there were a number of rooms, largely offices, all with filing cabinets. He came to the end of the corridor to which there was a lift. He went in and took it down.

As soon as the door opened, a gunshot rang out and Lechner ducked. He was relieved that the shot appeared not to be aimed at him. He looked down at the corridor before him and about 20 feet away he could see a reinforced door, which was open. He could hear laughter. Lechner cautiously moved down the corridor. This was where Fischer said the "invisible safe" was—what Dr. Cornelius had said was in fact a "force-field."

There were four guards inside, with a machine gun next to them. The room was circular, about 20-feet wide. Hans could see safes and cabinets of varying sizes, all with the K&K insignia on them. Right in front of him on the floor was a rectangular box about 1-foot wide and high. It was glowing a strange color; one he did not think he had seen before.

One of the guards was seemingly knocking a hammer against thin air.

"Simon!" said a Corporal. "Come to try and break in again and get the Emperor's riches? We've had no luck, but Hans here decided to shoot his way in again, almost killing us in the process," he said, pointing to a sheepish guard next to him and then to a hole in the wall where clearly the bullet had landed after ricocheting off the force-field. "Hans is new," he explained.

Lechner laughed and nodded. He then put his hands to the force-field. It was solid, like a strong wall. He started to move around it.

"It's still a square shape," the Corporal said. Lechner affected a coughing fit to cover his different voice and gasped, "Just checking," he replied. He noted that that the safes inside appeared to float on a centimeter of thin air, no doubt the floor of the force-field.

Before he could inspect it further, the sound of machine-gun fire could be heard. "Stay here and kill anyone is who not one of us," the Corporal said to the guard with the machine gun. "The rest of you, with me!"

Lechner also went with them. This sounded like serious trouble, and he had no intention of potentially being trapped underground. Getting out fast was his priority.

The Corporal charged up some stairs rather than using the lift, and they emerged on the ground floor. There was heavy gunfire coming from outside. Lechner held back, allowing the Corporal and the other two men to charge along the corridor towards the exit. *Let them get shot rather than me*, he thought.

The Corporal and his men got to the entrance. Ahead of them on the road outside were the bloodied bodies of four men lying on the floor. To the Corporal's side were the guards who were manning the entrance. "Looks like Red Guards, they tried to storm the building, but hadn't reckoned with old Pichler upstairs with his machine gun."

There was more firing from across the street, a gunman behind a street corner, clearly aiming at the machine gunner. Then, from the same corner ran three men, shouting as they came. The Corporal and his men picked them off easily.

It then went quiet. After a few minutes, some curious civilians started to move on the road, looking at the bodies. A few came from around the corner from where the shots were being fired – almost getting themselves machine-gunned, save for one of the figures being recognized as a guard. The man ran over to the Corporal. "I was in the pub. I heard gunfire. What happened."

The Corporal responded, "We were attacked. You came from where we were fired on. Did you see anything."

The guard nodded. "Yes, a group of armed men ran past me,"

The Corporal motioned to a couple of the men, and they ran across to check, coming back to report the gunmen had indeed gone.

"Given the slogans they were shouting, they appear to be those Bolshevik Red Guards," the Corporal said.

At that moment, a man on horseback appeared. He had a military uniform on—that of a Captain. Unlike the guards at the building, his unform still retained Imperial insignia. He got off his horse.

"Don't you salute an officer?"

"To hell with you. The Empire is finished. We'll be taking no orders from you."

The officer looked at the Corporal. He had experienced much of this of late. He decided to ignore the man's comments rather than threaten him, which he knew would result in nothing more than ridicule, and perhaps even violence.

"What has happened here?" he asked.

The Corporal obliged him with an answer. "Red Guards, trying to steal the riches here. We dealt with them."

Lechner quietly listened. He was sure Dr. Cornelius would want to know why an officer had stopped by. He was aware that the Doctor had someone watching this building at all times.

The officer appears to nod in approval. He reached inside his tunic and gave a piece of paper to the Corporal. "This is a direct order from the Emperor himself," he said.

The Corporal sneered. "I don't care. We work for Renner now," he said.

"Nonetheless, it is a legal order, whatever you might think. Renner is also being told. What will happen is that the Countess Irina Petrovska will soon arrive with the British military. All the men here are to give their complete cooperation."

"We will see what Renner says about that," responded the Corporal, to grunts of approval from the other men. The Captain decided that this would be a good time to leave. He had done as he had been ordered. He mounted his horse and rode off, to jeers from the guards.

Lechner made his excuses and left to report to Dr. Cornelius. However, he was not the only one to leave. One of the men with the Corporal slipped away. *Damn those fools*, the man thought. *What an insane attack! Did they not listen to me when I told them of the machine guns? How did they expect to take the materials from the invisible safe? Revolution will not be achieved in Vienna by such incompetence.* He was also angry that they attacked when he was present, putting him in danger. He would report back to the others on what had happened. Experienced military men were needed, not those such as the dead in the street were little more than local agitators—men who he presumed also did not believe his reports of the invisible safe. He would ignore the useless local comrade in charge and contact Von Bork directly. The spymaster would want to know of the involvement of this Countess.

Former Red Hand Safe House, Vienna

Dr. Cornelius listened to Lechner's report. "The Countess. Again," he said.

Lechner looked puzzled.

"A regular foe," the Doctor explained. "She seems to have cropped up at least once a year during this war. Even at the end of it, she still causes me trouble... The great Habsburg Empire she served now has to give its secrets to the British. However, given her mission, I would hazard a guess that she has some form of key to deactivate the force-field..." He looked over to Varga. "Where might the Countess be in Vienna?" he asked of him.

"Innere Stadt. She is a public figure due to her journalism and her nursing during the war, she receives prominent guests" he replied. "I can send some men to keep watch on her home?"

The Doctor shook his head. "No, we shall go with as many men now as we can. Time is against us. The British are on their way, and these Red Guards may yet cause further trouble."

The man turned to go to gather as many men as he could, when Dr. Cornelius stopped him. "Do you have links with these new authorities?" he asked.

"Indeed, I do," Varga replied. "I have done much business lately with one of his colleagues. "

"Can he delay the British?" he asked.

"For enough money, I am sure, although I suspect not for long. I have heard of a group of British troops heading towards Vienna. A diplomatic mission. it is being said."

"Pay him. I will recompense you later," Dr. Cornelius.

"This involvement of the British, could this be connected with the presence of a British Lord in the city?" asked Varga.

"British Lord?" the Doctor responded, immediately interested.

"A Lord... Buried?"

"Burydan."

"Yes, that's right. He's been seen in various pubs insulting people and waving a gun around."

"What else do you know of his activities?"

"Nothing, bar that. He is liable to get himself killed. He has already been in a number or fights, coming out on top."

Lord Burydan! Dr. Cornelius knew him well and was certain he knew why he was in Vienna. This British Lord was an old enemy. The Doctor was responsible for the man's hideous burns and scars, driving him more insane than he already was. The sculptor of human flesh later removed those scars, in return for this 'peer of the realm' working for him. The Doctor had told him a lie that the Countess was responsible for his burns. Lord Burydan had served him well—and even enthusiastically. The Doctor had no doubt as to why the Brition was in Vienna. With the war effectively over, he was here to take his revenge on the Countess.

"Find him and bring him here immediately," he ordered Varga. "Tell him I am here, and I know where to find the Countess. Tell him there is money in it too—and a bonus for you if he is here within the hour."

The Residence of Countess Irina Petrovska,
Innere Stadt, 11 November 1918, early evening

The Countess looked around her. Some of the most loyal people she had worked with were here. She had told them to go home, but with this final mission they wanted to stay. They seemed to be concerned about, as was she—as if trouble was in the air. She looked outside her window. She could see her old friend Lieutenant Mayr; he was taking a look around the street. He in particular was feeling uneasy. Up to recently, he was a Sergeant, but his services to the state earned him a commission to officer. The Countess had to help persuade him to take the commission, pointing out that the extra wages would help his family and the *Evidenzbureau* needed experienced men like him in authority, no matter how junior. That was a few months ago. His future, along with so many, was now uncertain. With her in the room was Captain Vuljanić, recently promoted from lieutenant, and Kata, an *Evidenzbureau* agent. She had been recruited in Sarajevo and acted as an assistant to the Countess, working as her maid as cover. Kata had ensured that the countess's children were transported safely out of Vienna to relatives.

The Countess's telephone rang. Kata picked it up. "Countess Irina Petrovska's residence" she announced.

She handed the receiver to the Countess. "The Emperor's diplomatic adviser," she said. The Countess took the phone and spoke to the adviser. She listened to what he had to say and then said, "See what you can do via diplomatic means. I will try and find out what is going on from this end. Goodbye."

She turned to her friends. "It would appear that Renner's men are blocking the British passage into Vienna. Their reasoning is that whatever agreement has been made with the British has no validity as Renner is in charge. The British force is only around 20 men and their vehicles, they cannot fight their way through and also have orders not to engage anyone in order to prevent any kind of incident—although Renner does not know that."

"Do they apply such logic to the armistice?" asked Kata.

"No. Something is going on. Others, perhaps, are after the archive." The Countess was concerned. The British were being delayed, the archive was in the hands of this man Renner and all she had were her friends here. Still, that had often been enough in the past.

Lieutenant Mayr burst in. "We may be in trouble," he said. "A group of men are approaching,"

"We are already here," said a voice behind him.

Everyone in the room saw a man enter, followed by others. He aimed his gun at Mayr's head.

"Greetings, Dr. Cornelius!" said Lord Burydan.

Dr. Cornelius was slightly startled. He and his men were just leaving their safe and boarding a lorry. Varga had brought him. The Briton patted his jacket pocket. "Only just holstered this. Your man could have been anyone, but glad to see he really does work for you," he said slapping the old man on the back hard enough to push him forward.

"I have work for you," said the Doctor, "however, I am curious to know why you are here," he asked.

Lord Burydan beamed, "Why, revenge of course! With the war effectively over, I have been able to move around Europe a bit more. It is past time to settle scores with the Countess. She lives here in Vienna. I see no reason to delay dealing with her. You wouldn't happen to know where she is? I always find getting around these foreign places a bit difficult."

Dr. Cornelius looked at this supposed peer of the British realm whose body he had restored. He knew full well the Briton was not of sound mind.

"Then I have good news for you, Lord Burydan. We are about to embark on a mission to her residence right now. I have something to collect from her. There may be resistance from her minions. Your undoubted skills of violence will come in useful. You will be paid well."

"Excellent," said Lord Burydan. "However, I have a condition—I must be allowed to kill the Countess."

"Of course," said the Doctor, "but only after I have got the item I need from her." Burydan nodded his assent. The Doctor gestured to the Briton to get into the lorry.

At the Countess's residence, It was the archive guard who earlier had left the archive building to report to Von Bork who was holding a gun to Mayr's head. The guard, a Private Brunner, was very pleased with himself. Von Bork, who was controlling this operation from somewhere out of the country. He had told the German spymaster—now a communist—of the incompetence of those in charge of this mission and how he, Private Brunner, could do better with his military experience. Von Bork let him take control. He, a mere private, would help bring the revolution to Vienna.

The Countess knew nothing of this, of course. She just saw some grubby-looking armed men in front of her.

With his gun still aimed directly at Mayr's head, Brunner said: "I will kill this man, if you do not comply with my orders,"

"Who are you?" asked the Countess, sternly.

"Who I am is of no importance, save that I serve the working class!"

Bolsheviks, thought the Countess. The Red Guards she had heard of. *Probably working for Von Bork*.

"And what the does the servant of the working class want?" she asked.

"You have the key to the invisible safe. Give it to me, and we will go. If not, your friend gets a bullet in the head."

The Countess went straight over to a desk. "It's in here," she said pointing to a drawer. "I shall of course take it out slowly lest you think I am reaching for a weapon." In fact, she, like all her friends in the room, had small weapons secreted about their person. The Countess slowly took the key the Emperor gave her from the drawer. Mayr's life was more important—they could retrieve the key later. However, she was concerned that these Red Guards may simply try to murder them all, at which point they would draw their weapons, come what may.

"Hold it out," said Brunner. The Countess did as ordered.

Brunner studied the key in her hand. It was clear to all that he had been briefed on how to recognize the key.

He held his free hand out. "Very well. Now, put it in my hand—carefully."

With the key handed over, Brunner moved his gun away from Meyr and aimed at the Countess. "I have heard, Countess, that before the war, you were friends with the Romanovs."

"That is the truth," she replied. "The war changed things. Then your people murdered them," she said bitterly. Whatever their faults, the Countess had some respect for them. Their murder at the hands of Lenin's men had a profound effect, convincing her that Bolshevism spelt nothing but horror for humanity.

"Murdered?" Brunner was angry. He had seen much horror fighting in the war. And then a fellow soldier told him of the revolution in Russia, how the workers had taken over and taken the country out of the war. He read the words of Marx and Engels, and became convinced, and decided to devote his life to world revolution. "No, they received justice, as all aristocrats and capitalists will get for starting this war. Including here in Vienna. Starting with you," he said, gun aimed straight at the Countess.

Everyone was thus surprised when Brunner's head appeared to explode. The three men with him looked startled.

Kata was first to collect her senses, grabbing her small pistol in her garter and firing at the nearest Red Guard. The Countess grabbed the key from the floor where Brunner had dropped it.

The surviving Red Guard hid behind a chair, firing in all directions—including at the doorway. Who was out there?

"Everybody out," she shouted, pointing at the stairwell. Her three friends ran down the stairs. She gave covering fire, shooting at the Red Guard, wounding him. She glanced at two men coming through the door—Dr. Cornelius and Lord Burydan, armed. She took a chance and headed for the stairwell.

Dr. Cornelius saw what must be key in her hand—it looked alien—and was about to shoot her, when Lord Burydan knocked the gun out of his hand.

The Countess disappeared down the stairwell, and an Austrian grenade came flying up from it and hit the floor.

Lord Burydan grabbed Dr. Cornelius and shoved him back out of the doorway. The grenade exploded, wrecking the room, but the two men were unharmed.

Exiting from the side of the building, the group of friends ran to *Elizabeth*, which was parked at the front. Two of Dr. Cornelius's henchmen were outside, looking the wrong way. They swung round with their guns, only to be shot down by the two *Evidenzbureau* officers. The four of them got into *Elizabeth* and drove away at speed.

Inside the residence, Dr. Cornelius was furious. "What did you do that for!" he shouted at Lord Burydan.

"I was saving your life, old man," the Briton replied nonchalantly.

"I meant, your preventing me from shooting the Countess."

"Our deal is that I kill her, not you. I was not going to let you cheat me,"

"You could have shot her yourself."

"You were in the way, old man."

Dr. Cornelius glared at him. The Briton was always arrogant. However, previously, his behavior had been tempered by needing the Doctor's serum to maintain his face. As a reward for good work, the Doctor let the man keep his features permanently—a decision he now re-gretted.

The Doctor silently walked downstairs. Lechner was outside. The henchman gestured to the road. "The Countess's work," he said. Many people were coming out of the other houses to see what the explosions were about.

"We must leave," said the Doctor. "Leave their bodies but get their guns." The three men got into the lorry, with Lechner driving. The Doctor and Lord Burydan got into the back.

"These silencer things of yours are pretty damn good," said Lord Burydan, pointing to his gun with a tube on the end of it, as did the other weapons the men had used. "Those men didn't hear the sound of their own deaths coming—very strange seeing that man's head explode. The Countess is in my debt, although I want to shoot her myself—and make sure she know it's me. She owes me her life. Ironic, no?"

Dr. Cornelius ignored him. He did not have the re-sources or time to plan things—he had no idea of the residence of the Countess, and not enough men. He had to find out where the Countess had gone.

In *Elizabeth*, the Countess congratulated Captain Vuljanić, "I think that grenade held off Dr. Cornelius and that mad Briton. Well thrown!"

"It is fortunate that you keep a supply of such weapons," he replied.

The Countess, driving, replied "Given the matters we deal with, it is best to be prepared. Although we were still taken too much by surprise. On some level, I still did not believe that my home could come under attack.

However, I never thought the Empire would collapse." The cab went silent.

They drove past the Archive, slowing to take a look. There were significantly more men outside the building.

"Let us see what the authorities have to say," the Countess said and drove on.

The authorities were less than helpful. "Countess, quite frankly you have no authority," said the man before her in a government building. "Neither you, the Emperor, let alone the British, have any right to issue orders or take documents. The archive belongs to the people of Austria."

"The archive belongs to all the peoples of the Empire," the Countess retorted angrily. "Only the Emperor has the authority to dispose of it—to the hands of those who will use it responsibly. I demand to see Karl Renner."

"Mr. Renner is busy governing."

"Does he not realize that there are armed groups trying to capture the archive?"

"We repelled the Red Guards. As for Dr. Cornelius, he has only attacked your residence, assuming that is true. Perhaps the police should detain you, to find out what is going on."

The Countess glared at him. "I shall go to the Emperor himself and we will take matters up with the British government. Let me remind you that they have won the war, and your lack of cooperation could well jeopardize the peace."

She turned and walked out. She went straight back to *Elizabeth*, where her friends were waiting.

"We must go to the Emperor at Schloss Eckartsau.[16] He has gone there as Vienna is not safe. Very wise, as we have found out tonight. The Red Guards, Dr. Cornelius and perhaps Renner's men are all targeting us."

The official came out and watched *Elizabeth* drive off. He had been paid well to hold up the British. He suspected that the money had originally come from this Dr. Cornelius. Perhaps the Doctor would pay also for the detail of the conversation he just had.

Schloss Eckartsau, 13 November 1918, morning

The Countess finished her breakfast. She had not slept well. They had arrived at Schloss Eckartsau She had contacted Professor Saxton and Dr. Wells. In the meantime, the Emperor had pursued his diplomatic lines. She looked around the table at her friends. They all looked tired.

Mayr spoke. "I have to say, I never thought I would be eating at the Emperor's table."

"Pity it's in these circumstances," said Captain Vuljanić. "It does feel like the end, doesn't it? I can't say I am keen on the British taking the archive, given they have been our enemies—especially Lord Burydan. However, better that then the current authorities. Apart from anything else, are they able to stand up to the Red Guards? No, let the British have it. I trust your judgement that your friends Saxton and Wells are honorable men, unlike Lord Burydan."

The Countess looked sympathetic. She knew he was worrying about his wife and their newborn child. "Have you heard from your family?"

---

[16] The hunting lodge of the Habsburgs, east of Vienna.

"Yes, the Emperor's staff were able to get me news. They are well, in Zagreb. However, the political situation is not good. There is talk of a state of Slovenes, Croat and Serbs, formed from within the Empire. That, I can live with, but this talk of uniting with Serbia… Given that country's role in starting the war, I can only view that with concern. The monarchy's authority is broken, alternatives are not being presented strongly enough."

The Countess nodded, "Yes, I have heard from my friends on the island of Brač. A bust of Franz Joseph in Supetar has found its way to the bottom of the harbor. In Poland, where I have already sent my children, there is turmoil. I shall join them soon. And what of you, Lieutenant Mayr and Kata?"

"I am stuck in Austria with Renner," said Mayr. "I may have to end with fighting with his men if the Red Guards become a serious problem."

"I shall be returning to Sarajevo," said Kata. "The Captain and I may well share the same fate as to who rules us."

"We shall stay in touch," said the Countess. "I have some thoughts on the future, and not just about Poland. I believe…"

She was interrupted as the Emperor Karl strode in. They all stood up.

"Please, sit down," he said. "I have been in touch with Renner's people. It appears the British government have made clear there will be consequences for non-compliance with our agreement. These have not been specified, but Renner has promised that the British will no longer be obstructed. Of course, he claims one of his staff was responsible and that he knew nothing about it. In any event, the handover is scheduled for 18:00."

"We will be there," the Countess said.

Outside Schloss Eckartsau, Dr. Cornelius and his depleted force had appeared in a car. The old man claimed there was no one available to replace the men who had been killed. The Doctor suspected that the man simply didn't want to hire men that would end up dead, damaging his reputation. He would have to make do with Lord Burydan and Lechner—Varga being too old for this. Still, Varga had at least got the information from his contact about the whereabouts of the Countess, even if he had only received the information in the early hours.

They were all dressed in the field grey uniforms of the Austro-Hungarian army. Dr. Cornelius wore the uniform of a Colonel, Lord Burydan as a Major and Lechner as a corporal. For a further fee, Lechner had retained the face of the guard they had kidnapped. That was to keep him quiet—the Doctor did not have time to bring back his old face at the moment.

The car drove slowly to the front of the hunting lodge. There were two guards at the gates. Dr. Cornelius walked up to them, striding purposefully with his hands behind his back. The guards looked at him suspiciously. They had strict orders not to let anyone pass. Yet, this man was clearly a Colonel. The Empire was falling apart, including the army, but these men would treat this officer respectfully. They did not salute, given they were holding rifles, but spoke to the Doctor respectfully. "I am sorry sir; we have orders direct from the Emperor himself – no entry to anyone not expected."

From behind his back, the Doctor brought out a gun with silencer and expertly shot both men dead, swiftly and to the head.

Lord Burydan bounded up. "Headshots! Just like me. Good to see you getting your hands dirty,"

The Doctor ignored him. He did this himself, rather than ordering one of them to do it in order to demonstrate that he was a force to be reckoned with, in case these two—especially the Briton—had any doubt.

Upstairs, the Countess left the breakfast room and headed to her bedroom to collect her things. She was planning for her group to leave early as she could sense the Emperor had much to deal with and she did not want to be in his way.

Dr. Cornelius's group entered the lodge. They walked around unchallenged. There appeared to be few people, no-one challenged them, presuming that as they were inside Schloss Eckartsau, they were supposed be there.

Soon, they came to the breakfast room. The Doctor motioned to his men to keep quiet. The Emperor was speaking. "Captain, take this folder to the Archive when you leave. It contains papers regarding alien interventions in the United States—which we knew about, but the American authorities did not. I had hoped there may be something in there to discuss with President Wilson, perhaps to win him over a little. Looking at them, however, I think it may be counterproductive."

Interesting, thought the sculptor of human flesh. He strode in, gun in hand just as the Emperor was putting the papers onto the breakfast table.

"Who the devil are you?" demanded the Emperor.

"As the others here will tell you, I am Dr. Cornelius Kramm. We met in Split. However, I am now wearing my own face. I see the Countess is not here. You will be good enough to tell me where she is, or, if you have the force-field key, I will simply take that."

The Doctor had no idea what he would do if he did get the key. However, a somewhat desperate plan was forming in his mind—perhaps poison gas to kill all in the archive, allowing him access? Varga could get such weapons—if money did not sway him, torture no doubt would. It was then that he noticed that Lord Burydan was not with him and Lechner.

The Countess emerged from her bedroom, with a bag of belongings in one hand and the key in another. The bag was a bit heavy. It contained her trusty Doppelpistole. She turned around a corridor, and ran straight into Lord Burydan. He raised his gun.

Dr. Cornelius was alarmed. Clearly, Lord Burydan had gone to look for the Countess. He did not care if the Briton killed her, but would he retrieve the key from her?

"Well?" he asked the Emperor.

"The key is none of your affair," said the Emperor, unwisely.

"It very much is," replied Dr. Cornelius. "Shall I kill you all one by one before you tell me where the Countess is?"

"I am here," said the Countess, walking in with her bag.

"The key," the Doctor said simply.

"It's already on its way to Vienna. We are going to be contacted when it arrives—at which point we can order it returned here, or wherever you want, provided you release everyone here."

The Doctor was suspicious but nodded his assent.

"No Lord Burydan?" asked the Countess.

"He is searching for you. Do not concern your-self—you will come to no harm if you cooperate," said the Doctor. In truth, once he had the key, he thought it best to simply let the Briton kill her.

"I take it he is still unaware that you pushed him in-to the flames of that burning ship in 1914, not me. Per-haps I will tell him that when he appears."

Dr. Cornelius laughed. "He won't believe you. He's insane. He believes you did it. And why not? Remember, technically he and I were on the same side. Why would I do that? Of course, I must confess that it was a moment of revenge for me, which worked out in the end with his working for me."

Dr. Cornelius's knee exploded. The Doctor screamed in agony, collapsing to the floor. He grabbed the tablecloth as went, pulling down some of the break-fast plates on him as well as the Emperor's folder.

Lechner collapsed next to him, dying from a shot to the heart.

Lord Burydan towered over the Doctor. "Insane, am I? You know, I really was on my way here to find the Countess. I was intercepted by a friend in British intelli-gence. He told me that you had pushed me in the fire, not the Countess—she has friends in London to whom she told this, apparently. He also told me you were working for the Americans, no need to tell me that, but we both are members of the same club. Of course, I had to find out, and he obligingly let me go on my way. I just sent the Countess in here to start a conversation on those events, so I could hear what you would say."

The Captain and Lieutenant grabbed the Emperor and shoved him outside the room. The Countess indicat-ed to Kata that she should go with them.

Through gritted teeth, Dr. Cornelius talked for his life. "Yes, I did. However, you are wealthier than you have ever been, having worked for me. You owe me!"

Lord Burydan laughed and aimed his pistol at his head. "I owe you a bullet," he said.

"Enough!" the commanding voice of the Countess made the Lord turn around. She had retrieved her Doppelpistole from her bag and was now aiming it at him.

"What do you care about him?" the Briton. "He wanted me to kill you in the past."

"I will not let him be killed in cold blood," she replied. "I intend to reveal to the press his presence in Vienna, and to hand him over to the Americans. They will, of course, deny employing him. He will have to be tried for his crimes and executed. Put your gun down."

"By jingo, he could be sent to that electric chair I've heard about! Perhaps I could even attend! Very well! Give him to the Americans," said Lord Burydan placing his gun on the table. Lieutenant Mayr took the gun away.

"It's all working out swimmingly," the Briton continued. "I don't care that you foiled my plan in 1914, Countess. You've lost. Your crappy little Empire is over and the Germans are out for the count. We have much to thank that man Princip for!" The Briton looked down at Dr. Cornelius. "Yes, old man, I have to say I did enjoy some moments working for you, great fun!" Dr. Cornelius, being attended to by Kata, simply glared at him.

"Your fun included to killing my friend in Split," said the Countess. She was recalling how Lord Burydan had shot and killed Captain Marić in Split, a brave man whom she had come to respect.

"Did I? Ah yes, I remember now. You must admit, it was a good shot on my part!"

The Countess still had her Doppelpistole aimed at him. She had had enough of this lunatic. She could feel the anger rise in her.

Lord Burydan saw the look on her face and felt cold fear. "Now, don't do anything hasty, old girl," he said, raising his hands slowly, his face now ashen.

The Countess was shaking with anger, and then she felt a hand on her shoulder.

"There has been enough death, has there not?" She looked around. The Emperor had come back in and was speaking to her. She regained her composure.

"Quite," she said.

Lord Burydan felt relief, but thought it best to say nothing further.

A short while later, the Countess went to see the Emperor in his office. Aside from the events at Eckartsau, a republic had been declared in Vienna and the Red Guards had mounted a failed attack on Parliament. *Quite a day*, she thought. "Your highness, we are leaving now," she said.

"Good," he replied, getting up from his desk. "Thank you, Countess. I would ask you to stay. I do have some hope that something of the Empire can be saved. However, I know you wish to go to Poland, and I will not make that difficult for you,"

"Thank you," she answered. She doubted that anything could be retrieved, except... "Your highness, my priority is indeed my homeland. However, there will be continuing threats from strange technologies, alien incursions, the supernatural and the likes of Dr. Cornelius. I intend to create a loose network of people across the former empire and Europe, some kind of defense. My friends with me will be part of it, as will others. And there will be close liaison with Professor Saxton and Dr. Wells."

The Emperor looked heartened. "Thank you, Countess. I am glad to hear that. If you need my help for anything, please do not hesitate to ask. Now, I have to prepare for a delegation arriving tomorrow from Hungary."

They made their farewells. She looked back as she left, seeing him seated at his desk, alone.

She would never see him again.

Vienna. 15 November 1918

The handover with the British went well. Renner's guards had simply melted away upon their arrival. The key worked perfectly, the force-field deactivated and the British soldiers efficiently took the papers.

The Countess and her friends discreetly ensured the key and force-field generator did not go with them. The deal was only for the papers, not the device, which the Countess considered could be of some use to her fledgling network.

Lord Burydan got on board the lorry with the other British troops. He had attempted to take command, but a Sergeant told him to shut up and sit down, giving the Countess some satisfaction. She watched the lorry drive off.

She turned to her friends. "We will meet again, because I have no doubt our specialist experience will be needed. For now, though we are all needed elsewhere."

They made their farewells and went their different ways.

US Army facility, France. 16 November 1918

Dr. Cornelius looked at the stern visage of the US Marshal who stood over him. The Countess had deposited him with trustworthy police. The press had indeed reported on his presence in Vienna—squeezed in amongst the major political news and by various means he had been taken to a US Army unit in France where he had been handed over to this Marshal. His leg had been saved, but he would not walk properly again—or rather until he had access to his own special surgical instruments. Now he was seated in a cell, handcuffed.

"Deal?" the Marshal said. "and you were supposed to steal documents about creatures from another world, strange sciences? You seem to be preparing for an insanity plea. The court will see right through that. You're going to fry."

Dr. Cornelius knew he had failed in his mission. However, he did have one last chance—something to show that he can be useful. "I am sure you have been told to report back whatever I say to your superiors." He was still wearing the army uniform he had at Schloss Eckartsau. He slowly, so as not to alarm the marshal, reached into his tunic—somewhat awkwardly given he was in handcuffs—and pulled out a folder.

They contained the papers the Emperor had consulted regarding the United States and which had fallen to the floor when Lord Burydan had shot him. The police had failed to search him properly, given his injuries and captured state.

"Give this to them," he told the Marshal, handing the folder to him.

The residence of Dr. Wells, Kensington, London,
August 1928

The Countess pointed to the newspaper on the table in front of her. "The Croatian politician Stjepan Radić has died from his wounds inflicted weeks ago by a gunshot from a Serb politician in Belgrade parliament. I met him during the 'Projector of Death' incident in 1916. He impressed me. The Yugoslav experiment is not going well, like much else in Europe."

Her friends Professor Saxton and Dr. Wells nodded in agreement. They were all seated in Wells' drawing room.

Professor Saxton leant forward, "In Germany, this man Hitler clearly spells trouble. He is clearly ludicrous. How can the Germans take this lunatic seriously?"

"The Versailles treaty has produced the conditions for such men to spew their bile," the Countess said.

Dr. Wells sipped his cup of tea. "And Russia—in the hands of communists. Their man Van Bork is gathering recruits to his supernatural division."

"My friends", the Countess said, "I know I have said this before, but it was a grave mistake for the Austro-Hungarian Empire to be completely dismembered. It was a protector of the small nations. Who knows how Germany may develop in the future, let alone Soviet Russia. Who will defend those nations?"

"Poland has its independence," said Dr. Wells. "We know you are pleased about that."

"Yes," the Countess replied. "I am, yet my country faces threats. Just a few years ago, we repelled a Soviet assault. How will the smaller nations fare in the future? We can all see the storm clouds forming."

"At least," said Dr. Wells, "systems are being put into place to deal with extraordinary threats. Within the British Empire, we have organizations and people ready to deal with alien threats and supernatural ones. Your pan-European network, Irina, has been very effective indeed."

The Countess nodded, "Yes, it was something salvaged from the Empire. Had he not died so young, I am sure Emperor Karl would at least have taken comfort from that. However, it will remain run by private citizens—the governments of Europe, I do not trust."

"I trust that does not apply to the British government," said Dr. Wells, smiling.

"Of course not," replied the Countess. "Provided you two remain in complete charge of such matters. I am grateful for your allowing the Vienna archive to be consulted by my people when needed. The governments of Europe and the Americas are setting up their own organizations, all in secret. The coming decades will see many such groups. I can only hope that there will be a high level of cooperation between them."

"Only to a degree," said Professor Saxton, "You won't get much help from the likes of Von Bork—he is likely to cause trouble in the Soviet quest for world revolution or whatever."

Their conversation was interrupted by the doorbell. The butler entered "A Dr. Cerral, sir," he announced to Dr. Wells. "He claims to be looking for an old friend at this address but will not say who."

"Dr. Cerral?" said the Countess. "That's a name of a surgeon of some notoriety—someone with questionable transplant procedures."

"Could he be armed?" Professor Saxton asked the butler.

"Very doubtful, sir. He is a wearing suit, with no apparent bulges indicating a firearm. Nonetheless, I am discreetly armed, and will be outside, should you wish to see him."

"I think we shall see what the fellow wants," said Dr. Wells. "We also have certain concealed defenses in here in any event."

The butler showed Dr. Cerral in. All three friends stood up to greet him.

Dr. Cerral was a thin man with a closely cropped haircut. "I am Dr. Wells, the owner of this residence" said Wells, and these are my friends, Countess Irina Petrovska and Professor Sir Alexander Saxton."

Dr. Cerral looked at them all. "I must apologize to you all; I am looking for an old medical friend, but I appear to have come to the wrong address." He looked at the Countess. "However, I think I recognize you—you are a journalist, are you not?"

There is something familiar about this man, the Countess thought. She felt uneasy. "Yes, I occasionally write articles for the European press about Poland," she said, glancing at her friends who understood immediately something was up.

"And you, Dr. Cerral, your name is also familiar."

"Ah" he said. "I am not *that* notorious surgeon," he replied. There was something about the emphasis on the word 'that' which made the Countess tense.

"As I say," said Dr. Cerral, "I was looking for an old friend, to say goodbye. You see, I have been working for an American medical firm since the war, most recently here in London, but my relations with them have broken down somewhat, and I am leaving for new horizons." He smiled at her. "I just wanted to pay my respects to my friend before leaving. I have taken enough of all your time. I apologize again for disturbing you."

With that, he promptly left.

The three friends looked at each other, and all swiftly went outside, only to see a car driving off in the distance. "I have the license plate number," said the butler, who was already outside.

"Please ask the police to try and find the vehicle and the driver. I doubt they will find him, but we must try," said the Countess.

"Use my authority to get them to do so," said Dr. Wells.

They went inside. "Well, Countess, what was that about?" asked Professor Saxton.

"I cannot be certain, but I think that may have been Dr. Cornelius Kramm. There was something in his manner."

"The Americans executed him," said the Professor.

"They said they did, after a brief trial in which he pleaded guilty. Let us recall that the Americans severely restricted those who could watch the execution. Your countryman Lord Burydan—who himself has hardly paid for his crimes—was most disappointed at not being allowed to see it."

"Why would Dr. Cornelius come here?" asked Dr. Wells.

"Just to make sure I know he is alive—and that I cannot do anything about it. Even if the police catch him, what could we then do? He has changed his face, how could we prove he is Dr. Cornelius, who is legally dead? The Americans would hardly admit to keeping him alive to work for them."

"There seems little we can do then," said the Professor.

"We can alert our networks. Assuming it is indeed Dr. Cornelius, it is best that he is considered a potential active threat—whatever the Americans say.

"Now, what say we go to one of London's finer restaurants?"

Meanwhile. Dr. Cerral drove through the Kensington streets. He was highly amused at his little farewell. After a short while, he parked the vehicle and left it—he had stolen it after all. He took out an envelope from inside his suit jacket and briefly checked the contents. Inside were tickets for voyage on a first-class liner to Bolivia.

New horizons, he thought.

Brian Stableford: *Malbrough s'en va-t-en guerre*

Oscar Tournesol had been on the Chemin des Dames ridge when the German bombardment began, but had somehow contrived to survive the initial shelling and the subsequent poison gas drop. When the *Sturm-struppen* divisions attacked, he was one of the few lucky enough to be able to join the retreat. His unit managed to reach the Aisne a matter of hours ahead of the Germans, and was initially ordered to reinforce the allied lines there. When the Germans smashed through that position too, what was left of his unit fell back toward the Vesle, and it was there that he was finally caught, albeit obliquely, by the blast of a shell fired from a tank.

He recovered consciousness just long enough to be vaguely aware of being loaded on to a truck, and to feel both the wound in his head and the shrapnel in both legs, before the blood-loss left him unconscious, just giving himself time to convince himself that he was about to die. He only caught the merest glimpse of the other bodies laid beside him in the back of the lorry, but it was enough to tell him that most of them were not going to get past the triage officer, and that he was, in effect, riding in a death-cart.

After that, there was no real consciousness at all for a long time—but there must have been some kind of delirium, because much later, when he became partially self-aware again, in the limbo of numbness that morphine sometimes cradles when one dose begins to wear off but another is not yet urgently necessary, he returned to that awkward state of renewed being dragging memories of a kind. Most of them evaporated swiftly, in the fashion that dream-memories do, but two of them stuck, and continued to serve as bright anchors for his semi-consciousness, which was as fugitive and flickering as a candle-flame.

One of the memories consisted of the opening lines of one of the songs that the British tommies making up the war-weary wreckage of the units assigned to "reinforce" the French along the Chemin des Dames had been singing in the trenches on the nights before the German push, which must have become fixed in his addled head like an earworm, repeating over and over again as his brain was maintained in muted activity by some kind of neural loop. Much of the song, he knew, was scabrous, but the two lines that had stuck fast in his head, taken in isolation, were simply plaintive: "Standing on the bridge at midnight/Throwing snowballs at the Moon."

Oscar continued to repeat those lines to himself, even when he was in a state closer to wakefulness, when the intermorphine limbo began to stretch and stabilize, and he was aware once again of who he was, and could, had he made the effort, have thought about something else. The two lines seemed somehow *safe*, all the safer because they were in a foreign language—albeit one that he knew well—and their incessant mental repetition seemed to be a valiant affirmation that he still existed, and of the continuity of time itself.

In principle, that existential anchor could have been the opening lines of any song—*Malbrough s'en va-t-en guerre/Mironton, mironton, mirontaine*, for example, which he had known since the earliest days of childhood, probably before emerging into self-awareness for the very first time, and which his fellow *poilus* had been singing valiantly since the Marne in '14—and it was probably just random chance that had given him that particular straw for his drowning mind to clutch. When a drowning and flickering mind has no choice, though, it clutches hard, and makes what brightness it can of what it finds.

The other memory that Oscar retained was that of Andrée Paganot's face, which he had seen not once but continually—or so it seemed. The first time he became conscious of having seen it before, repeatedly, since the shell-burst and the death-cart he instantly and unthinkingly took it as evidence that he was in Heaven—evidence, indeed, that there was a Heaven, in which he had never been able previously to believe—because he assumed that it was the face of an angel.

He did not make that assumption because he thought Andrée was dead—indeed, she was one of the few of his pre-war acquaintances of whose death he had not had news—but because he assumed, even in the arcane convolutions of candlelit delirium, that because angels had no form of their own, those who saw them had to give them a face, and for him, *the* angelic face had always been that of Andrée Paganot... or Andrée de Maubreuil, as she had been when her face first acquired that iconic status in his mind. That association was not in any way a betrayal of Regina, or any diminution of his wife's importance in the chronicle of his life, but a matter of history, a matter of his initial salvation, the first time he had required salvation... and, for that matter, the second.

It was the eventual realization that the face he had seen—obviously not the only one he had seen, while he hovered in suspension between life and death, but the only one he contrived to remember as his delirium eased—was actually real, and actually did belong to Andrée Paganot, that informed him that he was somehow still alive, having been directly in need of salvation yet again, and gave him hope that salvation might still be possible.

Possible, but not likely; self-awareness also brought him a limited ability to explore his existential situation, to explore his injuries, not so much in the silver currency of pain, which was still being eroded by morphine, but in the small change of petty inabilities: the fact, for instance, that he could not move his legs at all, and could hardly activate his tongue when he was fed by straw and spoon.

When his feeble hands finally attempted to explore his face and the top of his head, they found dressings. His ribs, he judged, had only been bruised, and his spine was still straight—that, at least, seemed a release of sorts; one potential nightmare less—but his skull and his thighs had obviously taken a battering.

His skull had been cracked before, and he had been hit more than once by bullets before the war even started, but he knew that such past experience had left him physically weaker, not stronger, like a patched pitcher more vulnerable to further breakage in going to the well.

Somehow, he knew, from the very beginning of his return to semiconsciousness, that he "ought" to be dead, that his survival was one of those million-to-one flukes that only happen in fiction.

There was nothing wrong with his jaws and throat, though, and almost as soon as he could think in a manner that was vaguely akin to "straight," he could talk, at least in clichéd monosyllables. For a time, the return of true consciousness was straightforwardly proportional to the return of pain, but that deadly link soon broke, and he was eventually able to remain not merely awake but alert for as much as an hour at a time, when it became possible to string together authentic dialogues, provided that his own contribution was minimal.

By then, he was able to remember other faces: nurses other than Andrée, orderlies, and the individual he had thought of, from the very beginning of returning thought, as "the bloodstained man," even though he knew that he had to be a doctor, an officer, and presumably a gentleman.

The first question to which he was able to get an answer—not from Andrée, but there didn't seem to be any point in waiting, in the hope of making some mysterious esthetic point—was: "Where am I?" Unfortunately, the answer he got wasn't very helpful. He had already deduced, obviously, that he was in a field hospital, and it really didn't matter where, although he was slightly surprised to hear that he was nowhere near Paris but somewhere in the vicinity of Rouen. In any case, that answer inevitably became confused with what his own mind was still doing of its own accord, in the background of his consciousness, and he couldn't be entirely certain that the honest answer to his question wasn't that he was standing on a bridge at midnight, engaged in the essentially ludicrous pastime of throwing snowballs at the pallid moon.

To save him the trouble of talking, though—not because it was costing him too much effort but because it was interfering with their attempts to feed him broth with a spoon—the nurses and orderlies gave him more information, in dribs and drabs.

The German advance had eventually been stopped fifty kilometers short of the capital. The whole point of Ludendorff's dash, apparently, had been one last desperate attempt to get to Paris before the Americans had landed enough troops to stop him, but the Americans had arrived in time: fresh-faced, well-fed mid-Western farmboys raring for a fight. The Boche offensive had been stopped, smashed and sunk. The war was as good as won. This time, it really would be over by Christmas… four Christmases late, alas, but even so…

Between spoonfuls of broth and not wanting to interrupt, it took Oscar quite a long time to form the questions he really wanted to ask, so he mostly let things drift, content, for a while longer—days, for sure, perhaps a week—to throw snowballs at the lunatic moon, and to try to salute the bloodstained man, and to try to smile at Andrée.

He didn't succeed in either of the more reasonable tasks, but the bloodstained man, in spite of being an officer, did seem to be a gentleman of sorts, and told him not to worry about protocol, or about anything. Only Andrée and the bloodstained man gave him injections, from which Oscar deduced that Andrée had the bloodstained man's full confidence—although that was only natural, since she was "Sister Paganot," not in the sense that she had taken Holy Orders, but in the sense that she was the senior nurse in the team, a veritable archangel: a seraph, perhaps, or at least a domination or a throne.

They all came and went, of course, just as his flickering candle-flame sense of self and reality came and went, and he was often alone—strangely in view of where he had to be and knew that he was—but it didn't matter, because he had his anchor to keep his mental ship in its protected haven; he was on that bridge, throwing those snowballs, knowing that when the bloodstained man and Andrée had finished their work, he would get to the second half of the verse, and eventually to the chorus, and real life would begin again. *Mironton, mironton, mirontaine.*

His intervals of lucidity were lasting far longer, and he felt that he was on the very brink of recovering not merely consciousness of his being but coherency and continuity: the true fabric of humanity.

At first, the question he asked most frequently was: "Andrée?" but whenever he had to ask it, the answer was, inevitably, something along the lines of: "She's asleep right now, but she's been looking after you. Not breaking rules, mind—no playing favorites—but for you, she's shed tears, and I never thought I'd see that."

A time came, however, when he was sufficiently together to ask why he, a mere sergeant, had a room to himself instead of being in some makeshift equivalent of a ward.

"It was Dr. Malbrough who insisted you got the room instead of being on the ward," was the answer to that. "He's allowed to play favorites. Something to do with experiments. Very big with the General Staff, Dr. Malbrough—not just Duchêne but the *high* High Command. He's Australian."

"Malbrough?" Oscar contrived to query. He already knew that General Duchêne was in command of the Sixth Army, and had been responsible for packing the trenches in the futile attempt to hold the Chemin des Dames ridge; had he given it a moment's thought, he would have deduced that Malbrough was the bloodstained man, but he asked anyway.

"As in the song." that particular orderly remarked. "It really is *Mal*brough, it seems, not *Marl-burrow*. Australian, as I said. Really has gone off to war—been in it since the start, they say: came halfway across the world in the first fortnight of August '14—just like you, Sarn't. Hasn't had a scratch, though." *Unlike you*, he didn't add, although the thought was readable.

Eventually, Oscar was able to hold himself together long enough to be told that he would soon be shipped out, no longer requiring to remain in the front trenches of the medical war. Ironically, it was only then that he was able to take stock of exactly where he had been for at least a week, maybe two: a tiny room, with no furniture except his own camp-bed, the stool on which the nurses or orderlies had sat to feed him and the blood-stained man—Dr. Malbrough—had sat to examine and inject him, and an empty ammunition-crate adapted into a table bearing a candle-tray, but a room nevertheless; the kind of privilege normally reserved for officers.

Oscar had worked his way up through the ranks, but not that far, and even that had been almost as much of a miracle as his being passed fit for combat in the first place. Standards were rumored to have fallen quite a way, cannon-fodder now beings in direly short supply, but in '14, people as puny as him had had difficulty getting passed fit, even if they were ex-members of the Gorilla Club, trained acrobats, and veterans of the storming of the Island of Hanged Men, who had come all the way from Florida because his homeland was in danger, and it was his duty.

Cynical as he was, he wouldn't have laughed or spat when he thought the word "duty," had he been capable of laughing or spitting.

The room also had a window, through which, on the eve of his being shipped out—or trucked out, now that he was capable of thinking pedantically—a slate-gray sky was visible; dusk was falling, very gently, behind a veil of cloud. There would be no visible moon that night—not that he had any snowballs to throw at it in any case.

He must have dazed off for a little, because it was dark when he received his next visitation from the angel—from *the* angel.

"No favorites," he said, trying to contrive a smile, but failing.

"To Hell with the rules," she said, leaning forward on the stool. "Even on duty, let alone off. You've been my special project for a decade and a half; I'm not about to let it slide. I'd go with you if I could, but I'm under orders."

He felt able now to ask the question that he had never dared ask before: "How bad is it?" He knew that he didn't have to add that he wanted the truth.

"It *was* about as bad as it could be," his angel said. "The triage officer wanted to leave you untreated as a hopeless case. I couldn't have stopped him—but Malbrough could, and did. He had supplies of some kind of artificial blood-substitute, and other tricks that aren't in the standard kit. He took one look at you and selected you out as a subject. Since then... well, there isn't any five-star treatment here, but you've certainly had his best attention, as you've doubtless noticed. Now...he's hopeful. Your head will heal, he says, and there's a good chance that you'll walk again. He won't put a percentage on it, but it's a good chance. Ask him yourself—he'll tell you. He can't go with you either, but I think he would if he could, and says that he'll come to see you when he can, in Kérity."

"Kérity? You fixed that?"

"Again, not me—Malbrough. You're one of his favorites, as I say, although he prefers to call them 'subjects.' His pride and his joy, anyway: his miracles. You're by no means the only one, but they're all precious to him. He's a saint."

"A saint as well as an angel," Oscar said, feeling a twinge of pain in his head that told him that he might soon need a booster shot of morphine. "I'm truly blessed."

He was, too; apparently, Andrée, with Dr. Malbrough's saintly help, had contrived to get him sent to Kérity-sur-Mer—to Frédérique Ravenel's home—instead of some crowded hospital in Paris or some recuperation facility in England. Eventually, no doubt, he would get back home to Regina, to Florida, but that might have to wait until the war really did end. In the meantime, Kérity was as close to Heaven as he could plausibly hope to get, even if Monsieur Bondonnat's Eden was running to rack and ruin again without him and Ravenel to tend it. That particular Tree of Knowledge was undoubtedly sick, and might not put forth leaves again for a long time.

"The saint's Australian?" Oscar remarked, repeating the only datum he knew about the bloodstained man whose experimental treatment had apparently save his life, and suddenly wanting to know more, now that he was to be sent away...at least until the bloodstained saint came to see him again, to check up on his "subject."

"Yes. He was with the Anzacs at Gallipoli, apparently; when they were disbanded in '16, he was redeployed to Flanders, and he's been up and down the Front ever since, performing emergency surgeries by the hundreds, maybe the thousand by now. Obtained a reputation as a miracle-worker, not just because of his scalpel skills—initially for new anti-infection agents, more recently with this artificial blood-substitute he's developed. Supplies are direly limited, for now, but if it can eventually deploy on a large scale... after the war..."

"The war has been such a spur to new ways of killing," Oscar observed, faintly. "Only fair that it should provoke new methods of healing too..." His head was feeling a trifle ominous, but standing on the bridge and throwing snowballs was still able to drown out the pain and hold his train of thought steady.

His angel leaned a little closer, perhaps worried by the weakness of his voice. Whatever she saw in his face must have been welcome, though, because the expression of reassurance in her blue eyes was worth more than any forced smile.

She too gave the impression of no longer being able to smile, but that was understandable, given that four years of war had cost her not merely her husband, killed at the third battle of Ypres, but her daughter, who had died of pertussis. After that, Oscar knew, she had enlisted as a nurse. Frédérique had been slightly luckier, in that her son was still alive, although Ravenel had been killed too, during the initial German invasion.

In a sense, Oscar knew, he and Frédérique were all that Andrée had left, although she couldn't really lay claim to him anymore, now that he was Regina's, or to Frédérique, who still had her own child to cherish. Even Pistolet was dead, simply having grown too old to keep on barking.

"I'm glad that Malbrough agreed to send you to Kérity," Andrée said. "For Frédérique's sake, as well as yours."

Oscar tried to nod his head, but it was beyond his present capacities. He was able to feel tears forming in the corners of his eyes, though, and he was glad that he was able to have these last few minutes with Andrée, before...

The door opened then, and the bloodstained man came in. He really was bloodstained, not having taken off the white smock he wore in the makeshift "operating theater." He rarely did, partly because he thought it unnecessary, given that it was impregnated with one of his own not-yet-patented anti-infection agents, and therefore posed no health-hazard, but mostly—or so Oscar suspected—because it was a badge of pride and status, his messy equivalent of the red cross of the Knights of St. John.

"It's all right, Sister Paganot," the bloodstained man said. "I'll sit with Sergeant Tournesol for a while. Get something to eat before you go back on duty. Don't worry—I'll make sure that he's all right."

Andrée didn't want to go. She had seen the tears in the corners of Oscar's eyes and she knew that it would be the last time that she would see him, until she too could get to Kérity. She wanted to be with him, for her own sake as well as his—but she got up, obediently. She made no protest. She had become used to taking orders, and the bloodstained man was an officer as well as a saint.

Everybody had become used to taking orders; the war had made automata of everyone, to some extent. It was a relief, in a way; taking full responsibility, in the present circumstances, was more than common souls could bear.

"I'll come back," Andrée promised, touching Oscar likely on the cheeks with angelic fingers. "If you're asleep, I'll make sure I'm there in the morning, to say goodbye when you leave." She left, closing the door quietly behind her.

Then Dr. Malbrough took her place, and inspected Oscar very carefully with his eyes.

The eyes in question were devoid of lashes, which made them seem reptilian, although there was also something raptorial about them. After the visual inspection, the bloodstained man reached out to check Oscar's dressings, and deploy his stethoscope in ritual fashion. Eventually, he nodded, in apparent satisfaction. He struck a match and lit the candle impaled on the spike of the tray on the ammunition-crate.

"How's the pain?" the bloodstained man asked, as the candlelight flickered in the eerie fashion that candlelight still retained, in a world from which electricity had not yet banished it completely. There was nothing particularly Australian about the Doctor's voice. It seemed free of any particular nationality, in fact: thoroughly cosmopolitan.

"Bearable, for now," Oscar answered, truthfully.

"I'll give you something to help you sleep," Malbrough said, although he didn't reach for the medical bag that he had set down beside the stool. For once, he didn't seem to be in a hurry. For once, he seemed to be hovering... waiting for something. Oscar knew how ungrateful it was for him to think "like a vulture," but just to make sure, he asked, aloud: "Am I going to recover?"

"I hope so. Your spine isn't damaged, so it's just a matter of letting your legs heal. You have every chance

278

of being able to walk, although you'll probably never work as an acrobat again."

Oscar knew that he had never mentioned his days with the Gorilla Club to the Doctor, but it was easy to suppose that Andrée might have done.

"Thank you," Oscar murmured, secretly throwing snowballs at the baleful moon of his increasing discomfort, but wanting to hold himself together, to prove to the saintly Doctor that he was a good subject, a worthy favorite.

"Don't thank me," said Dr. Malbrough. "Thank science—and luck. Experimental treatments don't always work. My work has cost as many lives as it has saved. And thank yourself. Considering what you've been through, before as well as during the war, you've been surprisingly resilient, and exceedingly patient. You have every reason to be proud of yourself."

Oscar thought, vaguely, about the chaos of his past tribulations: starvation, tuberculosis, injuries sustained by violence, and the series of operations that had straightened his crooked spine. Obviously, he really had been surprisingly resilient. Perhaps, he thought, he ought to have learned patience, but he was not at all sure that he had.

He was beginning to hurt now, and not just in his head, but in general. Dutifully, he reported that to Dr. Malbrough.

"I don't want to give you another injection immediately," the Doctor said, surprisingly. "It would put you back to sleep, and I'd rather you were as fully conscious as you can be for a while. I need to talk to you."

"All right," said Oscar, assuming that what the Doctor had to say was something to do with the experimental treatment to which he had been subjected. "I'll let you know if it gets to be unbearable."

The Doctor nodded. He looked around at the door, as if to make sure that it was shut. Then he leaned close to Oscar, and stared at him again, with a strange attitude of expectation. The candlelight danced over his clean-shaven face and caused the black fuzz of his razor-cut hair to gleam like something newborn... or something artificial. That gleam was nothing, though, compared with the intensity of the raptorial eyes.

"Do you know who I am, Sergeant Tournesol?" the Doctor asked, in a strangely affable fashion.

"Dr. Malbrough," Oscar said, thinking that it was a test. "Captain, I presume, or Major... sorry, I never asked."

The Doctor uttered an imperceptible sigh of disappointment. "I suppose we've never been formally introduced," he said, "and until you turned up on my doorstep here, you'd only ever see me at a distance—but I knew you, instantly. My memory rarely lets me down. Madame Paganot hasn't recognized me either. I wish I could claim full credit for that, but I can't. As you can probably imagine, it's infinitely easier to change the faces of others by surgical means than it is to change one's own appearance."

Having said that, the enigmatic Doctor waited, with evident expectation, for logic to take its course.

It did, but slowly—not so much because Oscar was intimidated by the incredible, but simply because the only thought that he seemed to be capable of holding in the forefront of his mind, for the moment, was that of standing on a bridge at midnight, throwing snowballs at an increasingly menacing moon.

Eventually, though, he responded to his cue. "Dr. Cornelius?" he said, trying to inject his tone with an appropriate degree of incredulity, for purely melodramatic purposes, although he wasn't sufficiently clear-headed, as yet, actually to feel astounded.

"The same," said Dr. Cornelius Kramm, alias Malbrough.

It suddenly occurred to Oscar that Dr. Cornelius must have chosen the name Malbrough as his pseudonym because of the popular song, and because he had imagined himself, in fleeing America for Australia after the catastrophic failure of his nefarious schemes, as yet again, stubbornly, "going off to war." And then the real war had come, and had brought him to France, where everyone who met him would see a completely different irony in his false name. *Mironton, mironton, mirontaine.*

Oscar would have laughed, had he been capable of it.

"I suppose you're wondering," said Dr. Cornelius, "why I saved your life?" He was still following the train of his own logical thought, unaware that the tracks in Oscar's brain had been scrambled.

"Yes," Oscar lied, obligingly. He was incapable of laughing, but he could still play ball. He was well aware of the fact that Dr. Cornelius Kramm had tried to kill him more than once—and Andrée too—most vilely and most recklessly by blowing up the Rochester railway bridge, but in actual fact, he didn't think it at least odd that in the present, very different, circumstances, the Doctor had saved his life instead, by means of the science that he prized far more highly than anything as vulgarly human as a desire for revenge.

"First of all," said Cornelius Kramm, scrupulously, like a man who always demanded order and hierarchy in

281

his arguments, "it was because I could. If you cast your mind back, you'll remember that I saved other lives too, even in the heat of our own little private war, because the challenge was there, and had to be met. If I'd killed Joe Dorgan, or allowed Fritz or Baruch to do it, I'd be one of the richest men in America now... but I needed him, as an experimental subject. Even if I hadn't... I saved Mademoiselle Bondonnat too, on the occasion when you and I saw one another for the first time in the flesh, simply because the challenge was there, and science had to meet it. If I had got to Burydan in time, on the Somme, I would have saved him, too... and if hazard presents me with further opportunities..."

"It won't," whispered Oscar, bleakly.

"Because all your friends are dead? Old Bondonnat, Burydan, Ravenel, Paganot, Noel Fless, even Kloum— but not quite all, Sergeant Tournesol. Pierre Gilkin is still guiding transatlantic convoys in the American merchant marine. Harry and Joe Dorgan are fit and well and disgustingly rich; Agénor Marmousier is in Paris; Bombridge is still breeding snails in Florida...and there are the ladies, of course: Andrée, Frédérique, Isidora, Dorypha... I kept careful track, you see, even when I was on the far side of the world, not because I was hoarding information for some future revenge, but simply because I'm a collector of data by nature and by habit. I still have agents in America, you know—dear old Leonello, the indestructible Slug, and a full dozen of my old hanged men. I always intended to go back, to start over."

"Pity about the war," whispered Oscar, wishing once again that he could laugh, if only to make it clear that he was being flippant, playing the gamin. The discomfort was increasing, and that always brought out the *gamin* in him, presumably in memory of the days when he really had been a street-urchin, living from hand to mouth, and leaving his mouth unsated more often than not.

"Do you think so?" said Cornelius, getting to his feet and going to the window to look out into the darkness, not because he wanted to see what was out there in the darkness, but because he was restless, unable to sit still for long. Officers were not immune to the automatism that claimed impotent souls like Oscar's and Andrée's, but they couldn't avoid their ration of responsibility, especially if they had to maintain steady hands for surgery. Officers developed all manner of neurotic symptoms, which made stillness difficult—even an officer like Dr. Malbrough, Oscar thought, whose mask of false identity hid the supposedly-imperturbable Dr. Cornelius Kramm, sculptor of human flesh and conscienceless master of the Red Hand. Or so it seemed. All this might, of course, be a nightmare.

"I suppose, in that," Dr. Cornelius continued, "you're in the majority. The war, almost everyone thinks, has shown us all how trivial everything else is—or was—by comparison. What were the few hundred people I killed in America by comparison with the tens of thousands slaughtered in a single day at Ypres or the Somme? What was the association of the Red Hand by comparison with the organized crime of the Boche war machine, of U-boats, mustard gas and zeppelin raids? What was the paltry scope of my insidious gathering of the experimental material of human flesh compared with the lavish provision of material laid on every day by bombardment and blast, flame-throwers and poisons, syphilis and staphylococcus?

"Flanders fields, you know, are among the most fertile in the world, enriched over centuries by animal and human manure—bacteria thrive there as nowhere else on Earth, and that's where the warriors of 1914 elected to dig their trenches, to bathe themselves in filth, to make absolutely certain that every wound they sustained, from barbed wire or machine-gun bullets, would become a crucible of infection... not merely a utopia of challenge for a man such as me but an ideal opportunity for an experimentalist like me to be hailed as a hero, or even a saint, and not condemned as a villain, or as a demon...

"Pity about the war? I don't think so, Sergeant Tournesol. If I were a lesser man, I'd say thank God for the war... but for all its wonderful advantages and opportunities, it's not what I want. Yes, all those mutilated bodies, all those men in the very jaws of death, almost beyond the reach of any possible snatching, are invaluable... and I certainly wouldn't want to be thought ungrateful... but it's not, at the end of the day, of any real significance. War is an inconvenience as well as a folly. The real challenge has to be fought on nature's battleground, against the everyday processes of aging and deterioration... and that's what I want, what I need, to get back to, in the fullness of time.

"Mending broken bodies and mangled flesh, like yours, is exhilarating, but at the end of the day, it's a distraction. I need to get back to experimenting on the healthy, not for the sake of repair but for the sake of improvement. I need to get past this stupid heroism, this repetitive fight to save lives that are hardly worth saving, to get back to the business of enhancement, the cultivation of the ultimate mutability of the flesh, the exploration of the further limits of possibility..."

Oscar wanted to tell the Doctor that his need for a morphine booster was now becoming acute, but all he could contrive as a kind of strangled grasp. The metaphorical moon, unintimidated by snowballs, was beginning to glare at him like a death's-head, for reasons that had nothing to do with Cornelius Kramm's compulsive confession.

In a way, the gasp worked. Realizing that his patient was in distress, Dr. Cornelius turned away from the window and came back to the candlelit bed. He sat down on the stool again, touched Oscar's forehead to test his temperature, and took his pulse—but he didn't want to be distracted, as yet, from what was on his own mind, from whatever crazy reasoning had led him to let Oscar in on a secret that he had surely not confided to anyone else.

"Don't worry," said the counterfeit Malbrough, "I won't leave you in distress much longer. I'm sorry—I've allowed myself to get carried away. But that's the point, you see. That's the second reason, the more important reason, why I saved your life. Because I need you, Sergeant Tournesol—may I call you Oscar? *I need you*, Oscar. Not so much now, while this stupid war is on, but afterwards, when I return to America, when I get back to work.

"The era of organized crime had only just begun, you see, before the war. Afterwards—and the German defeat can't be long delayed now; even setting propaganda and morale-boosting aside, this time, it really will be over by Christmas—afterwards, organized crime will really be able to take off, more so in America than anywhere else. It will be possible to make billions that way, and if billions are going to be made, it really will be far better that they're made by a man like me, who has a purpose in mind for them, rather than a decadent sensualist like my late brother Fritz, or a reckless hedonist like

Baruch Jorgell, or a smug wallower in pathetic luxury like any common-or-garden billionaire.

"Organized crime will provide a context for field-experiments on a scale that might not be quite as vast as the Somme, but will be far more amenable to planning, to control, for strategy..."

Oscar had been trying valiantly to interrupt for some time, but it wasn't easy, not so much because of Cornelius' volubility as because of his own deteriorating condition. He felt now as if he were on a Medieval rack, as if he were under torture—as, in a sense, he was. Hero-ically, he managed to say "Me?" and make it sound like a question.

"What has it got to do with you?" Cornelius echoed, quick on the uptake, as befitted a genius of his stature. "I'm sorry, my dear Oscar, I know that I'm not going fast enough for you, but you have no idea what a relief it is, finally to be able to speak to someone who knows who I am, someone who's studied me, someone who knows what I'm capable of doing, someone who *knows my measure*. That's why I need you, you see—that, above all else, is why I had to save *your* life, more ur-gently than anyone else's.

"Nobody else will know, you see, once the war is over and I return to America, what's really going on. From everyone else, I'll need to hide, as I'm hiding now, because I'll have to, in order to be able to carry out the kind of experiments that I want to carry out, not merely on volunteers like my precious hanged men, but on the healthy, on the contented and self-satisfied: people who would never volunteer to put what they have at risk for the chance of helping me, in the long run, to develop something better.

"From the world, I'll have to hide—not merely in the sense of remaining unseen, but unimaginable, beyond belief. But alongside that, in addition to that, I need there to be someone who *knows*, not merely that I'm there, but what I'm about, and what I'm capable of doing. I need an audience, Oscar, and not just any audience, but a specialist audience: an opponent, an adversary. Burydan might have done, if he hadn't got himself killed, Paganot, probably... even Ravenel... but they're all gone. You have no idea, my dear Oscar—although I'm doing my level best now to give you one—what high hopes I have for you, what I expect of you in terms, not merely of the intellectual comprehension of my endeavor but the esthetic appreciation of it.

"You see, my dear Oscar, in order really to exist, we all need someone who *knows* that we exist, who knows who and what we are—and for that reason, you need me as much as I need you. You have Regina, of course, and the angelic Andrée, but they don't really know you, and never will, because you love them far too much ever to let them see you as you really are, just as I would love a wife, if I were ever to marry, far too much to let her see what I really am. It's because you and I have been adversaries, Oscar, and because we can be adversaries again, that we can dispense with our masks and look one another in the face. It's because we've hated one another, and might do so again—in spite of the gratitude you're bound to feel and the quasi-paternal affection that I shall have difficulty henceforth keeping at bay—that we can rip away the veils of illusion, and confront one another as our true selves..."

He broke off then, even though Oscar could no more contrive a scream than a laugh, and bent down to delve into his medical bag for a Pravaz syringe. With practiced efficiency the fake Malbrough filled the in-strument, and plunged it into Oscar's flesh, near the hip.

Oscar felt the morphine rush almost instantly, but he knew—and knew that Cornelius Kramm knew it too—that he would still be capable of listening for a mi-nute or two more, before the numbness overwhelmed his brain, and took him away, at least to dream and delirium, if not to darkness...

Standing on the bridge at midnight, Oscar thought, or, at least, heard in his mind's ear, because he was inca-pable to real thought, *throwing snowballs at the Moon...*

"This is our secret, Oscar," said the bloodstained man, leaning forward yet again as if to soak up the frail, fleeting candlelight—and Oscar wondered, belatedly, whether he had begun to think of the man who had saved his life as "the bloodstained man" because somehow, deep below the surface of consciousness, he *had* recog-nized them man he had seen once before, at a funeral. "It's our secret, not because I'm forbidding you to tell anyone, but because I know that you can't, not so much to spare your reputation for sanity and to ward off the accusation that this is all a nightmare, but for Andrée's sake, and Regina's, because your instinct... your stupid, primitive, human instinct... is to protect them from the knowledge that the likes of Dr. Cornelius Kramm are haunting the world, and haunting *them...*

"But *you*'ll know, my dear Oscar. You'll know that this wasn't a mere fragment of delirium. You'll know, when the so-called war is over and the real war re-sumes—the war of all against all, the bloody war from whose agony true progress emerges, provided that there are men like me to make it—that I'm there, behind the scenes, immortal and unconquerable, doing my work. Perhaps you'll try to stop me—I hope you will, because nothing whets an appetite for progress like challenge and resistance—but whether you do or not, you'll know. You'll be on the lookout, ever-ready to read behind the lines of the news, ever-ready to say, of something anomalous and mysterious: 'That's Dr. Cornelius at work; that's one of his experiments, one of his sculptures, part of his quest to make human flesh malleable, and bring out the full potential, not merely of the clay of the body, but also of the clay of the mind.' And you'll..."

There was more. There was probably much more, in fact. Like all men who live in hiding, concealing their true selves—all men, in effect, and all women too—Dr. Cornelius Kramm, once having seized a rare opportunity to explain himself, wasn't easy to stop.

Oscar was no longer listening, however. Oscar was lost within himself, within the tide of chemical relief that was dulling his pain, dulling his consciousness, dulling his very being, his all-too-malleable clay. He could no longer hear Cornelius Kramm's passionate self-explanation and rebarbative boasting. He probably couldn't hear anything at all, in fact, but he thought, or dreamed, that he could. He thought, or dreamed, that he could hear a British tommy, on a ward somewhere down below, in some mysterious gulf, singing, no longer about hurling dirty snowballs at a sallow moon, but somehow having contrived, at last, to reach the plaintive and pain-racked chorus of his song: "It's the rich that get the pleasure/And the poor that get the blame/It's the same the whole world over/Ain't it all a bloody shame."

And Oscar thought, or dreamed, too, that he could hear an entire line of entrenched *poilus*, rising valiantly to that bizarre challenge, that crazy but stubborn resistance to the awful pressure of fate and circumstance, to counter anchoring gibberish with anchoring gibberish, by singing "*Malbrough s'en va-t-en guerre/Mironton, mironton, mirontaine…*"

Except that it wasn't gibberish, really, any more than the English song was really gibberish, because Malbrough really was going off to war, again...

Not that it mattered much, in the great scheme of things.

It didn't matter, because first thing in the morning, Oscar, conscious or unconscious, was trucking out. He would be on his way to Kérity-sur-Mer, to be cared for by Frédérique Ravenel: to the Earthly Paradise, doubtless damaged but not yet derelict, where he could rest and recuperate, if necessary until the war was over, when he could be shipped back to Florida, to Regina...

In the meantime, doubtless, he would see Dr. Malbrough again, having come to check up on his "subject," or the sharer of his secret. Now that he knew who Dr. Malbrough really was, it would no longer be a matter of saluting a saint, even mentally, but that didn't matter either—not so much because Cornelius Kramm now wanted him alive instead of dead, but because for him, Sergeant Oscar Tournesol, the war was over, and he was no longer on the bridge, but moving forward, into the future.

At the end of the day, and the beginning of the next, the future was all that really mattered, and all that ever would.

Mironton, mironton, mirontaine…

Afterword

The *Doctor Cornelius vs Countess Petrovska* series came about from a suggestion from my editor Jean-Marc Lofficier. I had concluded the Captain Vampire/Boris Liatoukine series. for the annual anthology *Tales of the Shadowmen* and we had been discussing what next. The *Tales of the Shadowmen* format was based on using classic Francophone fictional characters to create new stories. Non-Francophone characters could also appear alongside, but the French aspect gives the *Shadowmen* universe an identity all its own. Many of the characters that appear in this book are taken from fiction, both French and from elsewhere, or are historical, some of whom will be discussed later.

Jean-Marc suggested a series about Gustave Le Rouge's Dr. Cornelius and his criminal gang, the Red Hand. This appealed to me immediately, given that I had enjoyed writing the vampire Boris Liatoukine, another villainous character.

It immediately made sense to set the series during World War One, the original Dr. Cornelius series having been published—and likely set—during 1912-13. Further, the series would take place in each year of the war within self-contained stories. With the Red Hand having been destroyed in the original series, the Doctor would sell his services to whichever side in the war would pay the most. Brian Stableford had already written a Dr. Cornelius tale set during the war, included as an extra in this volume.[17] That story shows that he was up to a great deal during that time, beyond his activities as a criminal for hire.

Whereas Boris Liatoukine had a politically motivated element to him, mostly trying to keep on the right side of whoever ran Russia, Dr. Cornelius was a sadistic villain co-running a powerful criminal gang and did not have that extra depth that Captain Vampire had. Indeed, there was a full cast of heroes in the original Gustave Le Rouge stories that opposed him, who, more often than not, were the focus of the books. That set-up did not seem to me to be as suitable for a series of short stories starring the Lord of the Red Hand.

So I gave the Doctor a strong foil in the form of Countess Irina Petrovska. The character originated in the 1972 Spanish film *Horror Express*. She was created by Arnaud d'Usseau and Julian Zimet, and played by the Spanish actress Silvia Tortosa. I had previously used a descendant of the character as a heroine in the later Captain Vampire stories. The original version is more than a little imperious in the film. I softened her a little—but not too much—as she would otherwise not be of much use against the likes of Dr. Cornelius.

The film also suggested she was a Polish patriot. I dutifully incorporated that element and provided some extra background to the extent that her husband, Count Petrovski, was from the parts of Poland controlled by Russia, whilst she was from the Habsburg-controlled parts. After the events of *Horror Express*, the Countess resolved to combat such alien threats as the creature she faced on the Trans-Siberian Express. She became an adventurer, and also an occasional freelance agent for the

---

[17] Initially published in *Tales of the Shadowmen*, Vol. 10.

Evidenzbureau of the Austro-Hungarian Empire, as well as a journalist.

A number of *Horror Express* credits—including the BBC website—list the character as "Countess Petrovski," her surname being the same as her husband. However, in Polish her name would have the feminine ending of "ska," and so, for the purposes of this volume, I have used "Petrovska."

The first tale, *The Doctor of Sarajevo*, is set in the city where the assassination of Archduke Franz Ferdinand provided the spark for the First World War. It is not unusual to have World War One-themed science-fiction or fantasy stories. However, something set within the Austro-Hungarian Empire, and sympathetic to it, is hopefully a notion that is somewhat different from what has been done before. It also reflects my interest in those lands.

The first story touches on the nationalities issue throughout the Empire. Indeed, potential reforms that could have led to some kind of Slavic unity were unacceptable to the assassin Gavrilo Princip. His politics were a version of the Greater Serbia ideology that has caused so much violence in more recent decades.

Guest starring in the first story is the Frenchman Simon Hart, who first appeared, along with the Fulgurator weapon, in the 1896 Jules Verne story, *Facing the Flag*. Hart patriotically saves the day in that novel, and it made sense that he would be working for the French *Deuxième Bureau*, hiring—with the British, initially— Dr. Cornelius to handle sensitive and difficult tasks. He returns in a similar role throughout the series.

Lord Burydan, featured in the original Dr. Cornelius series as one of the *heroes* standing against the Red Hand, also returns, clearly as an unhinged villain. In these stories, we see this peer of the realm behave in a most questionable manner. At one point, he cold-bloodedly throws two of the Doctor's henchmen into a river to be eaten by alligators. I have no idea what Gustave Le Rouge was trying to say here about the British, if anything, but I thought it would be a good twist to take this characterization to its logical conclusion. He is not a hero, but a villain, or at least utterly amoral.

Lord Burydan's comment that Britain wished to encircle the Habsburg Empire was taken from a theory by the late American historian Paul Schroeder in a 1972 essay, *World War I as a Galloping Gertie*. It is not a mainstream historical view, but one that seemed appropriate for someone such as Lord Burydan.

The very name Sarajevo has a certain power due to its historical status, sadly with negative events such as the terrible siege by Serb forces in the 1990s, and, of course, the 1914 assassination. I've tried to depict it as it might have been at the time, and the characters of Mayor Fehim Curcić and Archbishop Stadler, who make cameo appearances, are real people. The fact that it is the location of a secret repository for alien and esoteric objects collected by the Habsburg Empire was, of course, my way of giving the city a different, albeit fictional, aspect.

The Telepath of Galicia came about due to the Countess's Polish patriotism. It would have made little sense for her to be operating in places such as Bosnia-Herzegovina and not helping her fellow Poles. Hence, as well as working as a journalist and sometime agent for the *Evidenzbureau*, I had her working as a nurse wherever Polish Habsburg troops were fighting—in this case, near the city of Kraków, just before the real-life Gorlice-Tarnów offensive. It also gave me an opportunity to further examine the Countess's political views. At the time,

Poland was split between Austria, Russia and Germany. Her vision—which was shared by some Polish politicians—was that of a united Poland under the Habsburg monarchy, which is why she is a willing agent of the Austro-Hungarian Empire.

The Lynx serum came from the eponymous novel *The Lynx*[18] by Michel Corday and Andre Couvreur, published in 1911. The serum, of course, would have ended up in the hands of Simon Hart, and then be stolen by France's erstwhile allies, the Russians. This provided a useful way of introducing telepathy into the war, a tool that would have had a devastating impact had it been real.

A number of characters featured in that story are real, historical figures, such as Russin spymaster A.V. Brune de St Hippolite and the Polish politician Władysław Jaworski. Most important of all was General Borojević. He was regarded as a highly competent officer, who always identified himself as a Croat. A lot of the action takes place in Kraków, which I had intended to visit prior to writing the story, but a certain pandemic intervened. I hope I have done the city justice.

The Deadly Projector over Split was originally published as *The Projector of Death*. The title was changed to fit in with the other titles which all mentioned the locations the story were set in so as not to stand out when collected in this volume.

My plan was always to bring back Lord Burydan, forced to work for Dr. Cornelius to maintain his restored facial features, with the extra twist that he thinks the Countess was responsible for his burns, not the Doctor. As we see, Lord Burydan finds it quite congenial work-

---

[18] Black Coat Press, ISBN 978-1-61227-273-3.

ing for the Doctor – again, in keeping with his dubious character. His appearance also gave me the chance to use the "Pig-Dog" translation of the "*Schweinhund*" so beloved by British war comics.

An early scene is set at Inverlair Lodge, Scotland. Enthusiasts of the classic 1967 TV series *The Prisoner*, will remember that the real-life Lodge was one of the influences on The Village, where spies and those with sensitive information were imprisoned.

For this story, I needed an Italian villain and some alien technology. Jean-Marc suggested I use Professor Marcus and the Saturnians from the classic Italian comic strip *Saturno Contro la Terra*, created in 1936 by Cesare Savattini, Frederico Pedrocchi and Giovanni Scolari. Set before the events of the comic, I made the Professor an Italian irredentist. This was feasible enough, given that time in Italian history. The story is set against the background of what in effect was an attempt by Italy to grab territory for itself in Slovenia and Croatia, a move resisted ferociously by the Austro-Hungarian Army. This Italian irredentism no doubt influenced the awful politics later pursued by Italy.

The story is Croatia-based, set in Dalmatia. I have connections with and have written about Croatia, so this story was an even greater pleasure to write. All the locations therein can be visited, Sutivan and Supetar, and even the Franz Joseph bridge as well as various locations in Split. Indeed, on a recent visit, I was looking at Diocletian Palace, recalling the final scenes with Professor Marcus and his projector.

Two more historical characters crop up. One is Stjepan Radić, of the Croatian Peasants Party. Croatian lands were split within the Empire, Croatia-Slavonia being under the Hungarian half, albeit with autonomy, and Dalmatia under the Austrian half. Croats aspired to some form of unification, possibly within some kind of third unit within the Empire. National aspirations were a major issue in the Empire, which did not go away during the war, whether it was the Poles, Croats, Czechs or the other nationalities. This is why this is such a strong thread throughout this series.

The other historical character who appears is Emperor Karl I. Franz Joseph I had died in 1916, and Karl, like Franz Ferdinand, had ideas for reforms and became an important character in the last three stories.

The projector's images of terror were influenced by the many real paintings during the war depicting specters of Death on the battlefield. Captain Marić's first scene in the story is based on the 1916 painting *Death Lying in Wait for a Cavalryman* by Lazić, held by the Croatian History Museum in Zagreb.

The Prisoner of Budapest, although the penultimate tale chronologically, was, in fact, the last story written and makes its debut here. *Tales of the Shadowmen* was coming to a natural end with volume 20, and so we decided to end the series properly with *The Secret Archive in Vienna* and insert this story here to ensure all years of the war are represented as planned.

Budapest was chosen to represent the Hungarian side of the Empire, otherwise, the series would have been too focused on the Austrian half. Saturnian technology reappears, this time being manipulated by Antoine de Grantaigle. The duplicating process comes from J.-H. Rosny *Aîné*'s *The Givreuse Enigma*[19] published in 1917, concerning a soldier who is found duplicated. Grantaigle does not appear in that story, his body is re-

[19] Black Coat Press , ISBN 978-1-935558-39-2.

ported as being found under the wreckage of his chateau. This revelation takes place later in the story, with it being a mystery earlier on, including the possibility he was captured by the Germans. It fits perfectly that he was duplicated, with one duplicate having indeed been captured by the Germans. Saturnian technology helps explain Grantaigle's ground-breaking technology.

The story features an appearance by Bela Lugosi, possibly the world's most famous Hungarian, and certainly one of the world's greatest actors. As related here, he volunteered to fight, was wounded and invalidated out of the army, returning to acting in 1917. Inserting him into the story was irresistible, and a high point for me in writing it, also providing me with an excuse to rewatch some of his greatest films.

Another real-life character was Prime Minister István Tisza. He did resign, as Dr. Cornelius related, due to tensions with the Emperor which plays a part in the story.

Finally, we come to *The Secret Archive of Vienna*. The last story was always going to be set in Vienna, with the end of the Habsburg Empire, and the looting of their alien secrets, by the victorious powers.

The Czech pilot Heinrich Kostrba was a real-life air ace. It is not clear where he served in 1917. This tale thus helps explain what he might have been doing in May of that year.

Within our universe, there was always the possibility that Germany and her allies would win, but in 1918, that was not the case, which gives the series its odd ending: our heroine is on the losing side, although at least she survived the war, to continue her adventures. Lord Burydan also survived, on the winning side as, it seems, did Dr. Cornelius.

However, the fates of some of our historical figures give an early warning of what is in store for Europe. Prime Minister István Tisza was assassinated by disgruntled soldiers in 1918. In 1928, the Croatian politician, Stjepan Radić, was shot in the Yugoslav Parliament by a Serb nationalist, later dying of his wounds. In 1922, Emperor Karl I died of heart failure brought on by pneumonia, at age 34, in exile in Portugal. General Borojević died in 1920 of a brain hemorrhage in Austria. The new Yugoslav authorities had refused to let him move to Croatia, even denying him a pension. The fates of these men symbolically signal that something important had been destroyed by World War One.

If the Habsburg Empire had survived the war, would it have solved the nationalities questions? I suspect there would be a fair chance that it might have been the case, given that Emperor Karl was open to reforms. However, the shock of the defeat made that impossible.

What would the Countess make of history as it unfolded? She would no doubt be appalled, but she would have plunged in to help Poland at every turn, especially in helping repel the 1920 Soviet invasion. Her daughter would have fought the Nazis in World War Two. In my *Captain Vampire* series, her granddaughter fought both the supernatural and communism. The Countess would be pleased to see Poland today as an independent state and also be proud to see her country helping its neighbor Ukraine against Russia.

Who knows, perhaps there is another Countess Irina Petrovska now, protecting Poland and Europe?

Brian Gallagher,
London, January 2024